Count Brühl

By Józef Ignacy Kraszewski

Translated by Guy Jean Raoul Eugène Charles Emmanuel de Savoie-Carignan, Comte de Soissons

Skomlin
House of Memory and Imagination

First Skomlin International Edition - October 2017

Skomlin
House of Memory and Imagination
For more information visit *www.skomlin.com*

A Skomlin Book
Melbourne, Australia

First published in Warsaw 1874
First English version, New York 1922
© Skomlin, 2017

ISBN: 978-0-9874014-1-0 *(paperback)*
ISBN: 978-0-6481826-0-3 *(eBook)*

A catalogue record for this book is available from the National Library of Australia

The paper used in this publication meets the minimum requirements of ANSI/NISO Z39.48-1992 (R1997) (Permanence of Paper). The paper used in this book is from responsibly managed forests. Printed in the United States of America, the United Kingdom and Australia by Lightning Source, Inc.

Count Brühl

One beautiful autumn day, towards sunset, the last flourishes of a trumpet calling the huntsmen together, resounded through a forest of beech trees. The group of court huntsmen passed along the wide highway that divided this ancient wilderness, accompanied by men armed with boar-spears and carrying nets; the horsemen wore green dresses with gold braid, and hats ornamented with black feathers: in the centre of the party were waggons laden with venison and adorned with green boughs. The hunt must have been successful, for the huntsmen were in high spirits, and from the waggons protruded the horns of deer, and the heads of boars with bloody tusks.

The retinue of the lord came first; there were beautiful horses, and several lady riders with lovely faces. All were dressed as for a festival, for hunting was a favourite amusement with Augustus II, who at that time ruled more or less happily over Saxony and Poland.

The King himself led the hunt, and at his side rode his eldest son, the prince then dearest to Saxony, and the one towards whom the eyes of the nation were directed with expectation. The King looked well, despite his advanced age, and rode his horse like a knight; whilst his son, who also looked well but whose face wore a sweeter expression, looked rather like his younger brother. A numerous and brilliant court surrounded the two lords. They were to pass the night at Hubertsburg, where the Prince would offer hospitality to his father, for the hunting castle belonged to him. The Princess Josepha, daughter-in-law to the King, and daughter of the Imperial house of Hapsburg, recently married to Frederick, awaited them at Hubertsburg. The King's court was so numerous that it was impossible to lodge it in the castle, and for this reason tents had been pitched in the grove for the greater part of the retinue. The tables were already laid for supper, and the moment the King entered the castle, the huntsmen dispersed to find the lodgings assigned to them.

Dusk began to fall; the tents were full of bustle and animation, the young men's laughter, hitherto restrained by the presence of the King, now resounded more freely. They were thirsty, and drinking commenced although the signal for supper had not been given. Soon they began disputing as to which was the prettiest lady, who was the best marksman, and to whom the King had shown most favour. The Prince was the hero of the day; a boar was rushing on him, and he had shot it in the forehead. Everyone admired his presence of mind as with steady arm he aimed and fired. When the huntsmen rushed forward to dispatch the wild beast with their hunting knives, it already lay on the ground bathed in its own blood. On this, King Augustus had kissed his son on the forehead approvingly, and the Prince had pressed his father's hand to his lips, but he remained as calm and composed after the victory as he had been before. The only sign of good humour he had shown was, that he ordered a pipe to be brought him, and blew forth a larger cloud than usual. In those times men had begun to use that now universal plant—tobacco. Augustus the Strong smoked a great deal, his son, Prince Frederick, was a passionate smoker. During a feast the men could not forego their pipes. At the court of the Prussian King, pipes were served out to everyone, and the man who felt sick from smoking was the laughingstock of the others. It was the height of fashion to suck at a pipe from morning till night. The women despised the habit, but their aversion did not prevent the men from indulging to excess in the fragrant weed. Only the youngsters were forbidden to smoke, the habit being coupled with such vices as gambling and drinking. Therefore there were no pipes under the tents.

The weary horsemen dismounted, and seated themselves wherever they could, some on the ground, some on benches, and others on rugs. Arrangements had been made for another hunt on the following day, in another part of the forest, and orders had been given for everyone to be in readiness.

Not very far from the groups of elderly gentlemen, a very handsome youth walked to and fro from the road leading to the castle. He might have been recognised by his dress as a page in the service of the King. His noble carriage, and slightly effeminate figure, attracted the attention even of the most indifferent. His dress was elegant, his wig carefully arranged; his pink and white face beneath was almost as beautiful as that of a girl about to smile; he had intelligent eyes that could be merry or sad, brilliant or dull; they could even express that which was not in the soul.

This beautiful youth attracted like an enigma. Almost everyone, the King not excepted, loved him, yet, while both polite and useful, there was not a more retiring person in the court. He never boasted, never attempted to show his superiority, but if asked to do anything he did it easily, quickly, and with exceeding intelligence.

He was a petty noble from Thuringia, the youngest of four brothers, the Brühls von Gangloffs-Sammern. Having sold his small mortgaged estate, his father became a councillor at the little court of Weissenfelds; and as he did not know what to do with his son he placed him in the service of the Princess Frederick Elizabeth, who generally resided at Leipzig. The Princess at that time came constantly to Weissenfelds for market days; Augustus the Strong was also very fond of these markets, and it is said that on one occasion the young page attracted the attention of the King by his beautiful face. The Princess willingly gave him to the monarch.

It was wonderful that a boy who had never seen so magnificent a court, so much etiquette, should understand his duties so well from the first day, that he surpassed the older pages in his zeal and ability. The King smiled kindly on him; he was pleased with the humility of the boy, who looked into his eyes, guessed his thoughts and worshipped the majesty of the Roi-Soleil.

Those who served with him, envied him, but were soon captivated by his sweetness, modesty, and readiness to serve them too. They had no fears; such a modest boy could never rise very high. He was poor, and the Brühl family, although, of ancient lineage, had so fallen, that its rich relations had forgotten it. The youth therefore had neither influence nor wealth to advance him, merely a sweet and smiling face.

And indeed, he was very beautiful. The women, especially the older ones, looked at him coquettishly, and he lowered his eyes bashfully. Malicious words, the wit of pages, characteristics these of the young men of the court, never escaped his lips. Brühl admired the lords, the dignitaries, the ladies, his equals, and even the King's lackeys, to whom he was invariably courteous, as though already aware of the great secret that the greatest things are often accomplished through the meanest persons, that lackeys have quietly overthrown ministers, whilst the ministers could do nothing against them. All this the lucky youth guessed through the instinct with which Mother Nature had endowed him.

At that moment, as Henry Brühl walked alone up and down the path leading from the castle to the tent, those who knew him might have said that he indulged in this solitary stroll to avoid being in the way of others, while, being seen of everyone, he would be in readiness for any service. Such persons are favoured by good fortune. As he thus walked aimlessly to and fro there came from the castle a young good-looking boy, about the same age, but different in dress and mien to modest Brühl.

It was evident that the new-comer was well satisfied with himself. He was tall and strong, his black eyes looked forth sharply. He walked swiftly with lordly gait, having one hand placed in his richly embroidered vest and the other hidden in the shirt of his green braided hunting dress. His features also were quite different to those of Brühl; the latter looked more like a courtier, the former like a soldier.

Everyone he met on his way bowed to him, and greeted him kindly, for from early youth he had been the Prince's companion. His name was Count Alexandre Sulkowski, he had been brought to the court of Frederick as a page, and was already a prominent huntsman. And this meant a great deal, for the Prince, to whom hunting was rather a serious occupation than a distraction, entrusted him with what he cherished most in the world.

Sulkowski was respected and dreaded, for although Augustus II with his health and strength seemed to be immortal, yet sooner or later the god was bound to die like any other mortal. Thus Sulkowski, in his relation to the new rising sun, was regarded as a star shining on the horizon of Saxony.

On seeing Sulkowski, the page assumed his modest mien, bowed slightly, smiled sweetly, and seemed as pleased as though he had met the most beautiful woman in the court of the King. Sulkowski received this mute and respectful greeting with dignified benevolence. He slackened his pace, and drawing near to Brühl, addressed him gaily:

'How are you, Henry? What are you thinking about in this solitude? Happy boy, you can rest, whilst I have much to do.'

'If the Count would order me to help him?'

'No thank you. I must fulfil my own duties! Work for such a guest as our gracious lord is agreeable.'

He sighed slightly.

'Well,' he continued, 'the hunt was successful.'

'Yes, very successful indeed,' replied Brühl. 'His Majesty has not been in such a good humour for a long time.'

Sulkowski bent close to Brühl's ear.

'And who rules now in the chamber?'

'I do not know. At present there is an interregnum.'

'That's impossible!' said Sulkowski laughing. 'Is it not Dieskau?'

'I don't know.'

'Is it possible, that you, the King's page, do not know?'

Brühl looked at him, and smiled.

'A faithful page should not know anything.'

'I understand,' said Sulkowski, 'but between ourselves—'

Brühl drew near the Count, and whispered some thing in his ear.

'Intermezzo!' said Sulkowski. 'It seems that after so many love affairs, that have cost our dear lord so much money, and caused him so much pain, intermezzo will do.'

Sulkowski was no longer in a hurry, either to go to the tents, whither his steps appeared to be bent, or to return to the castle. Taking Brühl's arm, an action which evidently gave the page great satisfaction, he walked with him.

'I must rest awhile,' said he, 'and although we are both too weary to converse, I am glad to be with you.'

'I do not feel tired,' replied Brühl, 'when I am in your company. From the first moment when I was so fortunate as to meet you, I conceived for you, my dear Count, deep respect, and permit me also to add, the most affectionate, friendship. Must I tell you the truth? Well then, I came here with a presentiment—with a hope—that I might have the pleasure of seeing you.'

The Count looked into Brühl's face, which was beaming with joy.

'I can assure you,' said he, 'that I am not ungrateful. In the court such disinterested friendship is rare, and if we help each other, we can rise to high appointments.'

Their eyes met, Brühl nodded.

'The King is fond of you.'

'Do you think so?' asked Brühl, modestly.

'I can assure you of it; I have heard it from his Majesty's own lips; he praised your zeal and intelligence. As for me, the Prince loves me, and I can say with pride that he calls me his friend. I doubt if he could get along without me.'

'Yes,' said Brühl with animation, 'you were so fortunate as to be the Prince's companion, from the time he was a mere boy, and you have had time to win his heart; and who would not love you if he knew you well? As for me, I am a stranger here, though I am thankful to the Princess for placing me at the King's court. I try to show my gratitude, but the parquetry of a court is very slippery. The more zeal I show for the lord, whom I respect and love, the more jealousy I excite. For every smile bestowed on me by the lord, I am repaid with the venom of envy. So one must tremble when one might be the happiest of mortals.'

Sulkowski listened with an air of distraction.

'Yes! That's true,' he rejoined quietly. 'But you have much in your favour and no reason to fear. I observe that you have adopted an excellent method: you are modest and patient. The principal thing at court is to remain passive, then you will advance; he who is restless soon falls.'

'Your advice is most precious,' exclaimed Brühl. 'I am indeed fortunate to have such an adviser.'

The Count seemed flattered at the exclamation, he smiled proudly, pleased at the acknowledgment of his own powers of which he was fully persuaded.

'Don't be afraid, Brühl,' he said. 'Go forward boldly and count on me.'

Those words seemed to arouse Brühl's enthusiasm, he clasped his hands as though in prayer, and his face was radiant; then he extended a hand to

Sulkowski in token of his gratitude. The Count magnanimously took it with the condescending air of a benefactor.

At that moment the trumpet resounded from the castle; the sound must have meant something to the young favourite, for signing to his friend that he must hasten, he ran towards the castle.

Brühl remained alone, hesitating as to what he should do with himself. The King had granted him leave for the evening, consequently he was entirely free. Supper had begun beneath the tents. At first he had intended to go there and enjoy himself with the others, but after looking on for a moment, he turned into a side path, and walked slowly and thoughtfully to the forest. Probably he wished to be alone with his thoughts, although his youthful eyes were not suggestive of deep speculation. It might be nearer truth to think that in a court full of love intrigues, he too had some love affair; but on his serene face no trace of such trouble could be detected. Brühl did not sigh, his look was cold and calm, he frowned, and appeared rather to be calculating something, than struggling against a particular sentiment.

He passed tents, horses, and packs of hounds; he passed the fires, built up by the people assembled for the hunt, who were eating the black bread they had brought with them in their bags, whilst venison was roasting for the nobles. The great majority of these were Slavs, called Wends, and they chatted quietly together in a tongue incomprehensible to the Germans. Several huntsmen kept guard over them, and whilst supper was prepared for the hounds, no one took the least trouble to ask these people if they had had anything to eat. Their supper of bread and water was soon finished, and they lay down on the grass to rest, that they might be in readiness for the work of the morrow.

Scarcely glancing at them, Brühl walked quietly forward. It was a lovely evening, peaceful and bright, and had it not been for the yellow leaves falling from the beech-trees, one might have thought it was summer.

Beyond the grove in which they were encamped all was still; the noise scarcely penetrated thither; trees concealed the castle; one could have imagined oneself far from the haunts of man.

Arrived here Brühl raised his head, and breathed more freely; his face

7

assumed a different expression; it lost its childish charm, and an ironical smile flitted across it. He thought he was alone, and was greatly surprised, almost frightened, at seeing two men lying beneath an enormous beech-tree. He retreated, and looked at them attentively. Those two men, lying beneath a tree not far from the King's camp, appeared to him suspicious characters. Beside them lay their travelling bags and sticks.

The dusk prevented him from seeing their faces very clearly, or noticing what clothes they wore, but after awhile Brühl was able to distinguish that they were young men.

What could they have been doing so close to the King? Curiosity, fear and suspicion, kept him rooted to the spot. He wondered whether it would not be right to return to the tents and give warning of the presence of two suspicious strangers. He changed his mind however, and drawn more by instinct than reason, moved forward, and approached so near to the strangers that they could see him. His appearance must have aston-ished them, for one of them rose hastily, and seemed about to ask what he was doing there.

Without waiting for this question, Brühl advanced a few steps further, and asked severely:

'What are you doing here?'

'We are resting,' replied the man. 'Is it forbidden here for travellers to rest?'

The voice was mild, and the speech indicated an educated man.

'The King's court and his Majesty in person are not far distant,' said Brühl.

'Are we in the way?' asked the stranger, who did not appear to be in the least alarmed.

'No,' answered Brühl with animation, 'but if you were noticed here, you might be suspected of evil designs.'

The man who remained seated laughed and rose, and when he came out from beneath the shadow of the trees, Brühl beheld a good-looking man, with long hair and a noble mien. By his dress he was easily to be recognised as a student from one of the German universities.

'What are you doing here?' Brühl repeated.

'We are wandering about that we may thank God by admiring nature and breathing the air of the forest, and that in this quiet we may lull our souls to prayer,' the youth said slowly. 'Night surprised us here; we should not have known of the presence of the King and his court, had it not been for the noise of the huntsmen.'

The words as well as the way they were pronounced struck Brühl. The man seemed to be from another world.

'Permit me, sir,' the student continued quietly, 'to introduce myself to you who seem to have some official position. I am Nicolaus Louis, Count and Lord of Zinzendorf and Pottendorf, at present *studiosus*, searching for the source of wisdom and light, a traveller, who has lost his way in the maze of this world.'

On hearing the name, Brühl looked at the stranger more attentively. The moon lit up the beautiful face of the student. They both remained silent for a time, as though not knowing what to say.

'I am Henry Brühl, his Majesty's page.'

Zinzendorf measured him with his eyes.

'I pity you very much,' he said sighing.

'Why?' asked the astonished page.

'Because to be courtier means to be a slave, to be a page means to be a servant, and although I respect the King, I prefer to serve the King of Heaven, to love Jesus Christ, our Saviour. You found us when we were praying, when we were trying to unite our thoughts with our Lord, who has saved us through His blood.'

Brühl was so astonished that he moved away from the youth, who went on pathetically, though sweetly:

'I know that to you, in whose ears the prattle and laughter of the court still ring, this must seem strange and perchance irreverent, but I consider it my duty, every time I have an opportunity, to speak as a Christian should.'

Brühl remained silent. Zinzendorf approached him.

'It is the hour of prayer ... listen, the forest rustles, glory to God on high!

The brook whispers the prayer, the moon shines forth to light the prayer of nature, why then should not our hearts unite with our Saviour at this solemn moment?'

The astonished page listened, and appeared not to understand.

'You behold an odd, whimsical fellow,' said Zinzendorf, 'but you meet many odd, whimsical society men, and you forgive their fancies; can you not then have some indulgence for an enthusiasm arising from the pure source of the soul?'

'Yes,' murmured Brühl. 'I am pious myself, but—'

'But you keep your piety hidden in the secret places of your heart, fearing to show it to profane persons. As for me, I show it forth like a flag, because I am ready to defend it with my life and my blood. Brother in Christ, if the life of the court weigh heavily on you, for I cannot otherwise explain your solitary evening wandering, sit with us, and let us pray together. I feel the need of prayer, and when it is made stronger by two or three praying together, it might reach the throne of Him who gave His blood for us worms.'

Brühl moved away, as though afraid the strangers would detain him.

'I am accustomed to pray alone,' he replied, 'besides my duties call me, you must therefore excuse me.'

He made a gesture in the direction whence noise could be heard.

'I pity you,' exclaimed Zinzendorf. 'If we could only sing a prayer—'

The page interrupted him: 'The grand huntsman, or some chamberlain might hear us, and order us to be put in prison, not here, for there is no prison here, but we should be taken to Dresden, and put in the Frauen-kirche guardhouse.'

He shrugged his shoulders as he spoke, bowed lightly, and would have departed, had not Zinzendorf barred his way.

'Is it true, that it is forbidden to be here?' he asked.

'Your presence might bring suspicion on you, and cause you some trouble. I advise you to be off. Beyond Hubertsburg there is an inn, where you would be more comfortable than beneath this tree.'

'Which road shall we take, so that we may not be in the way of his Majesty?' asked Zinzendorf.

Brühl pointed with his hand, and said:

'It would be difficult for you to find the highway but if you will accept me as your guide, I am at your service.'

Zinzendorf and his companion picked up their sticks and bags, and followed Brühl, who seemed by no means pleased at the meeting. Zinzendorf had had time to cool down from the state of enthusiasm in which the page had found him. It was evident that he was a man accustomed to the best society, for he had excellent manners. Having grown more calm, he endeavoured to excuse himself for the speech he had made.

'Do not be surprised,' said he calmly, 'we call ourselves Christians but in reality we are heathens, despite the promise we made at our baptism. I consider it the duty of every Christian to preach. The aim of my life is not only to preach, but also to set a good example. What is the use of preaching, if deeds do not follow our words? Catholics and Protestants, we are all heathens in our way of living. We do not worship gods, but we make sacrifices to them. A few priests quarrel about dogmas, but our Saviour's blood is wasted, for people do not wish to be saved.'

He sighed. At that moment they came in sight of the camp, where drinking was at its height. Zinzendorf looked towards it, and exclaimed:

'This is a veritable bacchanalia! It seems to me, that I hear *evoe*! Let us hasten! I have no desire to hear and see Christians enjoying themselves in so heathenish a way.'

Brühl made no reply. They passed by the camp, and soon reached the highway. Having pointed out the road to the student, he ran quickly to the lighted tent.

Zinzendorf's words were still resounding in his ears when he perceived a strange sight in the tent. It is true, that in those times it was nothing surprising, but very few people made such an exhibition of themselves in public, as did the military councillor Pauli that evening. He was lying on the ground in the centre of the tent; beside him there stood a large, empty, big-bellied bottle; his face was crimson; his dress unbuttoned and torn;

while beside him sat a hound, evidently his favourite, licking his face and whining.

Those who stood around were splitting their sides with laughter.

It was no unusual thing for the military councillor Pauli, whose duty it was to be near the King ready to write his letters, to be thus overcome with wine, but never was he so drunk or so much laughed at as on that night.

As soon as Brühl noticed it, he rushed to the unfortunate man and lifted him from the ground. The others, having come to their senses, helped him, and with a great effort they put the councillor on a heap of hay lying in the corner of the tent. Pauli opened his eyes, looked at the surrounding faces, and mumbled:

'Brühl, thank you—I know everything, I understand, I am not drunk— You are a good boy, Brühl, I thank you.'

Then he closed his eyes, sighed and muttered, 'Hard service!' and fell asleep.

The pages of Augustus II had rooms in the King's castle, where they awaited their orders during the time they were on duty. Their horses were always in readiness in case they might be sent on some errand. They relieved each other by turns at the door and attended the King in the antechamber, and often, when no other messenger was at hand, were sent to carry orders and despatches. Brühl always performed this arduous service with great zeal when his turn came, and even willingly took the place of others, so that the King, seeing him frequently, grew accustomed to his face and services.

'Brühl, you are again here,' he would say smiling.

'At your Majesty's command.'

'Are you not tired?'

'My greatest happiness is to look at your Majesty.' And the boy would bow, and the King would clap him on the shoulder.

Never was anything either impossible or too difficult for him; he ran immediately and fulfilled his orders at once.

They were waiting one day for the courier. In those days the post was often late; a horse would die on the road, or a river overflow, or a postillion become sick, and in consequence there was no fixed hour for the arrival of the post. Ever since the morning the military councillor Pauli, who used to write the King's letters, had been waiting for his orders.

Pauli, whom we saw drunk in Hubertsburg, slept during the night, rose in the morning, dressed himself and felt quite well except that he was still very thirsty.

He was aware that nature had provided water for him to drink, but he despised the simple beverage and used to say God created it for geese and not for men. Consequently he quenched his thirst with wine; he felt better and more lively.

He remembered that Brühl had come to his assistance in that awful moment of drunkenness, and from that moment a friendship sprang up between old Pauli and the young page.

Brühl, who did not despise anybody's favour, became attached to the councillor. Pauli was an elderly man, prematurely aged by his intemperate habits: he was very fat and could hardly walk, and, after dinner, would even doze standing up. Pauli's face was red, verging to purple, and his whole body seemed to be swollen.

But when he dressed in his best for the court, when he buttoned up, pulled himself together and assumed his official demeanour, one really could take him for a respectable person. He was so accustomed to the King and the King to him, that from one word, or even a look from Augustus, he could spin out whole letters, guessing the thought, grasping the style, and the King never needed to make any corrections. For this reason he was fond of Pauli, and requisitioned his services continually; for this reason too, he forgave him when he got drunk and was incapacitated from fulfilling his duties.

Then the lackeys were obliged to wake him up and the councillor would open his eyes, and murmur, 'Wait a minute! I am ready!' though he did not rise till he became sober. Then he would rise, wash himself with cold water, drink a big glass of strong wine, and go to the King.

Such things used to happen in those days, not to Pauli alone; the King's friend Fleming used to get drunk and many others too. People merely laughed at a drunken man for having so weak a head.

That day when they were waiting for the courier Pauli was sitting in the marshals' room, yawning. He selected a comfortable chair, stretched his legs, drooped his head a little and fell a-thinking. He could not doze. Who could travel with Morpheus into the country of dreams, not being prepared with good food for the journey?

The pictures that hung in the room were too familiar to his gaze to interest him. He could not look at them, so he yawned again, this time so outrageously that his jaws cracked. It was a heartrending sight to see such a respectable councillor yawn because he had nothing to eat.

The clock struck ten, then eleven, and still Pauli sat yawning and trembling on account of the emptiness of his stomach. At that moment he felt the most miserable of men.

At eleven o'clock Brühl, who was waiting for the hour of his service, entered. He was lovely in his page's dress, worn with great elegance; nobody could rival him in the freshness of the lace on his cuffs, the cut of his dress, and his exquisitely combed wig. As usual, he smiled sweetly. Everyone was conquered by his smiles, his words, and the grace of all his movements. Pauli, catching sight of him, put out his hand without rising.

Brühl ran to him and said:

'How happy I am to see you!' And he bowed humbly.

'Brühl, you alone can save me!' said Pauli. 'Just imagine, I have not yet had my breakfast! When will that courier arrive?'

The page looked at the clock and shrugged his shoulders.

'*Chi lo sa?*' he answered in that language which with French, was then used at court, for Italians were then quite numerous in Dresden.

'Eleven! and I have not had my breakfast! I shall die of starvation!' Having said this, Pauli yawned once more and shivered.

Brühl stood thoughtful, then he whispered in Pauli's ear:

'*Est modus in rebus!* Why do you sit here as though you were on a public road? There is a room with a door opening on the corridor leading to the kitchen; there I could manage to get you served with something.'

The councillor's eyes brightened, and he tried to rise, always a difficulty with him. He was obliged to put both hands on the arms of the chair, and leaning heavily on his elbows, at length succeeded.

'My dear boy,' he exclaimed, 'help me then, if you can.'

Brühl nodded and they disappeared through the door of the next room. Here, as though Pauli had been expected, some enchanted force had prepared a table. There stood a large chair, as if made for him, and on the snow-white table a soup tureen, a covered dish and a large bottle of golden wine.

Pauli, having perceived this, hastened to occupy the chair, as if afraid that someone else might step in before him, seized the napkin and stretched his arm towards the soup tureen; suddenly he remembered Brühl and said:

'And you?'

The page shook his head.

'It's for you, my dear sir.'

'May the gods reward you for this!' exclaimed Pauli enthusiastically. 'May Venus give you the prettiest girl in Dresden; may Hygiea give you a stomach with which you can digest stones; may Bacchus give you everlasting thirst and the means to quench it with Hungarian wine; may—'

But the tempting dishes did not permit him to finish. Brühl stood smiling at the councillor. Pauli poured out the first glass of wine. He expected an ordinary, light Hungarian wine, which they usually served at the court, but when he tasted it, his face brightened, his eyes shone, and having drunk he leaned back in his chair and smiled.

'Divine drink! My dear boy, you are working miracles! Where did you get it from? I know that wine, it's King's Tokay; smell it, taste it—it's ambrosia, nectar!'

'You must show your favour to the bottle, and not leave its contents to the profane, who would drink it without proper appreciation.'

'That would certainly be a profanation,' exclaimed the councillor, pouring out another large glass. 'To your health, to your success. Brühl—I shall be thankful to you till the day of my death—you saved my life. An hour longer and I should have been a dead man; I felt that my life was slipping away.'

'I am very glad,' said Brühl, 'that I have been able to be of service to you, sir. But pray, drink!'

Pauli drank another glass, smacked his lips, and said:

'What a wine! What a wine! Every glass tastes better than the last. It's like a good friend whom the more we know the better we love. But, Brühl, when the post comes, and his Majesty calls me, if it should be necessary for me to write a letter to Berlin or Vienna—'

In the meanwhile he poured out the third glass.

'Such a small bottle for you is nothing; it is only a *stimulans*.'

'Brühl, you are right. I have drunk more than that in my life.' He laughed. 'The worst thing is to mix the drinks. Who knows in what relation they stand to each other? There might meet two bitter foes, for instance, the French with German wine; they begin to fight in the stomach and head, and the man suffers. But when one drinks an honest, intelligent, matured wine, then there is no danger, it does no harm.'

Speaking thus the councillor ate the meat, drank the Tokay and smiled again. Brühl stood, looked, and when the glass was empty, he filled it once more.

At length the food having all disappeared, there remained only the wine.

Pauli sighed and mumbled:

'But the letters!'

'Would you be afraid?'

'You are right, if I were afraid, I should be a coward, and that is a despicable thing. Fill up! To your health! You shall get on! It's brighter in my head! It seems that the sun has come out from beneath the clouds, for everything looks brighter. I feel as if I could write more fluently than ever!'

Brühl filled the glass constantly.

The councillor looked at the bottle, and observing that it was larger at the bottom, promised himself that the wine would last still for some time.

'I have nothing to be afraid of,' said Pauli as though wishing to reassure himself. 'I don't know whether you remember or not. I remember once on a very warm day, when his Majesty was writing to that unfortunate Cosel, I drank some treacherous wine. It tasted as good as this Tokay, but it was treacherous. When I went out into the street my head swam. It was too bad, for I was obliged to write the letters. Two courtiers seized my arms—it seemed to me that I was flying; they put me at the table, they put a pen in my hand the paper before me; the King said a few words and I wrote an excellent letter. But if you killed me I could not remember what I wrote then. Suffice it that the letter was good, and the King, laughing, gave me a magnificent ring as a souvenir of that day.'

The wine was poured from the bottle to the glass, from the glass into the throat. The councillor smiled.

'Hard service,' he said quietly, 'but the wine is excellent.'

During the conversation the bottle was emptied. The last glass was a little clouded; Brühl wished to push it aside.

'Tyrant!' cried the councillor. 'What are you doing? It is the nature of the wine to have dregs, they are not to be wasted, but exist to hide the virtue which is in it,—the elixir, the essence.'

While Pauli was emptying the last glass, Brühl bent forward and took from under the table another bottle. Seeing it, the councillor wished to rise, but the sight rivetted him to his chair.

'What do I see?' he cried.

'It's another volume,' said the page quietly, 'of the work. It contains its conclusion, its quintessence. As you are fond of literature—'

Pauli bent his head.

'Who would not be fond of such literature?' sighed he.

'—I have been trying to get you a complete work,' continued the boy. 'I could not get both volumes of the same edition. The second volume is *editio princips*.'

'Ah!' exclaimed Pauli approaching the glass. 'Pour me only one page of that respectable volume.'

'But it will spoil. You must finish the bottle.'

'That's true! But the letters! The letters!' said Pauli.

'There will be none today.'

'Would that that were true,' Pauli sighed.

Brühl poured out another glass; Pauli drank it.

'This wine the King alone drinks when he doesn't feel well,' whispered Brühl.

'*Panaceum universale!* The lips of a woman are not sweeter.'

'Oh! oh!' exclaimed the youth.

'It is quite different for you,' said the councillor, 'but for me they have lost all sweetness. But the wine! wine is a nectar which, never loses its charm. Were it not for these letters!'

'You are still thinking of them?'

'Well, let the deuce take them.'

The councillor drank, but the wine was beginning to take effect. He grew heavier, he smiled, and then closed his eyes.

'Now a short nap,' said he.

'But you must finish the bottle,' said the page.

'Yes, it is the duty of an honest man to finish that which he began,' said Pauli.

Having poured out the last glass, Brühl brought forward a pipe and tobacco.

'Will you not smoke?' he said.

'You are an angel!' exclaimed Pauli opening his eyes. 'You remembered about that also. But suppose this herb intoxicates me further? What do you say?'

'It will make you sober,' said Brühl handing him the pipe.

'How can I resist such a tempting offer! Come what may, give it to me. Perchance the postillion will break his neck, and will not come. I don't wish him evil, but I would prefer that he stayed away.'

They both laughed. The councillor smoked assiduously.

'Very strong tobacco!'

'The King smokes it,' said the page,

'But he is stronger than I am.'

The tobacco evidently made him more intoxicated for he began to mumble. He smoked for a little while longer, then the pipe slipped from his hand, his head dropped, and he began to snore.

Brühl looked at him, smiled, went quietly to the door, and disappeared behind it. Then he ran straight to the King's ante-room.

A young, well-dressed boy, of lordly mien, also in page's costume, stopped him.

It was the Count Anthony Moszynski. He was distinguished among the other pages of the King, by his pale face, black hair, expressive although not beautiful features, eyes full of fire, but above all by his aristocratic bearing and stiff manners. He was with Sulkowski at the Prince's court, then he passed, to that of Augustus II, who, it was said, liked his liveliness and intelligence, and a brilliant career was prophesied for him.

'Brühl,' said he. 'Where have you been?'

The page hesitated to answer.

'In the marshals' room.'

'It is your hour now.'

'I know it, but I am not too late,' he answered, glancing at the clock.

'I thought,' said Moszynski laughing, 'that I should have to take your place.'

Something like anger flashed across Brühl's face, but it became serene again immediately.

'My dear Count,' said he sweetly, 'you favourites are permitted not to be punctual, but it would be unpardonable in me. I have often acted as a substitute for others, but no one has yet been substituted for me.'

'You wish to imply that no one is able to act as substitute for you,' said Moszynski.

'You are good-humouredly joking at my simplicity. I try to learn that in which you lords are masters.'

Moszynski put out his hand.

'It's dangerous to fight you with words. I would prefer swords.'

Brühl assumed a humble mien.

'I do not think I am superior in anything,' he said quietly.

'Well, I wish you good luck during your service,' said Moszynski. 'Good-bye!'

He left the room.

Brühl breathed more freely. He went slowly to the window, and stood there seemingly looking with indifference into a courtyard paved with stones. Beneath him swarmed a numerous company of busy courtiers. Soldiers in magnificent uniforms, chamberlains in dresses richly embroidered with gold, many lackeys and other servants moved quickly about; several post-chaises stood near the steps and yellow-dressed carriers waited for their masters; further there were carriages with German and Polish harness, hayduks in scarlet, kozaks, all constituting a variegated and picturesque whole. A chamberlain came out from the King.

'The post has not yet come?' he asked Brühl.

'Not yet.'

'As soon as it comes, bring the letters at once. Where is Pauli?'

'In the marshal's room.'

'Very well, he must wait.'

Brühl bowed and returned to the window, looking through it impatiently until he perceived, galloping in on a foaming horse, a postillion with a trumpet slung across his shoulder, and a leathern bag on his chest.

The page flew downstairs as fast as he could, and before the servants had noticed the postillion, he seized hold of the letters. A silver tray was in readiness in the ante-room; Brühl placed the letters on it, and entered the King's apartment.

Augustus was walking to and fro with the Count Hoym. Seeing the page, tray, and letters, he put out his hand and took the letters and broke the seals.

Brühl waited, while the King and Hoym read the letters.

'Ah!' exclaimed Augustus. 'Be quick, and call Pauli.'

Brühl did not move.

'Go and call Pauli to me,' repeated the King impatiently.

The page bowed, rushed out of the room and looked into the marshal's room. Pauli was sleeping like a log. Brühl returned to the King.

'Your Majesty!' stammered Brühl. 'Councillor Pauli—'

'Is he here?'

'Yes, your Majesty.'

'Then why doesn't he come?'

'The councillor,' said the page, dropping his eyes, 'is not well.'

'Were he dying, you must bring him here,' cried the King. 'Let him fulfil his duties, then he can die if he wishes to do so.'

Brühl ran out again, and entering the room, looked at the sleeping man, then returned to the King. Augustus' eyes burned with increasing anger, he began to grow pale, which was the worst sign; when he became white people trembled.

Brühl stopped at the door, silent.

'Pauli!' cried the King, rapping the floor with his foot.

'The councillor is—'

'Drunk?' Augustus guessed. 'Ah, the dirty old pig! Why could he not abstain for these few hours? Pour water on him! Conduct him to the fountain! Let the doctor give him some medicine and make him sober if but for one hour. Then the beast might die!'

Brühl promptly obeyed. He tried to wake up the councillor, but he was lying like a log; the only doctor who could bring him to his senses was time. Brühl, coming back slowly, seemed to hesitate, as though pondering something in his mind. He entered the King's room as noiselessly as he could.

The King stood in the centre holding the papers in his hand; his brows were contracted.

'Pauli!'

'It is impossible to awaken him.'

'I wish he would die! But the letters! Who will write them? Do you hear?'

'Your Majesty,' said Brühl humbly, 'my daring is great, almost criminal, but my love for your Majesty must be my excuse. One word from your Majesty—a small indication—and I will try to write the letters—'

'You, youngster?'

Brühl blushed.

'Your Majesty shall punish me—'

Augustus looked at him penetratingly.

'Come,' said he going to the window. 'There is the letter; read it, and give a negative answer, but you must hint that the answer is not definite. Let them think that there is some hope, but do not actually show it. Do you understand?'

Brühl bowed and wished to go out with the letter.

'Where are you going?' cried the King. 'Sit at this table and write at once.'

The page bowed again and sat on the edge of the chair which was upholstered in silk; he turned up his lace cuffs, bent over the paper and wrote with a rapidity that astonished the King.

Augustus II looked attentively, as though at a curious phenomenon, at the good-looking boy, who assumed the gravity of a chancellor and wrote the diplomatic letter as easily as he would have written a love-letter.

One might have thought, that the page, in accomplishing a task so important to his future, had forgotten about his pose.

Apparently he sat negligently and thoughtlessly, but the fact was, that as he bent gracefully to his work, the position of his legs, arms and head, was all carefully studied. His composure did not leave him for a moment though the work was apparently done in feverish haste. The King watched him closely and seemed to guess his intention. The page without thinking or losing time, wrote as if by dictation, he did not erase a single word, he did not stop for a moment. The pen stopped only when the letter was finished. Then he read it through and rose.

The King evidently curious and wishing to be indulgent came nearer.

'Read!' said he.

Brühl's voice trembled and was faint. Who would have thought that that fear was simulated? The King encouraging the boy, said kindly:

'Slowly, distinctly, aloud!'

The young page then began to read and his voice, which was at first faint, became sonorous. The face of Augustus depicted by turn surprise, joy, hilarity, and bewilderment.

When Brühl finished he did not dare to raise his eyes.

'Once more from the beginning,' said the King.

This time Brühl read more distinctly and more boldly.

The King's face became radiant; he clapped his hands.

'Excellent!' cried he. 'Pauli could not do better, not even so well. Copy it.'

Brühl bowing humbly presented the letter to the King, which was so well written that it was not necessary to copy it.

Augustus clapped him on the shoulder.

'From today, you are my secretary. I will have no more to do with Pauli; may the deuce take him! Let him drink and die!'

The King rang the bell, a chamberlain entered.

'Count,' said Augustus, 'give orders that Pauli is to be carried home; when he becomes sober express to him my great displeasure. I never wish to see him again! Brühl is my secretary from today. Discharge him from his duties as a page.'

The chamberlain smiled at the boy standing modestly aside.

'He saved me from a great trouble,' said the King. 'I know Pauli, he will be drunk till tomorrow, and it was necessary to send the letter at once.'

The King went to the table to sign the letter.

'Make a copy of it,' said he.

'I will copy it from memory,' said Brühl quietly.

'What a keen secretary I have now!' exclaimed Augustus. 'Pray give orders that he is to be paid the three hundred thalers.'

When Brühl approached to thank him, the King put out his hand to be kissed, an especial sign of favour.

A moment later a courier, having taken the sealed letter, conveyed it away at a gallop, blowing his trumpet. Brühl slipped out into the ante-room. Here the story of the letter and his unexpected promotion, told by the chamberlain Frisen, aroused curiosity and envy. When Brühl appeared all eyes turned to him, but in the new favourite of the King, one could see no trace of pride—on the contrary, he was as humble as if he were ashamed of his deed.

Moszynski rushed to him.

'What do I hear?' he exclaimed. 'Brühl his Majesty's *amanuensis*? When? How?'

'Let me come to myself from fear and astonishment,' said Brühl quietly. 'I do not know how it happened. Providence watched over me, *un pauvre cadet de famille*. My love for the King worked a miracle. I am dazed.'

Moszynski looked at him.

'If your good luck continues, you will soon be ahead of us all. We must recommend ourselves to your favour.'

'Count, be merciful, and do not mock a poor boy like me.'

Saying this, Brühl, as if he were tired, wiped the perspiration from his forehead and sat on the nearest chair.

'One would think,' said Moszynski, 'that he had met with the greatest misfortune.'

This was lost on Brühl, for he was deep in thought. All in the room dropped their voices to a whisper as they told the story of the lucky boy to those who came in. The news spread in the town and when in the evening Brühl appeared in the theatre among the pages, Sulkowski, who attended the Prince, came to congratulate him.

Brühl seemed to be very grateful and could not find words to thank him for his kindness.

'Do you see, Brühl,' whispered Sulkowski, looking upon him protectingly, 'I told you that they would appreciate you at your right value. I was not mistaken in thinking that our lord's eagle eye had singled you out in the crowd.'

They applauded the singer; Sulkowski also clapped his hands, but turning to his friend he said:

'I applaud you.'

The page bowed humbly, blushing.

After the end of the play he had a chance of disappearing, and the friends who looked for him in the castle and in his rooms could not find him. They thought it was his modesty; it was nice of him not to boast of his good fortune. On enquiry his servant told them that he had gone out.

The fact was, that after the opera Brühl stole into the Castle street and from it he went towards Taschenberg, where Cosel formerly lived, and which was now occupied by a daughter of the Emperor of Austria, Josepha.

Those who met him might have suspected that he was going to deposit his laurels at the feet of some goddess. It was very probable. He was twenty years of age, he was very good-looking, and the women, spoiled by Augustus, were very coquettish. It was evident that he was anxious not to be seen or recognised, for his face was wrapped in his mantle and every time he heard steps he hastened his own.

He entered the house next to the princess's palace, ran up the stairs, and knocked three times at the door.

There was no answer. Having waited a little while, he knocked again in the same way.

Slow steps were heard within, the door opened a little, and the head of an old man appeared. Brühl slipped in quickly.

The room into which he entered, lighted by one candle held by the servant standing at the door, was full of bookshelves and somewhat gloomy. The old servant, questioned in whispers, pointed to the door in lieu of an answer. Brühl threw off his cloak and going on tip-toe approached the door at which he knocked softly.

'Favorisca!'

The large room into which the page now entered was lighted by two candles under green shades. There were several tables loaded with books, between two windows there was a large crucifix, on the sofa a guitar was lying.

At the table leaning on one hand, stood an elderly, slightly bent man: his face was yellowish, bony; he wore a long beard; his eyes were black. By his features it was easy to recognise an Italian. There was something enigmatical about his thin, pale lips, but the whole face was rather jovial than mysterious. There was something ironical as well as kindly in it. A large hooked nose almost covered his lower lip.

On his closely-shaven hair he wore a black silk cap; his dress was long and dark; it indicated a priest.

He welcomed Brühl with outstretched arms.

'Ah! it's you, my dear boy! How glad I am to see you.'

The youth bent humbly and kissed his hand.

The host seated himself on the sofa, at the same time pointing to a chair for Brühl, who sat down, still holding his hat.

'Ecco! Ecco!' whispered the old man. 'You think you bring me news, but I already know about it. I am truly delighted. You see Providence rewards, God helps those who worship Him.'

'I am thankful to Him,' said Brühl quietly.

'Remain faithful to the creed to which you have opened your heart, and you shall see.' He raised his hand. 'You shall go far, far. I am telling you that. I am poor and humble, but I am the Lord's servant.'

He looked at the humble page, and having accomplished his pious duty, added joyfully:

'Have you been to the opera? How did Celesta sing? Did the King look at her? Was the Prince there?'

Padre Guarini was the name of the man to whom Brühl paid this visit; he was the Prince's confessor, confidant of the Princess, spiritual father of the young count, but he seemed to care as much about the opera as about the conversion of the young man sitting before him.

He asked about the tenor, the orchestra, the audience, and at length if the page went behind the stage.

'I?' asked Brühl with astonishment.

'I should think no worse of you for that, if for the sake of music, of art, you wished to see how those angels look as common mortals, divested of the glitter and sparkle of the stage. Celesta sang like an angel but she is ugly as a devil. There is no danger that the King will fall in love with her.'

And Padre Guarini laughed.

'And who rules over the King?' asked he. And without waiting for an answer, he said: 'It seems that, just as in Poland, the election is coming.'

He laughed again.

'But tell me something new; besides that you have become the King's secretary.'

'I have nothing to say, except that nothing can change my heart.'

'Yes, yes, I advise you to be a good Catholic, although secretly. We can't expect from the present King much zeal for the faith. We must be satisfied with him as he is, but his successor will be different; our pious lady Josepha will not permit him to leave the path of truth. The Prince is pious, a faithful husband, a zealous Catholic. When he becomes ruler we shall be mighty. Let us be patient and we will manage the Protestants. *Chi va 'piano, va sano—qui va sano, va lontano!'* He repeated the word *lontano* several times and sighed.

'As a souvenir of this fortunate day,' added he, 'I must bless you; it will bring you good luck. Wait.'

Padre Guarini pulled out a drawer and took from it a black rosary on which were a cross and medallion.

'The Holy Father blessed it; to the one who recites it every day, pardon is granted.'

Brühl murmured something indistinctly by way of thanks, kissed his hand and rose.

Padre Guarini bent over and whispered something in his ear. The page, having nodded in the affirmative, kissed his hand again and went out. The old servant awaited him at the door with a candle. Brühl gave him a thaler, wrapped himself in his mantle and descended the stairs. On reaching the door he looked cautiously down the street, and seeing no one pressed forward. Then he stopped, seeming in doubt as to where to go. He put the rosary which he was holding in his hand in a side pocket, and looked for a familiar house near St Sophia Church.

He glanced round once more. The door was opened. A little oil lamp gave a pale light. The spacious Gothic hall was quiet and solitary. Brühl rang the bell on the first floor. A female servant came and opened it.

'Is the minister at home?' he asked.

'Yes, sir, but he is engaged with visitors.'

'Visitors?' repeated Brühl, hesitating as to what to do. 'Who is there?'

'Some pious young men from Leipzig.'

Brühl was still hesitating, when a dignified middle-aged man appeared in the doorway and conducted him to a further apartment.

'I do not wish to intrude,' said the page, bowing.

'You never intrude,' said the host coolly and distinctly. 'The people will not crowd my house any more now. Pray, come in. In a Protestant country one enters a clergyman's house secretly, as the first Christians did into the catacombs. Glory to those who pass our threshold.'

So saying he entered with Brühl into a large, modestly furnished room. Here were two young men, and it seemed to Brühl that he knew the taller of the two. He could not however remember where he had seen him. The tall man also looked attentively at Brühl, and approaching him, said:

'If I am not mistaken, this is the second time we have met. I am indebted to your kindness that I did not fall into the hands of the King's servants and was not treated as a vagabond.'

'Count Zinzendorf—'

'Brother in Christ,' answered the youth, 'and were you Catholic, Aryan, Wicklyffite or of any denomination, I should always greet you as a brother in Christ.'

The host, whose face was severe and to whom bushy, contracted eyebrows gave a still more gloomy expression groaned.

'Count, let your dreams alone; the chaff must be separated from the grain, although they both grow on one stem.'

Brühl was silent.

'What news from the court?' asked the host. 'There does not seem to be any change; prayers in the morning, opera in the evening. But pray be seated.'

They all sat. Zinzendorf looked at Brühl piercingly, as though wishing to penetrate into his soul, but those windows, Brühl's beautiful eyes, through which he hoped to look within him, avoided meeting his.

'Is it true that they are going to build a Catholic church?' asked the host.

'I don't know anything definite about it,' answered Brühl.

'It would be scandalous!' the minister moaned.

'Why?' interrupted Zinzendorf. 'We complain that they are not tolerant; should we then retaliate? The glory of Christ may be sung in many ways. Why not by Catholics as well as by us?'

Brühl nodded in the affirmative, but as he did so he encountered a severe glance from the host; so he stopped the gesture, and changed his expression into a double-faced smile.

'Count,' said the minister, 'those are the ideas of youth, beautiful in your mouth, but impossible in life. As one cannot sit on two chairs, so one cannot confess two religions, for in that case, like some people in very high positions, we have no religion.'

The minister sighed; they all understood to whom he was alluding. Brühl pretended not to hear; perchance he was sorry he had fallen among these men, discussing such delicate questions. Zinzendorf, on the contrary, seemed to be perfectly happy.

'But how can we spread the truth and convert the people if we mix not with those of other creeds? Christ mixed with Pharisees and heathens and converted them by His kindness.'

'You are young, and you dream,' sighed the minister, 'but when you will be called upon to fight, and to change your dreams into action—'

'That's what I desire!' the young enthusiast cried, lifting his hands. 'Did I only love myself, I would go into the desert to seek for Christ in contemplation; but I love my fellow-man, everybody, even those who are in error; that is why I shall act and try to realise my dreams, as you put it.'

The minister, Brühl, and the other young man, each listened with quite different feelings. The first stood gloomy and irritated, the second was embarrassed although he smiled, and the other was filled with admiration for each of his friend's words.

'I think that your zeal,' said the minister, 'would diminish at court.'

'Shall we have the pleasure of seeing you at the court?' Brühl asked quietly.

'Never!' exclaimed Zinzendorf. 'I, at court? There is no power that could bring me there. My court is where there are poor people, my future is to apply Christ's teaching to my life. I go to preach Christ's love. At court I should be sneered at.—I shall search for another field in order to accomplish that whereunto I am called.'

'But your family, Count?' said the minister.

'My father is in heaven,' answered Zinzendorf. 'To Him alone I owe obedience.'

Brühl came to the conclusion that he had nothing to do there. Zinzendorf frightened him by his extraordinary speech. He took the minister aside, whispered with him for a moment, and took his leave. He bowed from afar in true courtly manner to the apostle and went out. It would be difficult to say whether he was more sincere with the Jesuit or with the minister, but the fact remains that although he visited both, he flattered Padre Guarini more than the Rev. Knofl.

In the street Brühl again hesitated. The Prince's palace was not far distant. Two guards were at the door. The young page went into the courtyard and ran to the left wing. The open door and the light in the window tempted him to try his luck at the court also. Here lived the Countess Kolowrath, lady in waiting to the princess, her favourite, a much respected and middle-aged lady; she was fond of the young page, who would bring her all the gossip of the court.

He could enter her apartments at any hour of the day, and took advantage of that privilege very freely, but in such, a way as not to be seen by the people, or to give them a chance to know about his intimacy with the Countess.

In the ante-room a lackey, in the court livery, opened the door and showed in the page. Brühl entered on tip-toe. The drawing-room was lighted with a few wax candles. To the right, through the half-opened door a stream of bright light was seen, and at the noise of Brühl's shoes on the shining parquetry floor, a child's head appeared.

Brühl stepped softly forward.

'Ah! it's you. Monsieur Henry,' said a fresh voice. 'Wait a moment.'

The head disappeared, but soon the door opened wide and an eight year old girl came to it. She wore a satin dress ornamented with lace, silk *à jour* stockings, shoes with high heels; her hair was curled and powdered, and she looked more like a doll than a child. She smiled to Brühl, curtseyed to him, as it was customary in the court and as she was taught by her *maître de ballet*, Monsieur Favier. She had the comically serious mien of those china figures made in Meissen.

Brühl bowed to her as he would have done to an elderly lady. The child looked seriously at him with a pair of big black eyes, but all at once her seriousness forsook her and she burst into laughter. The comedy was over.

'How do you do, Henry?'

'And how is her Excellency?'

'Her Excellency, my mother, prays with the Princess. Padre Guarini recites a litany, and I am bored. Listen, Brühl, let us play at court; I shall be the queen and you the great chamberlain.'

'I would do it willingly, my dear Frances,' but I must return to the King's service before playing.'

'You are not polite towards the ladies!' answered the little Countess with the air of an old lady, which made her very amusing.

'I will not love you, and should you ever fall in love with me—'

'Ah! yes, it will be soon,' said Brühl laughing.

'Then you will see how cruel I shall be,' added Frances.

Saying this she almost turned her back on Brühl, took a fan from a chair, inclined her head backwards, pouted her lips and looked at Brühl with contempt. In the eyes of that girl there was already reflected the frivolity of the times.

Brühl stood enchanted and the scene would perhaps have lasted much longer had it not been interrupted by the rustling of a silk gown and then by laughter.

'Francesca! Brühl, you are courting my daughter.'

The lady who said these words, was tall, majestic, still very beautiful, and above all had an aristocratic bearing. She was Frances's mother. Frances did not become confused, she repeated her curtsey and then ran to her. Brühl bowed humbly and then looked with ecstasy into the Countess's black eyes.

She was no longer young but her features were still very beautiful. The whiteness of her complexion was enhanced by black hair, that night innocent of powder, but carefully dressed. Her figure, notwithstanding its ample form, was still graceful. She looked at the page with half-closed eyes.

'Frances,' said she, 'go to Fraülein Braun; I must have some conversation with Henry.'

The girl looked roguishly at her mother and disappeared through the door. The Countess, rapidly moving her fan, walked to and fro in the room, then bending towards Brühl, spoke confidentially.

Brühl followed her respectfully, although sometimes he approached perchance too near.

Even the pictures on the walls heard not that conversation, and half an hour later the page was sitting in the King's ante-room, apparently dozing.

Ten years have passed since that prologue to Brühl's life, since that first scene in a long drama. Brühl was still that brilliant, affable, charming young man, whose fascination even his foes could not resist.

In the magnificent court of the Louis XIV of the North, whom the flatterer called Apollo-Hercules, the people and favourites were changed. A few days after that on which Brühl succeeded to Pauli's office, Augustus II's favourite became his aide-de-camp.

When old Fleming died, Brühl was placed in charge of the King's secret archives. Humble and exceedingly polite, Brühl succeeded in overthrowing two ministers: Fleming and Manteufel. Soon he was created a chamberlain, and promoted to wear a key, as badge of office; the key to the king's heart and exchequer he had already possessed for some time; at length he became a grand chamberlain and was given a new appointment created specially for him, that of *grand maitre de la garde-robe*. To this office belonged the care of the libraries, art galleries and other collections of Augustus II, who could do nothing without Brühl. Many others could not do without him either, and he, as if needing everyone himself, as if afraid of everyone, bowed, smiled, and respected even the door keeper of the castle.

King Augustus the Strong had changed a great deal since the days when he could drink so much. He still preserved the stature of Hercules but no longer possessed his strength. No more could he dig his spurs into his horse's flanks or saw his head off. Carefully dressed and smiling he would walk with a stick, and if he lingered for a longer time than usual to chat with a lady he would look round for a chair, for he felt pain in the toe, which the surgeon Weiss cut off, risking his head, but saving the King's life. The surgeon's head still existed, but the toe did not, and thus the King could not stand for long at a time. It was a glorious memory that tournament in which Augustus conquered the heart of Princess Lubonirski. The King's loves were scattered throughout the world. Even the last, Orzelska, now the Princess Holstein Beck, was a respectable mother of a family, for in the year 1732, during the carnival, she gave birth to the future head of the princely house.

The King would have felt lonely had not the Italian nightingale, Faustina Bordoni, brightened his gloomy thoughts by her lovely voice. The singer was married to the famous composer of those times, Hasse, whom however they sent to Italy, in order to give him a chance to cultivate his art and that he might not disturb his wife. Hasse composed masterpieces inspired by the yearning of his heart.

That year the carnival promised to be brilliant, but there was a lack of money, which the King could not bear: Brühl, who could manage everything, was the only man who could assure tranquillity to the King's mind. Therefore, during the carnival the King entrusted the modest Brühl with the portfolio of the minister of finance.

In vain the modest young official tried to excuse himself from such an honour, but King Augustus II would brook no refusal, would listen to no excuses, and commanded him to provide him with money. From that moment it was Brühl's duty to make the Pactolus flow continually with gold, although it would be mixed with blood and tears.

Brühl was no longer a humble page, but a man with whom the most influential dignitaries were obliged to reckon. The King would permit no word against him, and would frown threateningly if any were ventured. In him alone he found that for which he had formerly looked in ten other men. Brühl knew all about pictures, he was fond of music, he understood how to get money from those who were moneyless, how to be blind when occasion demanded, how to be dumb when it was prudent; he was always obedient.

Through the King's munificence he was then given a house near the castle, and he soon turned it into a palace.

The evening before Shrove-Tuesday the newly created minister was sitting in his palace; he was thoughtful, and seemed to be awaiting the arrival of someone.

The room in which he sat might have been the boudoir of the most fastidious woman spoiled by the luxury of the court. In gilded frames shone mirrors; the walls were covered with lilac-coloured silk; on the mantle-pieces, tables, consols, there was a perfect museum of china and bronzes; the floor was covered with a soft carpet.

Brühl, with his legs stretched out, lying back in the recesses of a comfortable arm chair, his hand shining with splendid rings, seemed to be absorbed in thought and perplexities. From time to time, at the sound of an opening door, he would listen, but when nobody came, he returned to his thoughts and calculations.

Sometimes he would glance at the clock standing on the mantle-piece, for a man burdened with so many duties was obliged to count his time as he counted the money.

Notwithstanding work and emotions, his youthful face had not lost its freshness, his eyes shone brilliantly as ever; one felt that he was a man reserved for the future, who had more hopes than reminiscences.

At the further end of the house doors could be heard opening one after another. Brühl listened—steps approached. The steps were those of a man, though cautious and soft; the tread of one person.

'It's he,' whispered Brühl, and rose from the chair.

The knock at the door was gentle and full of respect, as though the fingers that rapped were swathed in cotton wool.

'Enter!' said Brühl softly, and the door opened noiselessly. At the door stood a man, such as one could only find at the court, for they are born for the court; though cradled in a stable, their coffin would certainly be found in a palace. He was tall, strong and flexible in every movement as a juggler.

At the first glance one could read nothing in the man's face, for its features were insignificant, neither ugly nor comely, the expression was cold and vulgar. Clean-shaven, his lips closed so tightly that one could hardly see them, the new-comer stood humbly at the door and waited to be questioned.

His dress did not betray to what class he belonged. It was neither elegant nor striking. The coat he wore was grey with steel buttons; the rest was black; at his side hung a sword with dark enamelled hilt; on his head he had a wig, which was rather official and dignified than coquettish. Under his arm he held a black hat, innocent of galoons; and he had no lace round his sleeves. Brühl on seeing the man, rose quickly as though moved by a spring, and walked across the room.

'Hans,' said he, 'we have but half an hour. I sent for you about an unfortunate affair. Open the door and see that there is no one in the ante-room.'

The obedient Hans Henniche quickly opened the door, looked through it, and signed that there was no one.

'You know,' said Brühl, 'that his Majesty was kind enough to appoint me Secretary of the Treasury.'

'I wanted to congratulate your Excellency,' said Henniche with a bow.

'Don't trouble yourself,' said Brühl with the well-assumed mien of an embarrassed man. 'It's a new burden on my feeble shoulders.'

'Your Excellency is too modest,' said Henniche with a new bow.

'Hans,' said Brühl, 'do you wish to help me, to be my right hand? Will you swear to be faithful and obedient to me? Do you wish to go with me, even if we have to break our necks?'

'But you and I can't break our necks,' said Henniche, smiling cynically.

'Stronger people than we have done so before now.'

'Yes, but they were not so cunning as we are! Strength means nothing, if one does not know how to use it. I guarantee you that we shall succeed, provided I can do what I please.'

'Remember only,' Brühl said coolly, 'that these are not trifling words, but a solemn oath.'

Henniche raised his hand and said ironically:

'I swear—but on what, my lord and master?'

'On God!' said Brühl, bending his head piously. 'Henniche, you know that I am a religious man, you mustn't joke.'

'Your Excellency, I never joke. Joking is a very costly thing, and many people pay for it with their lives.'

'If you help me,' added Brühl, 'I promise to make you rich, powerful, important.'

'Before all, the first,' said Henniche, 'for riches mean everything.'

'You forget the one who although rich went to Königstein.'

'Do you know why?'

'Lord's disgrace. God's disgrace.'

'No, it's trifling with the sleeper,' said Henniche. 'An intelligent man ought to put a sleeper on the altar and pray to it: the women do everything.'

'But they fall also: Cosel is in Stolpen.'

'And who overthrew Cosel?' asked Henniche. 'If you look through a glass you will see the white fingers of the Countess Denhoff and a small sleeper, under which the great King was held.'

Brühl sighed but made no remark.

'Your Excellency entered on a new life yesterday, and ought to remember one word: woman.'

'I remember it,' Brühl said gloomily, 'but we don't have time to talk about it. Then you are with me?'

'For life or death,' answered Henniche. 'I am a man of no importance but great experience; and believe me that my wisdom is quite equal to those who bear silver trays to drawing-rooms. I need make no secret to you that for a long time I served as a lackey and used to open the door. But before that they opened to me. My first experience was in Lützen as a revenue officer.'

'That is why I need you. The King needs money and the country is already overtaxed. The people groan and complain.'

'Who would listen to them?' answered Henniche indifferently. 'They will never be satisfied, they will always complain. One must squeeze them as one squeezes a lemon for the juice.'

'But how?'

'We shall find the means.'

'They will complain.'

'To whom?' said Henniche laughing. 'Can we not close the road with bars, and send those who are too noisy to Königstein, or Sonnenstein, or Plissenburg, for the sake of the King's tranquillity?'

'Yes, that's true,' said Brühl thoughtfully, 'but it won't bring any money.'

'On the contrary, we must be severe, if we wish to obtain it.'

Brühl listened attentively.

'We need a great deal of money; the carnival will be costly.'

'Yes, and all that is spent at court does not sink into the ground, it returns to the people, therefore they can pay. We need money for the King and for ourselves.'

Brühl smiled and said:

'Naturally, we cannot toil for nothing.'

'And endure so many curses.'

'Well, when it is a matter of duty, one cannot pay attention to cursing. The King must have that which he needs.'

'And we, what is due to us,' Henniche added.

Brühl stepped before him and said after careful thought:—

'Then keep your eyes and ears open; inform me about everything, work for me and for yourself; I have already so much to do, that I can undertake no more without you.'

'Rely on me,' said Henniche. 'I quite understand, that while working for you, I work for myself. I don't promise you Platonic love; for thus if I mistake not, they call kissing the gloves, having no respect for the hands. One must clearly define the business. I shall remember my own interests; you and I will not forget the King.'

He bowed. Brühl clapped him on the shoulder.

'Henniche, I shall help you to rise.'

'Provided it's not too high, and not in the new market square,' whispered Henniche.

'You may be easy about that. And now, what would you advise me to do in order that I may not lose my footing at the court? It is easy to mount the ladder, but the question is not to break one's neck.'

'I have only one piece of advice,' said the former lackey, 'everything is done by the women.'

'Oh! Oh!' said Brühl,' there are other means too.'

'Yes, I know that your Excellency has Padre Guarini on his side.'

'Silence, Henniche!'

'I am already silent, but I must add all the same, that your Excellency must bear in mind the power of women, it will do no harm to have two strings to one's bow.'

Brühl sighed.

'I shall remember your advice.'

They were both silent for a few moments.

'How does your Excellency stand with the Count Sulkowski?' whispered Henniche. 'One must not forget that the sun sets, that the people are mortal, that the sons succeed the fathers, and Sulkowski the Brühls.'

'Oh!' said Brühl, 'he is my friend.'

'I would prefer that his wife was your Excellency's friend,' said Henniche. 'I put more faith in her.'

'Sulkowski has a noble heart.'

'I don't deny it, but the best heart prefers the chest in which it beats. And how about the Count Moszynski?'

Brühl shivered and blushed: looked at Henniche sharply, as though he would learn whether he mentioned the name with any design. But Henniche's face was placid and indifferent.

'The Count Moszynski is of no importance whatever,' hissed Brühl, 'and he never shall be of any importance.'

'His Majesty gave him his own daughter,' said Henniche slowly.

Brühl was silent.

'The people have evil tongues,' continued Henniche. 'They say that Fräulein Cosel would have preferred to marry someone else than Moszynski.'

'Yes,' cried Brühl passionately. 'He has stolen her from me.'

'Then he has done your Excellency a great favour,' said Henniche laughing, 'instead of one tool, you can have two.'

They looked into each other's eyes. Brühl was gloomy.

'Enough of it,' said he. 'Remember that you are mine and count on me. Your office will be here; tomorrow I shall send you an official appointment.'

Henniche bowed.

'And salary corresponding with my official position.'

'Yes, if you find the means to pay it with.'

'That is my business.'

'It is late; good-night.'

Henniche bowed and went out as quietly, as he came.

Brühl rang the bell; a lackey promptly attended.

'I must be in the castle in half-an-hour: my post-chaise!'

'It is ready.'

'Domino, masque?'

'Everything is ready,' and having said this the lackey opened the door and conducted Brühl to a large dressing-room.

Brühl's dressing-room was already considered one of the sights of the capital. Round it were large wardrobes of carved oak; between two windows stood a table and on it a large mirror in a china frame composed of cupids and flowers. Round the table, winter and summer, there were always a profusion of roses and lilies of the valley. And on the table were disposed such an array of toilet articles as might have belonged to a woman. The wardrobes contained dresses with shoes, swords, hats, and watches to match each, for the fashion demanded that everything should be in harmony.

For that evening the most important detail was the domino and not the dress. In a special wardrobe was everything necessary for fancy balls. Brühl was not quite decided in his choice of a dress. It was a very important matter, for the King was fond of difficulty in recognising his guests; and perchance Brühl did not wish to be recognised at all.

The lackey, walking after him with a candelabra, waited for the order.

'Where is that dress of a Venetian noble?' asked Brühl turning to the lackey.

The servant ran to a wardrobe standing in a corner and handed him the dress.

Brühl began to dress hastily. The dress was becoming to him; everything was black, even the sword. The only shining ornament was a heavy gold chain on which hung a medallion on which was the figure of Augustus the Strong. Brühl looked at himself in the mirror and put on a mask. In order not to be easily recognised he glued to his chin a little Spanish beard.

He changed the rings on his fingers and went downstairs.

At the door the post-chaise was in readiness.

The two carriers wore red woollen caps, short dark brown cloaks and masks. The moment Brühl entered the carriage and drew the green curtain he was driven to the castle.

In the principal gate the guards, gorgeously dressed, permitted only the lords' carriages and post-chaises to pass, thrusting back the curious crowd with halberds.

The court was already crowded with equipages, post-chaises and servants. The castle was profusely lighted: that day two courts were united, those of the King and the Prince.

Within the castle there were already numerous guests, all in fancy dress. Brühl's post-chaise stopped at the door and a Venetian nobleman stepped out gravely. Just as he was about to mount the stairs, there appeared another Italian but quite differently dressed. He was tall, strong, stiff, with a soldierly bearing, and was dressed like a bandit taken from Salvator Rosa's picture. The costume was very becoming to him. His head was covered with a light, iron helmet, on his chest he wore armour ornamented with gold, over his shoulder was thrown a short cloak, at his side he had a sword, and at his belt a dagger. His face was covered with a frightful mask, with long moustachios and a small beard.

Brühl glanced at the unpleasant mask and walked upstairs, but the bandit followed him.

'*Signore!*' he hissed, '*come sta?*'

Brühl merely nodded. The bandit came close to him, bent over him and whispered evidently something disagreeable in his ear, for Brühl drew aside impatiently. The bandit laughed and said:

'*A rivederci, carissimo, a rivederci!*' and continued to follow him.

One could already hear the music. When they both reached the rooms,

Brühl disappeared in the crowd. The rich, resplendent dresses of the women, were shining with precious stones. Everybody moved about, laughed, muttered, exclaimed, came and went.

In magnificent Polish dresses, their swords ornamented with precious stones, walked several senators who were easily recognised, for they wore only a small black strip over their eyes, in obedience to the King's order, that everyone should wear a mask. There were many Turks and Spaniards; several monks, women disguised as bats, many mythological goddesses and Venetians were to be distinguished among clowns, harlequins, and cupids with bows and arrows. There were also Queen Elizabeth, Mary Stuart, Henry IV, and many others.

The King, leaning on a gold-headed stick, walked slowly, talked to the women, and tried to recognise them. It was not difficult for him, he knew them all, at least those who were worthy to be known.

In one of the King's rooms were beautiful ladies sitting in the booths distributing refreshments. Beyond the King's apartments, the Princess Josepha and her court received the distinguished guests. Among her ladies in waiting the most brilliant was Frances Kolowrath, the same who, when but eight years of age, could so well play the rôle of a lady of the court. Now she was a beautiful young lady, coquettish, lively, proud, and covered with diamonds.

The Princess Josepha did not participate much in such amusements; she was there only to please her father-in-law and her husband. Her proud mien, severe and not beautiful face, cold manners, did not attract the people. Everybody knew she was not fond of amusements, that she preferred family life, prayers and gossip. Severe with herself she was the same with others, and looked sharply at those around her. Her surroundings were stiff and cold. Nobody dared to joke for fear of the lady's disapproval of any outburst of levity. Even during the fancy dress ball, Josepha did not forget that she was the daughter of an emperor.

Polite, affable, silent, the Prince Frederick stood beside her; he was good-looking but also cold and stiff like a statue. He was pleased that others enjoyed themselves, but took no part in the entertainment. One could see, that notwithstanding his youth, he was both physically and spiritually heavy, especially spiritually.

Splendidly dressed and lordly-looking, Sulkowski, the acknowledged favourite of the Prince, stood behind him, ready to carry out his orders. The Prince would often turn to him, ask some question and having received the answer, nod his head in sign of satisfaction.

On seeing them together, one could easily guess their relation to each other. The servant was much more lord than the lord himself, who merely represented his office but did not feel it. Sulkowski on the contrary assumed great airs and looked proudly on the people around him.

He was also better looking than the Prince, who notwithstanding his youthful age and good health looked like a common German.

Round Augustus the Strong's table a more joyful company was gathered. Bare-shouldered women tried to attract the attention of the King, who looked on their charms with indifference.

Brühl entered, as it seemed to him, without being noticed; he did not speak and seemed to be looking for someone. As he passed through the refreshment rooms he did not notice that the bandit was following him. His beautiful figure attracted the women and several of them tried to stop him, but he looked at them indifferently, and passed on. One or two tried to intrigue him but laughing he whispered their names and they let him alone.

The King looked at him and said to Frisen:

'If a Prussian prince were here, he would steal that man for his guard. Who is he?'

No one could answer the question for certain. The bandit disappeared behind the columns.

In the meantime Brühl was stopped by a gipsy. She was old, tall, leaning on a stick, and covered with a long silk cloak. Through the small mask could be seen the yellowish wrinkled face of the woman. She put out her hand and paling asked him to give her his that she might tell his fortune.

Brühl had no wish to look into the future and wanted to pass the gipsy, but she insisted.

'Non abiate paura!' whispered she. 'I will tell you of good fortune.'

Brühl put out his hand. The gipsy lifted it and having examined it, shook her head.

'A splendid future!' she said. 'You will be marvellously successful, but I cannot promise you much happiness.'

'How can that be,' said Brühl, 'to have success and not be happy?'

'For one can be happy but not successful,' exclaimed the old woman. 'And would you know the reason that you will lack happiness,—you have no heart.'

Brühl smiled ironically.

'You don't love anybody,' continued the woman.

'What more?' he asked.

'You are ungrateful,' she whispered, 'you are blind, you are only pursuing greatness.'

'I see,' said Brühl, 'that you take me for somebody else.'

The woman wrote on his palm; Brühl withdrew his hand, mixed quickly with the crowd and disappeared. Perchance he preferred to wander unknown among the guests. At length he noticed a woman who absorbed his whole attention.

Her fantastic, oriental costume, was meant to represent some queen, Semiramis or Cleopatra, it was difficult to say who, for its magnificence was greater than its historical exactness. The great thing in those days was to be magnificently dressed, not archaeologically exact. So the lady, who wished to appear a majestic ruler, succeeded by means of her dress which was made of gold brocade, over which a transparent veil fell from her diamond crown to her dainty feet; round her white neck hung a magnificent amethyst necklace; her girdle was set with diamonds; she held a sceptre in her hand; and her bearing was that of one who ruled not only over people, but also over their hearts.

Her hair was dark, covered with gold powder; the lower part of her face was of great beauty.

As she passed, everyone gave way to her, nobody dared to speak to her. She looked round indifferently.

Brühl stood near a column, hesitated for a moment, and then greeted her, touching the brim of his hat. She stopped. Brühl put out his hand and she gave him hers on which he wrote her name.

She looked at him attentively, and walked further on; Brühl followed her. She turned several times and seeing that he followed her, she stopped again. A bench nestled among some palms, and here the queen sat down. Brühl stood. She looked at him and when he gave her his hand, she wrote H. B. on it and laughed.

'It's no wonder, Countess, that I recognise you,' he said, 'for I could not mistake you, even were you not dressed like a queen. But I wonder how you recognised me?'

'By the dress of a member of the Council of Trent,' said the lady. 'And to whom would it be more becoming than to you?'

'Countess, you are beautiful.'

She accepted the compliment without paying much heed to it.

'But beautiful,' he continued, 'like a marble statue, and cold like the marble.'

'What more?' asked the woman. 'Say something more amusing, I have heard that so many times.'

'What else could I say to you?' said Brühl with trembling voice. 'Every time I look at you my anger is aroused, storms of vengeance and jealousy shake me.'

'Very pathetic,' whispered the woman. 'What more?'

'Had I the heart, I would curse the hour I first saw you,' said Brühl passionately. 'But a glance at you conquers me. You have a power over me possessed by no one else.'

'Is that true?' the woman coolly inquired.

'Is it necessary to swear it to you?'

'I do not need your oath. I merely wanted to be convinced, and very often an oath fails.'

She looked at him piercingly.

'But my love—' said Brühl.

The woman laughed.

'Brühl,' she said, 'I believe you were in love with me, I am not surprised at that. I was young, I had a good name and I could assure a splendid future to the man I married; but your love might have been that we see everyday, burning in the morning and quenched in the evening. I do not want such love.'

'I gave you proof of my constancy,' said Brühl with animation. 'My love for you began when I was a mere lad and was not quenched even when you took all hope away; it lasts although repulsed and despised.'

'Is it love or ambition?' asked the woman. 'For with you ambition dominates everything.'

'I do not deny that since I cannot be happy, my aim is now to be strong and to be feared.'

The woman looked at him and spoke slowly.

'I do not know what the future may have in store for us. Wait, be faithful to me. I will be frank with you; I was fond of you; with you I could have been happy; we are alike in character.—But things are better as they are. Husband and wife are two fighting enemies; we can be faithful friends to each other.'

'Friends!' said Brühl, 'it sounds like a funeral to my love for you. Your husband will be your lover and I your friend; that means a despised friend.'

'A husband a lover?' said the woman laughing. 'Where did you hear of that? Those two words swear at each other. My husband, I hate him, I despise him, I can't bear him!'

'But you married him.'

'My father, the King, married me to him; but believe me, it is well that it happened so. With him my heart is free, I am myself and shall preserve myself for the future. I believe in my star.'

'Will our stars ever meet?'

'If they are destined for each other, they will.'

'You say this so indifferently—'

'I always control my feelings, whether I love or hate. The sentiment that betrays itself, becomes the prey of the people.'

'But how can one believe in it, if one cannot see it?'

'Then what is faith?' said the woman laughing. 'The one who loves must feel, and he who cannot guess the woman's love is not worthy of it.'

Having said this, she very quickly, and before Brühl could realise it, disappeared.

He was standing thoughtfully, when a rather remarkable clown—for he had diamond buttons—appeared. He seemed to be looking for someone and seeing only the Venetian, stopped, gazing at him attentively. He bent down, wishing to look under the mask, but Brühl pressed it over his face with his hand.

'*Cavaliero nero!*' said the clown, what did the queen say to you? Do you know her?'

'*Sono un forestiere—Addio,*' hissed Brühl and made off, but the clown followed him. Presently he met the bandit to whom the clown whispered:

'Who is he?'

'Brühl.'

'Ah!' exclaimed the clown. 'I guessed it was he by the hatred I felt towards him. But are you sure it was he?'

'I? Who hate him more than you, Count? I would recognise him even in hell.'

The clown suddenly darted forward, for he caught sight of the queen. The bandit, thankful, wandered about without aim. The guests grew more and more animated and those who were searching for each other could hardly move among the dense crowd. Laughter and chatting were louder than the music. Brühl directed his steps towards the apartment where the Princess was receiving the people. A monk seized his hand.

'If you did not wish to be recognised,' said he in Italian, 'you have not succeeded. Who would not recognise you, the Secretary of the Treasury?'

And he laughed.

'How could they recognise me?' asked Brühl.

'By your way of walking and by your beautiful dress.'

Brühl could not be sure that he recognised the monk; he disappeared in the crowd. He could have sworn it was Padre Guarini, but could he suppose that a Jesuit would be at a fancy dress ball?

A little disappointed, he found himself in a room lighted with alabaster lamps. Here a tall woman struck him with her fan. He recognised her and had no doubt that she knew also who he was.

'Brühl, accept my congratulations,' said she.

'What for?'

'You have already mounted very high, but be careful, for *non si va sano*. You must lean on the arm of a woman, who often raises a man as though he had wings.'

Brühl sighed.

'I know for whom you sigh,' she continued, 'and what there is in your heart. But you must forget the ungrateful queen and look for another.'

'To search, in order to be repulsed and despised!'

'Only the one who is unworthy of you could despise you, and such a woman is not to be regretted.'

She bent close to his ear, and having whispered something in it, disappeared in the crowd. He passed on. Opposite him was Frances Kolowrath's table, surrounded by young men. The girl laughing, her parted lips showing her teeth, handed the glasses of wine. He looked at her from a distance. She was tempting and graceful, but her cool coquettishness frightened him. He stood for a long while deep in thought, and then turned aside.

Hardly had he sat down on a chair, in order to rest for he was tired, when the bandit sat beside him.

'Not long ago,' said he, 'you were flirting with a queen, and now you are thinking of that young girl. Am I not right?'

Brühl shook his head without answering.

'She is a rich girl, and she has plenty of diamonds.—Are you not fond of them?'

Brühl turned his head away and did not answer. But the bandit spoke further.

'Look, what dainty hands, what round arms, what a fresh face. It's a bite for a minister if not for a king; but Augustus II is too old, and the Prince is too pious,—you may have her. And after that, I don't know what might happen, for look how she smiles on twenty young men, and it's dreadful what her eyes are saying! She is the very wife for such a man as you. They married Hasse, a great musician, to Faustina; such an artist as you must marry Frances Kolowrath. See how admirably she already plays her part and what a success she will have in the rôle of *la grande coquette*!'

One could see by an impatient movement that Brühl was terribly annoyed, but he did not lose his head, he did not change his position, he did not look at the bandit; he rose and went off. His tormentor searched for him in vain, he was no longer in the palace.

The music played and the masqueraders danced till daybreak.

The last couple still whirled in the King's apartments, while, in the chapel of the castle in Taschenberg, Padre Guarini put ashes on the young Prince, his consort and the Catholic court.

Notwithstanding the carnival, notwithstanding the enormous buildings in course of construction with which the King tried to amuse himself, notwithstanding the magnificence by which he was surrounded, Augustus II began to be wearied. They wanted him to marry for the sake of distracting his thoughts—he yawned and laughed; he had no wish for a wedding, for they were expensive, and the wedding worthy of such a monarch was bound to cost much. His foot pained him, he was sad. The world had no interest for him; he tasted of so many pleasures, that at the bottom of the cup, there remained only dregs. The most beautiful girls ceased to attract him, in his memory there passed in review an endless number of lovely forms, shining for a moment and withered so quickly. The Princess Tubonirska was old, the Countess Cosel locked up, the others scattered throughout the world. Unable to be happy, he wanted to be great. Therefore he sent servants to Africa and built.

Enormous barracks were built in New City, rebuilt by him in the Old City, the Catholic church and palaces were in course of erection.

The King would go to Königstein to look at the walls and find them gone; he would go to Hubertsburg and be wearied; he would give orders that he was to be driven to Moritzburg and there find nothing to interest him. Dresden simply bored him. Had anyone suggested it to him, he would probably have ordered the town to be fired, in order to build it again, though the idea was not new.

While he was in Poland his affections were with Dresden, but when he was in Dresden he was longing after Warsaw. November the second, the day of St Hubert patron of hunting, was always celebrated with a great display; the two courts, that of the King and that of the Prince went to Hubertsburg. The grand huntsman of the court was Herr von Leibnitz, the grand falconer the Count Moszynski.

But the King found St Hubert too old-fashioned and the hunting monotonous. He was seized with restlessness. On New Year's day the market at Leipzig attracted him; the horse dealers promised to bring splendid horses, but the King found they were hacks; and the actresses brought from Belgium had false teeth.

On the sixth of January Augustus returned to Dresden for the opening of the carnival, and at the first ball he perceived that the faces of the women were withered, that their eyes lacked fire, and their lips were pale. He thought that he would enjoy Poland better, therefore he left the carnival, for the Prince and Padre Guarini and ordered the carriages to be got ready to convey him to Warsaw.

Brühl was in constant attendance. Others had disappeared, changed for fresh faces; but he, who from a page had become the minister, was indispensable to the King. The money flowed to the Treasury, the heavy taxes filled the coffers.

The noblemen grumbled, but there was a remedy: the court was filled with foreigners, Italians, Frenchmen, Dutch, Danes, Prussians, Bavarians flourished at the court and the Saxon noblemen returned to their estates to make money for the King.

Brühl's opinion was that his Majesty was right in maintaining that those made the best servants whose whole career depended on the favour of the King.

On the tenth of January the courtyard of the castle was full of horses, carriages and people. The Polish and Saxon courts were ready for the journey. The rooms were filled with those who were to accompany the King. Augustus II was taking leave of his son and his wife.

The former majesty in his face was replaced by impatience and weariness. The Prince was tender towards his father, while his wife, the Princess Josepha, was majestic. Frederick looked into his father's eyes and smiled sweetly. Brühl entered: there were some papers to be signed and money to be taken for the journey.

The King looked sharply towards the Secretary of the Treasury and asked:

'Brühl, have you the money?'

'Yes, your Majesty!' answered he bowing.

The lord's face brightened.

'Look,' said he to his son, 'what a servant! I commend him to you—he is the man who relieved me of my money troubles. Remember! I am indebted to him for the order that prevails.'

Frederick looked into his father's eyes, as though wishing to show him that he promised to obey.

'Had I a few more men like him in Poland,' continued the King, 'I should have restored order in the republic and introduced the same system as I have in Saxony. Ah, those Polish, so-called friends and faithful servants, suck as Lipski, Hozynsz and others, are all afraid of the nobility, and they fool me. But let us be patient, I shall end all that, several heads shall fall off and then everything will be quiet. I cannot bear a public that dares to murmur when I command.—-Enough of it.'

The interrupted leave-taking was continued: Frederick kissed his father's hand. Lackeys, pages and servants were ready in the ante-room. The officials and clergy stood quietly in a corner. The King smiled to all. He repeated to the huntsmen his order to take care of the twelve bisons brought from Bialowiezer and kept in Kreirn near Moritzburg and moved towards a carriage standing ready.

The postillions were already mounted; in the courtyard stood bareheaded burghers, at whom the King only glanced and whom he commanded to pay their taxes: a moment later everything was quiet in the castle and in Dresden.

Everyone had plenty of time to rest until the King returned, when it would fall to their lot to amuse him again.

The whole retinue, escorted by a detachment of cavalry, had already reached the bridge, while Brühl's carriage still stood in the courtyard of the castle. The King's favourite came out thoughtfully and saw Sulkowski. Brühl's face brightened at once; he seized Sulkowski's arm and conducted him to one of the nearest rooms.

Brühl's face expressed the tenderest friendship. Sulkowski was indifferent.

'How happy I am,' said Brühl, 'to be able once more to win a place in your affections.' And his voice was as sweet as his words.

'Brühl, listen!' Sulkowski interrupted. 'I also remind you of our agreement. In good fortune or bad, we shall remain friends.'

'Do you need to remind me?' exclaimed Brühl. 'I love you, I respect you, I am grateful to you, I am your friend.'

'Give me a proof of it.'

'As soon as I have opportunity! Pray, give me that opportunity! Dear Count, I am yours! Do not forget me! You know what I mean—'

'Fräulein Kolowrath!' said Sulkowski laughing. *'Grand bien vous fasse*, you shall have her. Her mother is in your favour.'

'But she?'

'Oh! don't be afraid, nobody will stand in your way. One must be as brave as you to attain to such bliss.'

'I missed a greater and the only bliss,' said Brühl, sighing.

Sulkowski slapped him on the shoulder and said laughing:

'I see that Moszynski is right in hating you.'

'Nonsense!' protested Brühl.

'Oh! don't deny it. It's difficult to conceal anything at court. You and the Countess Moszynski are better friends than if you were married.'

Brühl shrugged his shoulders. 'My heart owns only Frances Kolowrath.'

'Her hand is waiting for you.'

'Her mother herself will propose her to you. And it is time that Frances was married, for her eyes shine strangely.'

'Like stars!' Brühl exclaimed.

'What would the Countess Moszynski say to that?'

Suddenly Brühl seized Sulkowski's hand.

'Count,' said he, 'do not forget me and speak in my favour to the Prince. I fear whether I sufficiently showed my respect and attachment to him, as well as towards the pure and saintly Princess —-Tell him—.'

'You speak for us to the King,' interrupted the Count, 'and I will do the same for you with the Prince. And then, my Brühl, you will not be without protectors. Padre Guarini tries to convert you, the Countess thinks of you as her future son-in-law, and I should not be surprised if you had still another friend at court.'

'All that is nothing if you are not with me,' said Brühl. I would give up Guarini and Kolowrath in your favour.'

'But you would not give up Moszynski,' said Sulkowski laughing. 'And now good luck to your journey; remember me in Poland to all my countrymen.'

'Not to their wives and daughters?'

'Yes, should some of them ask after me—but I doubt it. I prefer German women.'

'I too!' said Brühl.

They had already reached the door.

'*Eh, bien, à la vie, à la mort!*'

They shook hands. Brühl hastened towards the carriage. At the farther end of the courtyard Padre Guarini was standing, making the sign of the cross over Brühl as he drove off, following his master to Warsaw.

It was the beginning of January 1733. In the morning Prince Frederick returned from hunting at Hubertsburg. Sulkowski was with him. In the evening the incomparable Faustina was going to sing in the opera. The Prince was as great an admirer of her voice and beauty as his father. The singer would tyrannise over her competitors, would persecute those who had not the good fortune to please her, and when she deigned to sing there was quiet in the hall as in a church; if anyone dared to sneeze he might be sure that she would become his bitterest foe. The opera called 'Cleophia' was announced and Prince Frederick enjoyed the prospect.

In the afternoon, the Prince, dressed in a splendid *robe de chambre*, was sitting in an armchair, digesting with that pleasant feeling produced by a strong stomach and excellent cooking.

Sulkowski stood opposite him. From time to time the Prince would look at his friend, smile, and smoke on in silence.

The friend and servant looked with pleasure on his happy master, sharing his happiness silently.

The Prince's face beamed, but it was his habit, when in a happy mood, to speak very little and to think. Nobody knew about what. Sometimes he would raise his drooping head, look at Sulkowski and say:

'H'm! Sulkowski?'

'I am here.'

Then he would nod and that was the end of it. A quarter of an hour would elapse and the Prince would call him again by his Christian name, or caressingly in the Italian language. The Count would reply as before that he was there and the eloquent silence would follow.

The Prince spoke but little and only when obliged to do so. He disliked anything unexpected. His life must flow quietly, monotonously. The afternoon hours, when he only received his most familiar friends, were those he enjoyed best. In the forenoon he was obliged to give audience, to listen, to talk, to sign papers. After such efforts the afternoon siesta was delightful to him. When there was no opera he would go to Princess Josepha, listen to some music, and the day would end with a supper.

Never before did the courtiers have a lord more easy to entertain. He was satisfied though one day resembled another as two drops of water.

That day the afternoon siesta had just begun; the Prince was smoking a second pipe, when Sulkowski, noticing something through the window, hesitated a moment and then went towards the door. The Prince's eyes followed him.

'Sulkowski!' he said softly.

'I return at once,' answered the Count, opening the door and disappearing through it. In the anteroom two pages and some servants were waiting.

'Don't let anybody in without my special permission,' said Sulkowski.

All heads bowed.

Sulkowski went out, rushed down the stairs, and stopped in the doorway petrified.

'Brühl? You, here?'

Wrapped in a fur cloak covered with snow, cold, tired, pale and troubled, there stood the favourite of Augustus II. In the courtyard one might have seen a carriage with two tired horses; the postillions had already dismounted and were also so tired that they could hardly keep on their feet.

Brühl did not answer: he made him understand by his look that he wished to enter and to rest. This sudden arrival had something so mysterious about it, that Sulkowski, being very much troubled about it, led the way to a room situated on the ground floor. The servants recognised Brühl, and pressed forward, but he dismissed them with a wave of the hand and entered the room with Sulkowski. Brühl quickly divested himself of his furs. The Count stood waiting.

'For Heaven's sake, Brühl, what news do you bring?'

Brühl sat down on a chair as though not having heard the question, and leaned his sorrowful head on his hand. The favourite of the Prince, uneasy and impatient, stood before him, but pride prevented him from insisting—. He waited.

Brühl rose and sighed, looked around, wrung his hands and cried:

'My most gracious lord, the King, is dead!'

Over Sulkowski's face there passed like lightning an expression difficult to define—fear and joy mixed. He moved as though about to run, but stopped.

'Nobody come before me from Warsaw?' asked Brühl.

'Nobody.'

'Then the Prince knows nothing?'

'No, he does not even suspect anything,' said Sulkowski. 'The Prince must be notified at once,' continued the Count. 'But tell me, how was it? The King was in good health.'

Brühl sighed pitifully.

'On the sixteenth we came to Warsaw,' he said quietly. 'The road was most abominable: in some places snow drifts, in others mud. The King was tired and impatient, but catching sight of Warsaw, his face brightened up. We sent couriers ahead; the reception was splendid notwithstanding the wretched weather, the cannons boomed, the regiment of musketeers was splendid. The carriage stopped at the door of the Saxon Palace. As the King alighted he knocked his foot against the step, in the place which has troubled him continually since Weiss amputated his big toe. We noticed that he grew pale and leaned on his stick. Two pages ran to help him, and leaning on them he entered the palace, where the clergy, the lords and the ladies awaited him in large numbers. The King was obliged to sit down immediately and he told the Grand Marshal to shorten the reception as he did not feel well. As soon as he entered the chamber he ordered Dr Weiss to be called, complaining that he felt his foot hot and wet. They cut the boot; it was full of blood. Weiss grew pale: the foot was already swollen and discoloured; yet notwithstanding that—'

'Cut it short,' cried Sulkowski. 'Someone might tell the Prince that you have arrived.'

Brühl came near to him.

'Count,' said he, 'I—we should come to some understanding before we venture to do anything. The Prince loved his father dearly, the shock he will receive—will it not be necessary to prepare him for the news?'

'Yes, but how?'

'My advice is,' said Brühl, 'that we should do nothing without first consulting Padre Guarini and the Princess.'

Sulkowski looked at him with ill-disguised discontent.

'But it seems to me,' said he, 'that the Prince needs neither the Princess's help nor the spiritual consolation of his confessor.'

'I should think—' said Brühl, and suddenly confused he looked towards the door which opened and Padre Guarini appeared. It was difficult to guess how he could have learned so quickly of Brühl's arrival. He walked straight to him; his face was sad although it was difficult for him to change its naturally cheerful expression; he opened his arms as though he would like to embrace him. Brühl would probably have kissed his hand had there not been a witness. Therefore he only advanced and drooping his head said:

'The King is dead.'

'*Eviva il re!*' answered the Jesuit quietly, raising his eyes. 'God's designs are impenetrable. Does the Prince know it?'

'Not yet,' said Sulkowski drily, looking at the Jesuit askance.

Guarini purposely averted his gaze.

'My wish,' said Brühl, 'is to spare the Prince's feelings and take the advice of the Princess.'

Guarini nodded and Sulkowski shrugged his shoulders and looked at Brühl with discontent.

'Then let us all go to the Princess,' he said, 'for there is not a moment to be lost.'

Brühl glanced at his travelling clothes.

'I can't go as I am,' said he. 'You both go to the Princess; I shall order my clothes to be brought here and dress first.'

Sulkowski agreed in silence to the proposition, Guarini nodded in the affirmative, and they turned towards the door. Brühl threw himself into a chair, as though unable to stand on his feet.

Sulkowski followed the Jesuit quite unwillingly, leaving Brühl who leaned his head on his hand and became thoughtful.

This resting and thinking did not last very long; as soon as the two disappeared in the dark corridor of the castle, Brühl rose quickly, hurried to the door, opened it, and looked into the ante-room.

There stood a lackey as if waiting for orders.

'Send page Berlepsch at once to me.'

The servant went off and five minutes later a boy, wearing the uniform of the King's pages, rushed in out of breath.

Brühl, standing near the door, put his hand on the boy's shoulder.

'Berlepsch, I hope you have confidence in me; don't ask any questions but go to the Prince's apartments, and on your own responsibility, understand, on your own responsibility tell the Prince that I have arrived. Listen! If anything prevented you all would be useless.'

The intelligent boy looked into Brühl's eyes, did not say a word, and went out. Brühl again sat at the table and covered his face with his hands.

It was quiet about him, but he trembled at the slightest noise. There was some stir and bustle on the upper floor, and on the stairs one could hear someone rushing down; a good-looking man, with an ironical smile, appeared in the doorway, and said:

'His Royal Highness, the Prince, having learned by an accident about your arrival, commands you at once to bring him the dispatches.'

Brühl pretended to be embarrassed.

'I am not dressed.'

'Come as you are.'

'Such is the order?'

'Word for word.'

Brühl rose as if he were forced, but he was satisfied inwardly.

They both went silently upstairs.

The door opened, Brühl entered slowly with such a sorrowful expression on his face, that the Prince dropped his pipe and rose.

The door closed and Brühl fell on his knees.

'I bring to Your Majesty the saddest news, but first bow down at the feet of the new King. Our most gracious lord, the King, is dead.'

Frederick stood for a while as if turned into a block of stone; he covered his face. There was a moment of silence; at length Frederick gave Brühl his hand to be kissed and made a sign to him to rise.

'Brühl, how and when did it happen?'

'On the first day of February, the King Augustus the Great died in my arms and entrusted me with his last will, with the jewels of the Crown and secret papers. I, myself, brought the jewels and the papers and I deposit them at the feet of your Majesty.'

Frederick again gave him his hand to be kissed; Brühl bent very low and pretended to be crying; covering his eyes with a handkerchief, he sobbed. The new King also took out a handkerchief and began to weep for his father, whom he loved and respected.

'Brühl, tell me, how did this misfortune occur?' he said quietly.

In a muffled voice, trying to master his emotion, Brühl narrated the circumstances of the illness, its course, and told of the King's patience and peace at the moment of death. At length he took out a letter and handed it to Frederick, who impatiently tore open the envelope. After having read it, he kissed it.

The letter contained the blessing and recommendation of his most faithful and best servant, the messenger of his last will. Frederick looked at Brühl and sighed.

'I will do as my father advises and commands me.'

The letter was still lying on Frederick's knees, when the door leading to the Princess's rooms opened, and there entered Josepha dressed in black, Sulkowski and Guarini.

How surprised they were at seeing Frederick crying, Brühl in his travelling clothes standing at the door, and the opened letter!

Frederick, still sobbing, threw himself into his wife's arms; she began to cry also, according to the Spanish etiquette prescribed to rulers and their courtiers as the form of sorrow and expression of grief.

Sulkowski looked at Brühl with disapproval and whispered to him:

'You told me, you would wait for me.'

'Someone betrayed the secret of my arrival; they called me; I was obliged to obey.'

'Who did that?'

'Watzdorf.'

Sulkowski seemed to be trying to remember the name.

The five people gathered in that room made an interesting group. Frederick alone was really sorrowful. Accustomed to respect and love his father, overwhelmed by grief and the fear of the burden that now fell on his shoulders, Frederick's face was very much changed. Usually serene and quiet, it was now twisted with grief which he could not conceal. Josepha's sorrow was more simulated than true; she never forgot for a moment her dignity and etiquette. Sulkowski was thoughtful and gloomy, as a man who, coming into power, calculates how to begin. His great self-esteem never left him even in the presence of the lady, to whom his respect was due.

Padre Guarini bent his head, closed his eyes, and twitched his face with an expression well assumed for the moment. Brühl while not forgetting that he should appear to be overwhelmed by sorrow, could not abstain from glancing from time to time at those present, especially at Sulkowski. He seemed to see an adversary.

While the Princess tried to comfort her husband, Sulkowski mustered up courage and coming nearer proposed that he should call the dignitaries for a council and announce to the capital and the country, by ordering the bells to be rung, that Augustus II was dead.

Josepha looked at the intruding adviser with some aversion, whispered something to her husband, and majestically directed her steps towards the same door through which she had entered a short time before, Guarini following her.

Those who remained were silent for a time. Brühl waited for orders which the new King did not dare to give; Sulkowski gave Brühl to understand that he had better leave them.

Brühl hesitated, and then he left the room. Frederick did not notice him go out. They remained alone, till suddenly Frederick took the handkerchief from his eyes and said:

'Where is Brühl?'

'He went out.'

'He must not leave me. Pray command him to stay here.'

Sulkowski wished to protest, but then he opened the door, whispered through it and returned.

'One must bear God's will as a man and king,' said he familiarly. 'The King has no time for sorrow.'

Frederick only made a gesture.

'The council shall be called at once.'

'Then go and preside at it; I can't,' said the King. 'Call Brühl here.'

'But why is Brühl necessary?' said Sulkowski in a tone of reproach.

'He? In his arms my father died. Father recommended him to me, I wish to have him, let him come.'

'They have sent for him,' Sulkowski said shrugging his shoulders impatiently.

'Joseph, don't be angry,' said Frederick in a plaintive tone.

As he said this the bells began to ring mournfully in the churches of the capital of Saxony. Frederick kneeled and prayed. Sulkowski followed his example. One after the other the bells rang out, the solemn sounds forming a gloomy choir, accompanied by the whispering of the people, whispering to each other the sad news.

While the preceding events were taking place in the castle, preparations were in progress at the opera for the performance of 'Cleophila.'

The splendour with which the operas were put upon the stage, a hundred horses and camels appearing with numberless artistes in gorgeous oriental costumes, and the fairy-like effects produced by elaborate machinery, combined to attract as large an audience as did the charming voice of Signora Faustina Bordoni.

Faustina, the first singer of those times, famous for her victory over the equally famous Cuzzoni, was prima donna in the full meaning of the word, on the stage, behind the scenes, and beyond. Signora Bordoni, although married to the great composer, Johanet Hasse, could forget him. The marriage had been broken the next day by command of the King, who sent the musician to Italy to study there.

As the carriage bringing Brühl and the sad news of the death of Augustus the Strong neared the castle Faustina was sitting in the small drawing-room arranged for her near the stage, and having removed her furs was about to issue her orders.

The prima donna was not very young, but notwithstanding her Italian beauty, which blossoms and withers quickly, she preserved her voice, the charm of her figure, and the beauty of her face, the features of Juno with which nature had endowed her.

She was not a delicate woman, but strong and majestic, with the form of a statue, as though made from one block by the energetic chisel of Michael Angelo.

Her beauty was equal to her voice. Everything was in harmony with her character; her head of a goddess, bosom of a nymph, hand of a Bacchante, figure of an Amazon, hands and feet of a princess, abundant black hair like the mane of an Arabian horse. In her face, notwithstanding the classical beauty of her features, there was more strength than womanly sweetness. Not infrequently her black eyebrows contracted in a frown, her nostrils dilated with anger, and behind her pink lips her white teeth gleamed angrily.

Her manner was that of a woman accustomed to command, to receive homage, fearing nought, daring even to hurl her thunderbolts at crowned heads.

The drawing-room was elegantly furnished with gold, the furniture upholstered with blue satin, and the dressing-table, covered with lace, was loaded with silver and china. The wardrobes for her dresses were ornamented with bronze, and from the ceiling descended a china chandelier like a basket of flowers.

Three servants stood at the door waiting for orders. One could recognise that two of them were Italian women, for they had not given up their national coifure. Faustina glanced at the clock, threw herself on the sofa, and, half leaning and half sitting, played with the silk sash of her large, silk *robe de chambre*.

The servants were silent.

There was a knock at the door. Faustina did not move, but glancing towards a good-looking young man who appeared in the doorway, greeted him with a smile.

It was the tenor, Angelo Monticelli. It was easy to see that he was also Italian; but while Faustina was the personification of Italian energy and liveliness, he was the embodiment of almost womanly charm. Young, remarkably handsome, with long black hair falling over his shoulders, he seemed to be born for the rôles of *innamorati*, of lovers and gods. The classical Apollo, playing the lute, could not have been more charming. Only he lacked the pride and energy of the god.

He bent to salute Faustina, who hardly nodded to him.

'Angelo!' said Faustina, 'you run after those horrid German women—you will lose your voice. Fie! How you can see a woman in those German girls! Look at their hands and feet!'

'*Signora!*' said Angelo, placing one hand on his chest and looking into a mirror, for he was in love with himself. '*Signora, non è vero!*'

'You would tell me, by way of excuse,' said Faustina laughing, 'that they run after you.'

'Not that either; I am longing for the Italian sky, Italian faces, and the heart of an Italian woman—I wither here—'

Faustina glanced at him and made a sign to the servants to leave the room.

'Ingrato!' whispered she. 'We all pet you, and yet you complain.'

Then she turned her gaze to the ceiling taking no notice of Monticelli's devouring eyes.

'Has Abbuzzi come?' she asked.

'I don't know.'

'You do not wish to know about Abbuzzi!'

'I don't care about her.'

'When you are talking to me! But I am neither jealous of her nor your Apollo-like beauty; only I hate her, and I can't bear you.'

'Why not?'

'Because you are a doll. Look at the clock and go and dress.'

As she spoke a new face appeared in the doorway; it was the cheerful Puttini.

'My humblest homage,' said he. 'But perchance I interrupt a duet; excuse me.'

He glanced at Angelo. Faustina laughed and shrugged her shoulders.

'We sing duets only on the stage,' said she. 'You are all late today. Go and dress.'

She jumped down from the sofa; Angelo moved towards the door; Puttini laughed and remained where he was.

'My costume is ready, I shall not be late.'

The door opened noisily and in rushed a man dressed in black; his round face, with small nose and low forehead, expressed fear.

Faustina who was in continual dread of fire, shrieked:

'Holy Virgin, help! Fire! Fire!'

'Where? Where?'

The new-comer, much surprised, stood still. His name was Klein, a member of the orchestra, Faustina's great admirer, a friend of the Italians, and an enthusiastic musician.

His Christian name was Johan, Faustina changed it into Giovanni and called him Piccolo.

'Piccolo! are you mad? What is the matter with you?' she cried.

'The King is dead! King Augustus the Strong died in Warsaw.'

At this, Faustina screamed piercingly, covering her face with her hands; the rest stood silent. Klein left the door open and the actors began to crowd in. The great majority of them were already half dressed for the performance of 'Cleophila.' Abbuzzi rushed in with naked bosom. Her beauty was striking even when compared with Faustina; only she was small and still more lively.

Catherine Piluga, with a crowd of Italians and French, half dressed, with frightened faces, followed Abbuzzi. All pressed round Faustina exclaiming in all possible voices: *'Il re è morto!'* Their faces expressed more fear than sorrow. Faustina alone was silent, and did not seem much afraid of the news. All looked at her hoping that she would speak, but she would not betray her thoughts.

The bells resounded throughout the whole city.

'There will be no performance tonight, go home!' she cried imperatively.

But they did not obey her; frightened, they stood as though rivetted to the spot.

'Go home!' repeated Faustina. 'We have nothing to do here; we shall not play for some time.'

The crowd began to withdraw, murmuring. As soon as the last had gone, Abbuzzi also disappeared, and Faustina lay on the sofa not seeming to notice an elderly gentleman standing quietly apart.

He coughed softly.

'Ah! It's you?'

'Yes,' said the German, indifferently.

It was Hasse, Faustina's husband.

'What are you thinking about? About a new Requiem for the dead King?'

'You have guessed almost right,' answered the composer. 'I was wondering if the mass: *Sulla morte d'un eroe*, which I composed some time ago, would be suitable for the funeral service. I am a musician, and even grief turns with me to music.'

'But what will become of us now?' sighed Faustina.

'*Chi lo sa?*'

They were both silent; Hasse walked to and fro, then stopped in front of his wife.

'I think we need not fear,' said he, 'for there is hardly anyone who could be put in my place, not even such a one as Popora, and there is absolutely no one to rival Faustina.'

'Flatterer,' said the Italian. 'Faustina's voice is like a candle that burns brightly—it will be extinguished one day.'

'Not very soon,' answered the thoughtful German, 'you know that better than I do.'

'But that quiet, pious, modest, ruled-by-his-wife new King—'

Hasse laughed.

'*E un fanatico per la musica, e fanatico per la Faustina.*'

'*Chi lo sa?*' whispered the singer thoughtfully, 'Well, if he is not all that you say, we must make him so.' A bright idea flashed through her brain, 'Poor old Augustus is dead,' said she in a lowered voice. 'I should like to make a beautiful speech over his grave, but I can't.'

Hasse shrugged his shoulders.

'There will be plenty of funeral speeches,' he said almost in a whisper, 'but history will not be indulgent to him. He was a magnificent tyrant and lived for himself only. Saxony will breathe more freely.'

'You are unjust,' Faustina exclaimed. 'Could Saxony be more happy, more brilliant, more favoured? The glory of that hero is reflected in her.'

Hasse smiled painfully.

'He may have looked like a hero, when from his box in the opera, covered with diamonds, he smiled upon you, but the whole country paid for those diamonds with tears. Joy and singing resounded through Dresden, moaning and crying throughout Saxony and Poland. In the capital there was luxury, in the country misery and woe.'

Faustina sprang to her feet, she was indignant.

'*Tace!* I will not permit you to say anything against him; your words betoken horrid jealousy.'

'No,' said Hasse quietly, looking at her. 'My love was absorbed by the music, I loved the beautiful Faustina for her voice, and was entranced when I heard it or even thought of it.'

At that moment the door opened a little way, and then closed again immediately, but Faustina had perceived who was there and called him in. It was Watzdorf, the same who had called Brühl to the Prince. His figure and movements resembled those of the bandit of the fancy dress ball. For a courtier the expression of his face was unusual, an ironical smile, merciless and biting, overspread his features, which were illumined by piercing eyes.

'I thought,' said he, entering and smiling to Faustina, 'that you had not yet heard what had happened.'

'But it was announced *urbi et orbi* by the sound of the bells,' replied the Italian approaching him.

'Yes, but the bells ring all the same for funeral or wedding; you might even suppose that a princess was born and that they called you to rejoice.'

'Poor King,' Faustina sighed.

'Yes,' said Watzdorf maliciously, 'he lived long, had at least three hundred mistresses, scattered millions, drank rivers of wine, wore out plenty of horses' shoes, and cut off many heads—was it not time after such labour to lie down to rest?'

None ventured to interrupt the speaker; Hasse eyed him furtively.

'What will happen next?' asked Faustina.

'We had an opera called *Il re Augusto*, we shall now have a new, but will it be a better one? The daughter of the emperors, Padre Guarini, Padre Salerno, Padre Toyler and Padre Kopper. Faustina shall sing as she used to sing before; Hasse shall compose operas as he composed before. It will be worse for us court composers when the first rôles are taken by foreign pages and foreign lackeys.'

Hasse bowed and said in a low voice:

'Enough! Enough! Suppose someone should be listening at the door. It is dangerous even to listen to such a speech as yours!'

Watzdorf shrugged his shoulders.

'Where were you in March last year?' asked Faustina carelessly.

'I? In March? Wait—well—I don't remember.'

'I see you were not in New Market Square where the drama entitled *"Major d'Argelles"* was played.'

Watzdorf said nothing.

'Don't you remember that d'Argelles who spoke the truth invariably, sparing no one? I could see him from a window. I pitied the poor man whom they put in the pillory surrounded by the crowd. The executioner broke a sword over his head, gave him two slaps on the face, and thrust into his mouth a bunch of his libellous writings. Then he was incarcerated in Kaspelhouse in Dantzig till his death.'

'An interesting story,' said Watzdorf ironically, 'but I pity more the man who acted so cruelly towards Major d'Argelles.'

Watzdorf looked at Faustina triumphantly and continued,

'Signora Faustina, during the morning you will be able to rest and get strength for your voice so as to be able to charm the new king and rule over him as you ruled over the deceased. And I can tell you that it will be an easier task. Augustus the Strong was a great seducer, whilst his son is fond of smoking the same pipe; when they hand him a new one he shakes his head, and if he could he would be angry.'

He laughed and continued:—

'Well, I am not needed here, you know all about it, and I must hasten to get my mourning suit ready for tomorrow. I must show my sorrow outwardly if I cannot within; no one can see into my heart.'

'I have forgotten,' said he suddenly turning from the door to Faustina, 'to ask you how you stand with Sulkowski? Tomorrow he ascends the throne, and tomorrow also Brühl will either return to Thuringia or accept the position of a lackey in order to overthrow him at the opportune moment. Brühl and Padre Guarini are the best of friends.'

Hasse called 'hush!' Watzdorf suddenly covered his mouth with his hand.

'Is it not allowed? I am silent then.'

Faustina was confused. 'Signore,' said she, coming near him, 'you are incorrigible. Be careful.'

She placed a finger on his lips.

'I fear nothing,' said Watzdorf sighing. 'I have no other ambition than to remain an honest man, and should they put me in Königstein I will not be tempted to change my opinion, it is worth something.'

'I hope you may not be your own prophet,' said Hasse clasping his hand. 'Think what you please, but say nothing.'

'There would be no merit if I did not try to spread my thoughts among people,' answered Watzdorf already at the door. 'I wish you a very good-night.'

And he disappeared.

'There is no doubt that he will end in Königstein, or if there should be no room for him there, then in Sonnenstein or Pleissenburg.'

And Hasse sighed.

The next morning one could hardly see any signs of grief or mourning in the town, but a general feeling of uneasiness and curiosity had been aroused.

Small groups of people might be seen near the castle and in Taschenburg trying to guess what was going on.

There was unusual animation but the order of changing guards was unchanged. Carriages with drawn curtains and closed *porte-chaises* went to and fro through the streets. It was a quiet, subdued animation, however. The official signs of mourning did not yet appear, and there was no grief visible on any face. Every courier on horseback was an object of curiosity to the crowd who tried to guess his errand. The people whispered but did not dare to speak aloud. Königstein was near, and it seemed that at the head of the government the same officials would remain, carrying out the same policy, for the Prince, the present Elector, out of respect to his late father would not introduce any strangers, and he was too fond of peace and quiet to be bothered with changes. They guessed only that Brühl might fall and that Sulkowski would rise above all. But no one knew how he would exercise his power.

Round Brühl's house situated in the New Market Square everything was quiet. They only knew that, the day before, he had brought the crown jewels and the King's secret archives.

The whole day passed in this apparent quiet. The smaller officials did not know to whom they should bow or whom avoid.

Henniche, Brühl's confidential man, that ex-lackey whom although promoted to the rank of councillor the people still called by that name, was sitting in his house situated near that of his protector.

At the time of his marriage Henniche never dreamt of how high he might rise, for he had married a servant, whose only claim to his favour was youth and some slight beauty. Today, when both had disappeared, Henniche's wife although a good woman was a veritable torture to her husband, for she bore such evident traces of her low origin, that he could not bring her forward. Notwithstanding her love for her lord and master, she tormented him by her talkativeness and petty ways. He had only just got rid of her and yawned leaning on his elbows, when there entered his room, without being announced, a good-looking man, elegantly dressed—although already in mourning—and evidently a courtier.

From, his face one could not guess much more than that he was an intelligent and cunning man, two qualities necessary for a life among intrigues, which, like the wheels of passing carriages, might catch and crush a man.

The new-comer threw his hat on a chair, took out a snuff-box and handing it to Henniche, who looked at him inquisitively, said:

'Well, what do you think, how will it be?'

'I don't think anything; I wait and watch,' answered Henniche quietly.

'You think, Brühl?'

They looked into each other's eyes.

'What does the world say?' asked Henniche.

'Everybody says that which he wishes for; some say that Brühl will be driven away and perhaps imprisoned; others say that Brühl will remain and drive out the rest. And what do you think?'

'I told you, I don't think anything,' answered Henniche. 'Should they succeed in overthrowing Brühl, I shall help them: should Brühl be successful in overthrowing them, I shall help Brühl. Thank God, I am not yet in so high a position, as to break my neck, should I fall down.'

The new-comer laughed.

'The fact is that the only safe policy is to wait and not mix oneself up in anything.'

'Yes, yes, my dear councillor Globig,' said Henniche rising, 'it's dangerous to go forward as well as to remain in the rear; the wisest course is to remain in the middle. But, between ourselves, I wager you anything you like—even my wife against another better-looking one, for she tried me today by her prattle—that Brühl will not fall and that nobody will be able to rival him: from today begins the reign of Brühl I, and let us pray that it lasts as long as possible. We shall both be satisfied. But you must have come from the castle? What news there?'

'Nothing, quiet as the grave; they prepare for mourning, that's all. Padre Guarini passes from the Prince to the Princess; Sulkowski watches them closely, and as to Brühl, I don't even know what has become of him.'

'He will not be lost,' said Henniche.

'It seems that the Princess will not be satisfied if she becomes only the wife of an Elector.'

'Brühl shall make her a Queen,' said Henniche laughing.

At that moment horses' hoofs resounded in the street; both men rushed to the window, in time to see a detachment of cavalry gallop to the castle. A court lackey entered the house. Henniche ran to the door; Globig took his hat. There was a knock and the lackey appeared holding a letter in his hand. Henniche glanced at it and Globig looked inquisitively at the message but could not read it, for their host put it into his pocket and dismissed the lackey.

Again they remained alone.

'There is no secret,' said Henniche smiling, 'a great deal of money is needed. It is not forthcoming but must be had.'

Globig advanced towards the door; Henniche took up his hat.

'Henniche, I hope we shall always pull together.'

'Even if we have to fall,' said the host smiling ironically.

'That is not necessary,' answered Globig quickly. 'On the contrary, if one of us should fall, the other must remain and help him to rise. We must climb together.'

'And if we fall, push each other down.'

'No, we should require no help from each other for that.'

They shook hands.

Henniche was just going out when he met a new-comer in the ante-room; this was a tall man with thin arms and long legs and an ugly but intelligent face.

'Look, he is here also,' said Henniche laughing.

The tall man entered bowing.

'Well, what news? Do we fall or rise?'

'You must be patient and wait,' said the host.

'When there is the question of our skins!' answered the newcomer.

'My dear councillor Loss, our skins sown together would not cover a comfortable seat. Everything rests on someone who has broader shoulders than ours. Have you heard anything?'

'Just what everyone expected; Sulkowski is prime minister.'

'Very interesting indeed!' Henniche hissed. 'Sulkowski, being a Catholic, cannot preside at state councils in Protestant Saxony, unless he becomes a Lutheran, and should he do this the Prince would spit in his face, not to speak of the Princess.'

'You are right,' said Councillor Globig, 'I never thought of that.'

'You forget,' said Loss showing a row of long teeth, 'that his majesty can change the law.'

'Without convocation of the diet?' asked Henniche.

'Yes, here he is ruler,' replied Loss, 'and Saxony is not Poland, where the nobles do as they please and the King is obliged to bow to their will.'

Henniche cleared his throat, for steps were heard at the door and at that moment there appeared a large, fat man, who without taking off his hat, looked at the three men.

He was another councillor. Hammer.

'What is it, a diet?' said he slowly uncovering his head.

'This is quite unexpected,' said Henniche angrily 'speaking frankly, one would think that we conspire.'

'Who does anything today? The work will not begin till tomorrow,' said Hammer. 'Today everyone thinks of himself and makes a compromise with his conscience, lest he should seem to be against the rising sun by saluting the setting one; it is well known that if one turns one's face towards the West, one turns something else to the East.'

They all laughed.

'Hammer,' said Globig, 'you who know everything, tell us, what news have you?'

'Bells, bells, bells!' answered Hammer. 'Even if I knew anything I would not say, for who knows today, who is his friend and who his foe? One must be silent, one must cry with one eye and laugh with the other and be silent, silent! Henniche has his hat,' said he after a pause, 'are you going out?'

'I must,' said the host, 'duty!'

Yes! it is the most important thing,' said Hammer. 'Today, everybody serves himself—there is no more exacting master.'

'Don't you know anything new?' said Globig in a low voice coming near Hammer.

'On the contrary, I have much news, but I shall not tell it, except one item.'

All drew nearer.

'We Saxons do not count at present, Poles are the most important. They are sure of the succession to the principality of Saxony, but to get the Polish crown Sapiechas, Lipskis, Czartoryskis, Lubonirskis, Moszynskis, and Sulkowskis are necessary.'

'You have put Sulkowski last?'—asked Loss ironically.

'For this reason, that he should be at the head,' said Hammer; 'and now, gentlemen, I wish you good-bye.'

He put on his hat and went out first followed by the others. The host remained behind evidently wishing to go alone.

At the door of the house everyone of them looked round cautiously, and they all went in different directions.

In the square could be seen groups of people and soldiers marching. The same curiosity was aroused in other houses of the capital of Saxony, but until the evening nobody could say anything for certain.

The dusk was falling, when a *porte-chaise* stopped at the house in which Padre Guarini lived. He was in the same room in which we saw him previously with Brühl. Here, the confessor to the Prince and Princess, the most powerful although the most modest man in the court, received his friends. The modest old man would have contented himself with a couple of rooms, but as he was obliged to receive many distinguished guests, he occupied the whole house. According to the rank of his visitor, he received him either in his study or his drawing-room, the latter being beautifully furnished and ornamented with pictures by old masters.

A tall man alighted from the *porte-chaise* dressed in dark clothes and wearing a sword. By his face one could see he was a foreigner; his features were delicate, aristocratic but faded. A sweet smile brightened his face. His forehead was high and white, his eyes were large and dark; a Roman nose, thin lips, and a clean shaven face showed that he was a man of gentle birth. He wore a black cloak and white lace cuffs to his dress.

He ran upstairs, rang the bell, and when Guarini's old servant opened the door, he entered without asking any questions and without giving his name. The old servant hastened to open not the door of the study but that of the drawing-room.

The room was dark and unoccupied, but Padre Guarini entered almost at the same moment; not a little surprised at seeing the new-comer, he bent his head humbly and crossed his arms on his chest.

The stranger drew near and they kissed each other's shoulders, Guarini bending almost to his hand.

'You didn't expect me,' said the guest, 'I did not know myself that I should come today. You can guess what brings me here—the present situation is of the greatest importance.'

'Yesterday I sent a letter asking for instructions,' answered the host.

'I have brought them to you. Lock the door. We must be alone.'

'It is not necessary,' answered Guarini, 'we are quite safe here.'

'Then let us not waste time! How do things stand? What is going to happen? Are you afraid of anything? Do you need any help? Speak and let us be advised beforehand.'

Guarini became silent, weighing that which he was going to say. Although the stranger wore civil dress, he said to him:

'Most Reverend Father, you know as well as I do the state of affairs at the court. The Prince is a zealous Catholic, the Princess, if it were possible, is still more zealous. The first favourite Sulkowski is also a Catholic. Everyone about them confesses to our holy faith.'

'But Sulkowski! I heard that he will be the most important figure in the future. The Prince is good, of weak character, and lazy, consequently someone must rule for him. Can we trust Sulkowski?'

Guarini became thoughtful, looked into the eyes of the stranger, put one hand on his mouth and shook his head.

'He is a Catholic,' said he after a pause, 'but he is cold, his ambition is stronger than his faith; his longer influence would be perilous both for us and Catholicism. There is no doubt.'

'But, as far as I know, it is impossible to overthrow him,' said the guest. 'Is the Princess strong enough?'

'By her face and character?' whispered the Jesuit. 'Do you think, then, that in that quiet nature of the Prince, there will ever arise the blood and the passions of Augustus the Strong? Is it possible? Then of what account would the Princess be? Sulkowski will suggest other women to him, in order to rule through them.'

The stranger frowned.

'Your views are too gloomy,' said he 'we must find some remedy.'

'I have thought it over beforehand,' began Guarini seating his guest on the sofa and taking a chair beside him. 'We must have near the Prince a man whom we can be sure will serve us, who would also depend upon us. Frederick is lazy, we must make him a soft bed, provide him with his favourite amusements, give him operas, hunting and pictures. Who knows, perhaps something more,' said he sighing.

Again the stranger frowned.

'It is too bad,' he interrupted, 'that for so great a purpose, we must use base means; it is sad—'

'*Cum finis est licitus, etiam media licita sunt,*' quoted Guarini quietly. 'We cannot limit the means: they are different in every case.'

'I understand,' said the guest, 'it is of the greatest importance that we do not expose ourselves to calumny. The question is about the salvation of our souls, about holding our position here, where previously Luther was omnipotent. We have tools, it would be sinful if we dropped them for the sake of scruples, we must rather lose one soul than sacrifice thousands.'

Guarini listened humbly.

'Father,' said he quietly, 'I have told myself the same a hundred times, and that is why I serve as best I can, not always in the direction conscience would direct, but often like a *pulcinello* of the Prince, like an impresario behind the stage, like a councillor there, where advice is necessary. When the question is how to take a stronghold, and when one cannot take it by force of arms, one takes it by strategy. *Media sunt licita.*'

'We don't need to repeat that to each other,' said the guest. 'Tell me all about your plans.'

'We must act with caution,' began Guarini. 'You must not be scandalised at our actions; sometimes you will have cause to sigh over our wickedness, but weak people must be guided by the cords of their own passions.—We are sure of the Princess; our first duty is, if possible, to make her influence stronger. But that most pious lady, I am forced to admit, is the most unbearable in private life, and the King must have some distraction, for he could not live without it. If we do not furnish it, he will supply it for himself—'

He paused and then continued:

'Sulkowski will not listen to anybody, he will sacrifice everything for himself; in order to keep the King under his domination, he will give him everything he wishes for. We never can be certain of him; we must overthrow him.'

'By what means?'

'I shall come to that; Providence has given us a tool. We have a man. Brühl is that man.'

'Protestant,' said the stranger.

'He is a Protestant in Saxony and publicly; but in Poland and in his private life he is a Catholic. We must permit that; you know what our Maldonatus says:—*Onando vobis dissimulantibus religio vera aliquod detrimentum acceptura sit aut aliqua religio falsa confirmaretur, alias ittam dissimulare licet, aliqua causa legitima interveniente.* Brühl shall be or rather is a Catholic. We shall find him a Catholic wife, whom he will accept from the Prince's and our hands; we shall help him to overthrow Sulkowski; with Brühl we are lords here. Nobody will suspect that we have had a hand in the matter, for nobody could suspect us of helping a Protestant against a Catholic.'

'But are you sure of him?'

Guarini smiled.

'He shall be dependent upon us; should he attempt to betray us, he would fall tomorrow; we have plenty of means to accomplish that.'

'I cannot deny that the plan is excellent,' said the stranger after a moment of thought, 'but the execution of it seems to me doubtful.'

'Yes, just at present,' said Padre Guarini, 'it may take us one or perchance two years' work, using all possible means, but with God's help victory is certain as far as in human affairs one can be certain of anything.'

'Do you count on the Prince's character?'

'Yes,' answered Guarini, 'having been his confessor for so many years I know him well.'

'What about the Princess?' asked the guest.

'She is a worthy lady and a saint, but God has not endowed her with any feminine charm. She will not satisfy the Prince.'

'For God's sake! I hope you will not persuade him to lead the lascivious life that his father did!'

'We need not restrain him from that,' said Guarini, 'his natural disposition will not allow him to create a public scandal, but it would be impossible to put a bridle on his passions. They will be secret but stubborn. We must overlook many things in order to make him remain a Catholic.'

The stranger became sad.

'What an awful thing it is to be obliged to soil oneself for the sake of the holy truth!'

'Well, there must be some scapegoat, such as I,' said Guarini jocosely. 'The people envy me—'

'Not I,' interrupted the visitor, 'not I!'

'What are your orders?' asked Guarini.

'Your plans shall be considered by our council,' answered the stranger. 'In the meanwhile you must act. We shall send you our instructions soon.'

'Brühl shall remain. The Prince, with tears, has promised his wife to fulfil his father's last wish. Sulkowski shall only be the apparent ruler, Brühl shall be the true one, and then—'

'You think you will be able to overthrow him?'

'We are certain; we all act against the man, who has not the slightest idea of danger, and Brühl's ambition is the best weapon in our hands.'

'But Brühl!'

'He is a devil in human form, but a devil who prays and is equally ready to crush his enemy, and suffers from no qualms of conscience. Then he is sweet, polite and winning to the highest degree.'

They became silent, the stranger thoughtful.

'Any progress in conversion?' asked he after a moment's pause.

'In this nest of heresy?' said Guarini, 'here, where Protestantism dominates? The progress is very small, and the souls, which our fishermen's nets pull to the shore, are not worth much. Their descendants may pay for our labour. And then there is a new heresy spreading rapidly, the fight against which may be more difficult than against the others.'

'What is it?'

'Nothing new, any more than other heresies; but the apostle of it is a powerful, exalted, self-satisfied man. We have to fight not only a dogma, for with him dogma is of secondary importance, but a new social organisation, which he proposes to build. Falsehood takes the brightness from truth. In the woods beyond the town, the committee of the Moravian Brothers, something like a monastic order without any rules, was organised and prospers.'

'Tell me more about it,' said the guest, with animation. 'I have heard nothing about it.'

'A strange fanatic, not of religion but of the social organisation and the way of living, attempted in the name of Christ and his teaching, to create a new State. Christ is the King of that republic. Separated, but living in the same spot, there dwell troops of women, girls and children. They are united by joining in common prayers and meals. The powerful lord, Count Zinzendorf, granted land to the community and became its minister and preacher. Work and prayer, strict discipline and brotherly love, rule over the Moravian Brothers of Herrnhut.'

The stranger listened attentively.

'And you permitted the spreading of heresy?' he exclaimed.

'I tried to stop it, but in vain,' said Guarini. 'Investigations were made, and I hope Zinzendorf will be banished.'

'But they must have committed some abominations!' said the guest.

'The most careful investigations failed to discover anything vicious. Those people confess different creeds, but they are united in one strange community, in which there is no private property, no poor people, no orphans; they constitute one family, the father of which is Christ.'

'*Horrendum!*' exclaimed the stranger. 'And the marriages?'

'They are strictly observed, but as they believe that they are directly ruled by Christ, you may guess how marriages are contracted. The young men draw their wives by lots and the couples live an exemplary life.'

'You tell me of strange things. But may they not be false rumours?'

'I was there myself, and I saw the praying bands of maidens with purple sashes, of married women with blue, and of widows with white.'

The guest sighed.

'I trust you will not suffer the sect to grow.'

'We must cut off its head,' said Guarini. 'Zinzendorf shall be banished, then the community will scatter.'

'Have you seen this Zinzendorf?'

'Yes, several times, for he does not avoid the Catholic priests: on the contrary, he discourses willingly with them, not about theology, however, but about the first Christians, their life and our Saviour's love, the axle-tree, according to him, round which the Christian world ought to revolve.'

At this moment the old servant appeared in the doorway. Padre Guarini, having excused himself, went to the ante-room where he found one of the King's lackeys. The Prince had sent for his confessor.

It was necessary to take leave of the guest, to whom paper, pen and ink were given, and he settled himself to write as though in his own house. Padre Guarini took leave of his guest and preceded by the lackey, hastened to the Prince.

Frederick was sitting in the same room in which he had learned about his father's death. He held a pipe, his head drooped, and he was silent as usual. Only the wrinkles of his forehead indicated that he was thinking hard.

When Padre Guarini entered the Prince wished to rise, but the Jesuit held him gently to his chair and kissed his hand. At a little distance stood Sulkowski, who would not leave his master even for a moment. His face was beaming triumphantly but he tried to be sad officially.

Padre Guarini could take more liberties; he knew that notwithstanding the official mourning, a little distraction would be necessary; consequently his manner was almost jovial, he took a stool and sat near the Prince, and looking into his eyes, spoke in Italian with animation.

'We must pray for our late King, but it is not proper to mourn too much over that which is natural and necessary. Too intense grief is injurious to the health, and then your Royal Highness has no time for it. It is necessary to rule and to keep in good health.'

The Prince smiled.

'I saw Frosch the fool in the ante-room,' continued the Jesuit, 'he looks as if someone had put him into vinegar; he cries because he cannot play tricks on Horch. They sit in opposite corners and put out their tongues at each other.'

'It must be very amusing!' whispered the Prince: 'but it would not be decorous for me to see it; it is the time of mourning.'

The Jesuit was silent.

'Frosch is very amusing, and I like him,' added the Prince, and looked at Sulkowski, who walked softly to and fro. The Padre tried to read the Count's face, but saw only pride and self-satisfaction. The Prince pointed at him and whispered—'Good friend—all my hopes are centred in him—but for him I could not have peace.'

The Jesuit nodded in sign of approval

Sulkowski knowing that to prolong the conversation would bore the Prince, came to him and said:

'It is difficult to find amusement for your Royal Highness amid so many troubles.'

'I think,' said the Jesuit, 'that with your good-will everything can be done.'

'Yes, in Saxony,' answered Sulkowski at whom the Prince was looking and nodding affirmatively, 'but in Poland—'

'Our late King left many friends and faithful servants there. What does Brühl say?' asked Guarini.

The Prince looked at Sulkowski as if authorising him to answer. The Count hesitated a moment, then said:

'Brühl assured us that our friends there will work zealously at the coming election. But who knows that Leszezynski, France and intrigues will not stand in our way? For that we need money.'

'Brühl must furnish it,' said the Prince. 'He is very able at that.'

Sulkowski became silent.

'We shall all do our best and put the crown of a king on the head of our gracious lord.—'

'And Josepha's,' added Frederick quickly. 'It is due to her; she cannot remain the wife of the Elector of Saxony.'

Both men nodded; the Prince smoked his pipe and became thoughtful. It seemed that he would talk further on the same subject when he bent to Guarini and whispered:

'Frosch sitting in the corner must be very amusing; you say they showed each other their tongues?'

'I am certain I saw two red tongues, but I don't know whether they showed them to each other or to me.'

The Prince, forgetting himself, laughed aloud, then he put his hand to his mouth and became silent.

And it was not until after a long while that Frederick bent again to Guarini's ear and whispered:

'Have you seen Faustina?'

'No,' answered the Jesuit.

'Ah? No? Why? Assure her of my favour, only she must take care of her voice. I appreciate her very much. *E una diva!* She sings like an angel! No other can rival her. I shall be longing to hear her. Now she must sing in church, there at least I may listen to her.'

Sulkowski disliked that whispering: he moved aside, and then came near the Prince. Frederick again pointed him out to the priest.

'He will be my prime minister—my right hand.'

'I am glad to hear such good news,' said Guarini, clapping his hands softly. 'Saxony is to be congratulated at having at her head such a man and such a good Catholic as the Count.'

The Prince looked round.

'If my Saxon subjects object to having a Catholic as my prime minister, Brühl will do whatever I command.'

'I have nothing against Brühl,' said the Jesuit, 'but he is a stubborn Protestant.'

To this the Prince answered: 'Pshaw!' and waved his hand.

Sulkowski looked suspiciously at the Jesuit, who assumed a humble and quiet mien.

At that moment Moszynski was announced, and the Prince ordered him to be shown in.

'I wished to take leave of your Royal Highness,' he said bending to kiss Frederick's hand. 'I am going to Warsaw: we cannot neglect the election.'

'Very well, go then,' said the Prince sighing. 'Although Brühl assures me—'

'Brühl knows neither Poland nor the Poles,' said Moszynski with fervour. 'It is our affair.'

Suddenly, Frederick rose, and exclaimed as if he had recollected something:

'By the bye! You are going to Warsaw! Pray remember about those hounds that were left in Wilanow. I must have them! Send someone by *porte-chaise* with them. There are no better hounds than they are. You know—'

'Yes, they are black,' said Moszynski.

'Jupiter, Diana, and Mercury,' enumerated the Prince. 'Pray send them to me at once.'

'I think they had better stay there,' said Moszynski. 'When the Prince becomes King——'

'My dear Count, send me also Corregio's Madonna! Take it from the Saxony Palace and send it! It is a masterpiece!'

Moszynski bowed.

'Any further orders?' asked he.

'Greet the musketeers; my father was very fond of them.'

The remembrance of his father made him gloomy, he sat down. Sulkowski, always anxious that his master should have that of which he was fond, went to tell a lackey to bring a fresh pipe. The Prince seized it quickly and began to smoke.

All were silent. Guarini looked attentively at Frederick; Moszynski waited in vain, for the Prince was so much absorbed in his pipe that he forgot about everything else.

At length Moszynski kissed the Prince's hand and took his leave. Frederick smiled on him affectionately, but said not a word more.

Sulkowski conducted Moszynski to the ante-room; the Prince remained with Guarini. Hardly had the door closed when the Prince turned to the Jesuit.

'That's nothing,' he whispered, 'when they only show each other their tongues, but when Frosch begins to abuse Horch, and the latter begins to kick, and then when both go under the table and fight, then one can die of laughter.'

Guarini seemed to share the Prince's appreciation of the comical attitude of two fighting fools.

'No,' continued the Prince, 'one cannot let them into the dining-room tomorrow; but later on, for they must not forget their excellent tricks.'

Guarini got up; it seemed that he was hastening to return to the guest he had left at his house. The Prince changed the subject of conversation, and said:

'Don't be angry, that I propose to make Brühl a minister although he is a Protestant. He shall be quickly converted, for he is an intelligent man, and I shall command him—you shall see.'

Guarini made no answer; he bowed and went out.

During the reign of Augustus the Strong, Dresden was not lacking in beautiful women. Notwithstanding sad experiences of the King's instability, every beautiful woman hoped to be able to attract his attention, although they well knew that it would not be for long. Among the young ladies there was not however, one more beautiful, more coquettish, more vivacious, or better able to please, than the young Countess Frances Kolowrath, the same who, several years before, received Brühl in the Taschenberg Palace, the same, whom we saw in one of the booths during the fancy dress ball in the castle. The high rank of her mother, who was the principal lady-in-waiting at the court of the Princess, gave her the privilege of precedence before all other ladies except the princesses of the ruling houses: the favours of Princess Josephina, hopes of a brilliant future, her family name, all made the girl proud and self-willed. The older she grew the more difficult it was for her mother to control her. An only child and much petted, notwithstanding the Princess's severity, she was able to throw off the court etiquette, and form many acquaintances and love intrigues. She did not seem to care much about the future. She looked upon matrimony as upon freedom from a yoke which she could not bear.

A few days after the news of the King's death, when the court was obliged to go into mourning and all amusements were stopped, Lady Frances was bored more than ever. The black dress, which she was obliged to put on, was becoming to her, but she disliked it very much. That evening she stood in her room before her mirror and admired her beautiful figure and features.

As dusk fell she rang the bell and ordered lights to be brought. She was alone, for her mother was at the court, and she did not know what to do with herself. Walking to and fro she noticed a box and took it from a little table. She brought it near the light and opened it with a little key she carried in her pocket.

The box was full of small jewels and pieces of paper. One could guess that these were letters addressed to herself.

Some of them she put aside with a smile, the others she read and became thoughtful. Then she locked the box and lay down on the sofa, looking at a little ring that glistened on her finger. It was an old, black enamelled ring, with an inscription in gold on it: *A hora y siempre.*

In the young lady's room, besides the door leading to her mother's apartment, there was another little door concealed in the wall, leading to some side stairs. Just as she became thoughtful over the ring, the door opened quietly and someone looked through it cautiously: the young lady turned her head, saw who it was, and rose from the sofa with an exclamation. The good-looking young Watzdorf stood before her. We saw him at Faustina's comically joking, and ironically sneering. Today his face, usually ironical, bore quite another expression; it was almost sad and thoughtful.

The beautiful Frances, as if afraid at his appearance, stood silent.

Watzdorf seemed to beseech her forgiveness with his eyes.

'Christian, how could you!' she said at length, with a voice in which there was true or artificial emotion. 'How could you do this, when there are so many people about? Someone will see you and tell about it. The Princess is severe, and my mother—'

'Nobody could see me,' said Watzdorf coming nearer. 'Frances, my goddess! I have been waiting for hours under the stairs, in order to see you alone for a moment. Your mother prays with the Princess, there is nobody in the house.'

'Ah! those stolen moments!' cried Frances. 'I don't much like such secret happiness.'

'Patience, till the other comes,' said Watzdorf taking her hand. 'I hope—'

'Not I,' interrupted the girl, 'they will dispose of me, against my will, as they would dispose of a piece of furniture. The Princess, the Prince, my mother, Padre Guarini—I am a slave.'

'Then let us run away from here!'

'Where?' asked Frances laughing. 'To Austria, where we shall be caught by the Emperor's police: to Prussia, where the Brandenburgian would stop us. Let us run! That is all very well, but how and with what? You have nothing, except your salary at the court, and I have only the favour of the Prince and Princess.'

'But your mother's heart—'

'That heart will search out happiness for me in diamonds—it understands no other.'

'Frances, my goddess! How cruel you are today, you take all my hope from me!'

'I can't give that which I don't possess myself,' said the girl coolly and sadly.

'For you don't love me.'

The lovely girl looked at him reproachfully.

'I never loved anybody but you!' said she. 'I shall never be able to love anybody else, and because I love you, I should like to speak frankly with you.'

Watzdorf cast his eyes on the floor.

'I understand,' he muttered, 'You wish to convince me, that because you love me, you cannot be mine, and that I must give you up. Such is the logic of love in courts. Because you love me, because I love you, you must marry another man—'

'Yes; I must marry the first one they give me; but that man shall not have my heart.'

'It's hideous!' interrupted Watzdorf. 'You do not wish to sacrifice anything for me.'

'For I do not wish to bring evil on you,' said the girl. 'They would catch us tomorrow if we fly today, you would be sent to Königstein, and they would marry me to the man whom they have selected for me.'

'I think I shall go to Königstein in any case,' said Watzdorf. 'I cannot shut my mouth looking at this horrible life, at this despotism of a lackey. I say what I think, and that is, as you know, the way to get there, where one speaks only to four walls of the prison.'

'Listen, Christian, instead of talking, we ought to be silent,' said the girl, 'instead of wishing to improve them, we ought to despise them and rule them.'

'Giving in to their fancies, and lying for a lifetime, cheating them, and soiling oneself—' said Watzdorf. 'What a lovely life!'

'Then is it better to give up everything?' said the girl laughing. 'I, a woman, I am not so tragical, I take life as it is.'

'I despise it,' muttered Watzdorf.

The girl put out her hand to him.

'Poor enthusiast!' she sighed. 'Ah! how I pity you and myself; there is no hope for us—and if we could catch a moment of happiness, it is amidst falsehood and lying.'

She came near him, put one hand on his shoulder, and the other she put round his neck.

'Ah! this life!' she whispered, 'one must be drunk in order to bear it.'

'And be a cheat!' added Watzdorf, who seized her hand and kissed it passionately. 'Frances, you don't love me; you love the life more than me; the world and the golden fetters.'

The girl was silent and sad.

'Who knows?' she said. 'I don't know myself. They brought me up, cradling me in falsehood and teaching me how to lie, in the meanwhile arousing in me a desire for sensation, distraction, luxury and enjoyment. I am not certain of my own heart, for I was corrupted before I began to live.'

'Love ought to make us both better,' said Watzdorf looking into her eyes passionately. 'I was also a courtier before I loved you—by that love I became a man; I became purified in its flames.'

The girl laid her head on his shoulder and spoke to him in a whisper; they both seemed to forget about the whole world. Their eyes spoke more than their lips; their hands met and joined.

They forgot themselves to such a degree that they did not notice that the same door by which Watzdorf had entered opened, and the threatening, pale and angry face of the girl's mother appeared through it.

Seeing her daughter with a man whom she did not recognise at once, she was struck dumb. She made a step forward and pulled Watzdorf by his sleeve. Her lips trembled and her eyes were full of awful anger; the girl turned and perceived the thunder-bolt look of her mother. But she was not afraid. She retreated a step, while Watzdorf not knowing yet who had disturbed them, mechanically searched for his sword.

Only when he turned and saw the Countess did he become pale and stood silent like a criminal caught red-handed in the act.

The Countess could not speak, because of her great anger: she breathed heavily, pressing her bosom with one hand, with the other pointing imperiously to the door.

Watzdorf before obeying bent over the girl's hand and pressed it to his lips; the mother pulled it from him, and trembling continually pointed to the door.

Watzdorf looked at the pale girl and went out slowly. The Countess fell on the sofa—her daughter remained cold and indifferent like a statue. The Countess cried from anger.

'Shame on you!' cried she, 'you dare to receive that man in your room!'

'Because I love him!' answered the girl calmly.

'And you dare to tell me that!'

'Why should I not say what I feel?'

The Countess sobbed.

'And you think that because of your stupid love for that good-for-nothing man, who is hardly tolerated in the court, I shall sacrifice your future? Never!'

'I did not expect that I could be happy and honest,' answered the girl coolly.

'You are mad!' cried the mother.

The girl sat in the chair opposite her mother, took a flower from the bouquet standing on the table, and raised it to her lips. Cold and ironical resignation was depicted on her face; the mother looked at her and was frightened.

'Happily, he could go out without being noticed,' she murmured to herself. 'Tomorrow I shall order that door to be fastened, and I shall lock you in like a slave. Could I ever have expected to see such a thing?'

The girl, biting the flower, seemed to be ready to listen to any reproaches her mother might heap on her. The disdainful silence of her daughter made the Countess still more angry. She sprang from the sofa and walked rapidly across the room.

'If Watzdorf shall dare to speak, or look at you, woe betide him! I shall fall at the feet of the Princess, I shall pray Sulkowski, and they will lock him up for ever.'

'I don't think he would like to expose himself to that,' said the girl. 'To-day I took all hope from him. I told him that I may not dispose of myself; that they would treat me like a slave; that I shall marry the man they destine for me, but that I shall not love him—'

'You dare to tell me that!'

'I say what I think. The man who would marry me, will know what to expect from me.'

The Countess looked at her daughter threateningly but she was silent. Suddenly she wrung her hands.

'Ungrateful!' she cried more tenderly. 'The moment I try to secure for you with our lady the most brilliant future, you—'

'I am quite aware that I shall be led like a sacrifice, dressed in brocade,' rejoined the girl laughing bitterly. 'Such a future is unavoidable.'

'Yes, for you know that you cannot resist the will of your mother and that of the Princess and the Prince.'

'Who has no will whatever,' said the girl ironically.

'Silence!' interrupted her mother threateningly. 'I came to tell you about happiness, and I found shame!'

'It was not necessary to tell me of that which I was aware. Sulkowski is married, consequently I must marry the other minister, Brühl. I expected that. Indeed, it's a great happiness!'

'Greater than you deserve,' answered her mother. 'What could you have against the nicest man in the world?'

'Nothing whatever; I am as indifferent to him as if he were the most stupid and the most horrid. He or another is just the same to me, if I can not marry the one whom I love.'

'Don't dare to pronounce his name: I hate him! If he dares to make one step he is lost!'

'I shall warn him: I don't wish him to come to nought: I wish him to avenge me.'

'Don't you dare to speak to him! I forbid you!'

The girl became silent. The Countess, having noticed that she was five minutes late for her duties at the court, said:

'You come with me; the Princess commanded you to come. You know how you should behave.'

A few minutes later both ladies went out. It was supper time. The strict etiquette introduced from the Austrian court and severely observed by the Princess Josephine did not permit anyone to sit at the same table with the Prince and Princess, except the ministers. The other dignitaries of the court, who were present during meal times sat at another table in a separate room. That day the Prince supped alone with his consort. Padre Guarini sat on a stool apart to keep them company. Before the court went into mourning he would amuse the Prince by joking with Frosch and Horch, who usually would fight, while the Prince would laugh to encourage them, and be in his best humour. The new mourning did not permit the fools to perform, but in consideration of the necessity of distraction for the Princess, Guarini allowed Frosch and Horch to be present in the dining-room, but they were not permitted to play their usual jokes. They were placed in such a way that the Prince would notice them immediately.

The table was set magnificently and lighted profusely. Frederick entered with his consort whose common features were in striking contrast to the serene and beautiful although cold face of her husband. The type of the Hapsburgs was not well represented in Josephine, who although still young had none of the charm of youth; the hanging lower lip, gloomy expression, something common and severe in her face, made her repulsive.

Whilst Padre Guarini recited the *benedicite*, the Prince and Princess stood with piously clasped hands, the servants waiting. As Frederick sat down he caught sight of Frosch and Horch who had assumed such a dignified and pompous mien that they were more ridiculous than ever.

Frosch was almost dwarfish; Horch tall and thin. They were both dressed alike. Although the court was in mourning the fools wore red tail coats and blue trousers. Frosch's wig was curled like a sheepskin, while Horch's hair was flat. Frosch stood in the position of the Colossus of Rhodes, with hands placed behind his back. Horch stood stretched like a soldier, with arms straight down his sides. Both were very amusing.

The Prince having noticed them smiled. While eating and drinking with a famous appetite, Frederick looked from time to time at his favourites; he was sorry he could not permit them to play their jokes, but they would have been too noisy. The sight of them alone made the Prince happy, but he had another source of happiness in that Sulkowski and Brühl were such good friends. Brühl willingly resigned his appointment as Grand Marshal of the court, which dignity the Prince bestowed upon Sulkowski, and was content to be the president of the ministers and Secretary of the Treasury. It was only a matter of form, as Sulkowski was expected to keep everything under his own control.

But the future was not certain.

Brühl seemed to be Sulkowski's best friend, and the latter being sure of the Prince's favour did not fear him as a rival.

Having put the whole burden of ruling on these two men, the Prince felt at ease to lead his own monotonous life. He only longed after the opera, after Faustina, and after hunting. But all that was bound to return after the mourning was over. In Poland the Count Moszynski, the Bishop Lipski and others were working hard to assure the Prince's election as King, and Brühl guaranteed that it would be done.

A few days after the news of his father's death, Frederick declared that he would not change anything. But Saxony expected some improvements, and was soon disillusioned and informed that she must not expect anything. The taxes were as heavy as ever.

That evening when the Prince went to his apartment, Sulkowski and Brühl followed him.

In another room some courtiers were grouped round Josephine, and between them was the joking Padre Guarini. The Princess, having remained to talk to them for a time, retired to her own room followed by the Countess Kolowrath, who told her daughter to follow her.

Josephine stood in the centre of the drawing-room as though expecting something. The young girl entered without the least sign of fear. The Princess asked her to come near and said:

'My dear girl, it is time to think of your future—I am willing to do something for you.'

The mother fearing some improper answer said:

'We shall ever be thankful to your Royal Highness.'

'I know that you are a good Catholic,' continued the Princess, 'therefore, I must assure you before all, that your future husband, although not born in the Catholic faith, shall embrace it. Consequently you shall have the merit of gaining one soul for God.'

The girl listened quite indifferently. The Princess looked at her but failed to see any emotion in her face.

'I congratulate you,' added she, 'on the choice made for you by myself and your mother; the man destined for your husband is very pious, of great character and keen intelligence—it is the Secretary of the Treasury, Brühl.'

Josephine looked again at the girl, who stood silent.

'You must permit him to approach you, so that you may get to know each other, and I hope you will be happy.'

The mother pushed the girl towards the Princess; Frances resented being pushed, bent her head and moved aside.

Thus the day ended, memorable in the life of the girl, who looked so indifferently on her future.

The next day, probably by permission of the Countess, Brühl paid his respects to the young girl who was sitting alone. After a moment's reflection she allowed him to be shown in. She received him in the same room in which yesterday, leaning on Watzdorf's shoulder, she had said good-bye to happiness.

The mourning was very becoming to her: her beauty seemed still greater on the dark background of her black dress. Besides paleness there was no other sign of suffering on her face; cool and brave resignation lent something imposing to her features.

Brühl, who was one of the most refined dandies of his time, attributed great importance to dress, and was dressed that day with particular care. The sweet smile did not leave his too delicate face even for a moment. In the same proportion that the young lady wished to be sober and thoughtful, did he wish to be joyful and happy.

He advanced quickly to the table behind which she was sitting; she nodded slightly and pointed to a chair standing near.

'I see,' said Brühl, 'that you have assumed a sad expression to be in harmony with your mourning, while I—'

'You are more lively today than ever,' interrupted the young lady. 'May I ask what makes you so happy?'

'I hope you are aware of the cause,' said Brühl raising his hand to his heart.

'Let us not play a comedy,' said Frances, 'neither you can deceive me, nor I you. They commanded me to marry you, while I love another man; they command you to marry me, while you love another woman. Those are not very joyful things.'

'I, in love with another?' said Brühl, with well-assumed surprise.

'For a long time you have loved, and passionately, the Countess Moszynski; of this both she and her husband and everyone else, is aware, and you think that I, living in the court, do not know it?'

'If you wish me to confess that I was in love with her—'

'Oh! the old love is lasting.'

'But you tell me that you love.'

'Yes, I don't conceal that I love another man.'

'Whom?'

'There is no need to betray his and my secret.—Suffice it that I am sincere when I tell you of this.'

'It is very sad news for me!' exclaimed Brühl.

'It is still sadder for myself. Could you not find another woman, with whom you could be happy?'

She looked at him: Brühl grew confused.

'It is the will of the Prince and Princess.'

'As well as Padre Guarini's,' said the young lady. 'I understand. Is it then irrevocable?'

'Madam,' said Brühl, 'I hope that I shall win your regard—I—'

'I have no hopes, but as our matrimony is inevitable, it would be well to prepare ourselves for that which we must expect.'

'I shall try to make you happy.'

'Thank you, but I think I had better take care of my happiness myself, and you of yours. I don't forbid you to love Moszynski, for even were I to forbid you to do so, it would be useless. Cosel's daughter inherited her mother's beauty and power—which unfortunately, I don't possess.'

'You are cruel.'

'No, I am sincere, that's all.'

Brühl, notwithstanding a great faculty for conversation, felt that words failed him. His situation became painful, while the young lady did not show that she was disturbed in the least.

'Notwithstanding all, I am not in despair,' he said after a pause. 'I have known you ever since you were a mere child, I have been your admirer for a long time; that which you said about the Countess Moszynski was only a fancy, already passed and forgotten. My heart is free, and it is yours. I hope you will be able to throw off your aversion to me.'

'I have no aversion to you; you are a matter of perfect indifference to me,' the young lady interrupted.

'Even that means something.'

'It means, that you might awaken my aversion, while wishing to awaken love.—It is very possible.'

Brühl rose; his face was burning.

'Perchance never a wooer met with a worse reception,' he said sighing. 'But I shall be able to overcome this impression.'

'Do as you please, but remember, that if I become a victim, I shall marry you, for I must, but you know now what awaits you.'

Having said this, she rose; Brühl smiling as sweetly as he could, wished to take hold of her hand, but she withdrew, and said:

'I wish you good-bye.'

The secretary left the room: his face was sweet and serene as ever, and nobody could have guessed his defeat.

While walking with elastic step across the drawing-room, he met the Countess Kolowrath, who, before speaking, looked at him sharply—but discovered nothing.

'Have you seen Frances?' she asked.

'I return from her.'

'How did she receive you?'

Brühl did not answer at once.

'As one receives someone who is not welcome,' he said at length.

'Ah! you have plenty of time.——For many reasons I should not care to hasten the wedding.'

'I am not of your opinion, for I know that it is easiest to conquer the heart, when one is sure of the hand,' said Brühl. 'The approach of the wedding would give us a chance to know each other, and I hope that your daughter knowing me better, and my sentiment—'

The Countess smiled.

'Enough for today,' said she, *cela viendra*. Frances is so beautiful that it is impossible not to worship her, but she is proud and high-spirited like a goddess. If our old King were living, I should fear for her, for she could make an impression even on him.'

Brühl, having made some further remark, left her with a sweet smile. When he entered his *post-chaise*, waiting for him at the door, his face became gloomy.

'I should like to know,' said he to himself, 'whom she loves. She had always so many admirers, and was so sweet to them all, that it is impossible to guess who succeeded in winning her heart, but her beauty is necessary to me. Who knows! The Prince may not always be faithful to his wife,—and in that case—'

He finished his thought with a smile.

'She may not love me, but our common interests will make us friends. Then they know about Moszynski; it is difficult to conceal love.'

Drowned in his thoughts, Brühl did not notice that his *post-chaise* had stopped before the door of his house.

Numerous servants waited for him. The moment he alighted his face was sweetly smiling.

He ran upstairs. Henniche was waiting for him. The faithful servant looked better and more healthy than usual. His face was smiling ironically. Brühl entered the office, where he found Globig, Hammer, and Loss. All rose to greet his Excellency, followed by Henniche.

The secretary was ready to look through some papers, when Henniche whispered.

'You are wanted there.'

And he pointed to the door of the drawing-room. There, Padre Guarini, dressed in a grey coat was walking to and fro.

The Prince could rest quietly; in Poland numerous adherents were working for him, in Dresden Sulkowski and Brühl, equally ambitious, though the former was more sure of his position. The Prince loved him and, what was more important, was accustomed to him. He had been with Frederick ever since they were mere boys. Together they received their first impressions, together they became men. Sulkowski knew his master, for he had watched him as he grew. Brühl divined him.

When Augustus II became a Catholic in order to get the Polish crown, the Pope Clement XI, made every effort that the son might not follow his mother, a zealous Protestant, but that he should follow his father's religion, a matter of indifference to the King who did not believe in anything. For Augustus the Strong was an irritating problem to the Church.

It was uncertain which way the election would go in Poland; in Protestant Saxony Catholicism was an obstacle and a peril. Then the mother, Queen Eberhardin, née Beirenth, and the grandmother Anna Sophia, the Danish Princess, watched that the son and grandson might not follow his father. Both ladies were Protestant fanatics. But this is certain, that Augustus II, in his efforts to make a hereditary monarchy of Poland, even if he were obliged to sacrifice part of it, was inclined to make his son a Catholic—otherwise it was immaterial to him. Urged by the Pope, Augustus the Strong on the 4th of September 1701 swore that his son should be brought up a Catholic, and on February 8th 1702, he assured the Saxon states that his son should be Lutheran. The fact was that he did not know which policy was the best.

When Frederick was yet a mere boy, his grandmother appointed Alexander von Miltitz as tutor. The man was not fitted for the position. The contemporary documents say that the grandmother had not much judgment; she was ruled by Protestant motives, and after dinner knew less than in the morning what she was doing. The little Frederick was taken from the Queen Eberhardin and placed in the care of the grandmother. Alexander von Miltitz being pedantic, avaricious, dull and lazy, could not have had any good influence. As he was indifferent in the matter of religion, the Protestant clergymen surrounded the young Prince, and did not permit him to come in contact with Catholics. Furstenburg notified the Pope about it and an admonition came from Rome.

When Frederick was twelve years old he was taken out of the women's hands and sent with a tutor to travel, but he soon came back. Both queens, being afraid that he might be made a Catholic, ordered him, when fourteen years of age, to make a public confession of Protestantism and then he received confirmation. The King, who was then in Danzig, wrote to the Pope about it, assuring him that were he not hindered by certain circumstances, he would have those who had dared to take such a bold step without his knowledge, punished.

The circumstances then were such that Augustus was obliged to smooth matters over with Rome by promising that Frederick should be converted. General Koss was brought from Poland and appointed the Prince's instructor. Sulkowski was already with the Prince.

In 1711 Augustus took his son to Poland from whence they went to Prague and here the consultation with the Pope's nuncio Albani took place. The result of it was that they determined to change the Prince's whole court, and to surround him with Catholics. Frederick knew nothing about it and on his return to Dresden he went to a Lutheran church.

Then General Koss, by the King's command, dismissed Baron von Miltitz together with the other members of the court, with the exception of the physician and the cook, and the Jesuit father Salerno took the Prince's education in hand. In the meantime Augustus II sent his son to travel, commanding him to go first to Venice. In those days the Venetian carnivals held in St Mark's Square were still very famous. In January 1712 they started on the voyage which, in order to keep the Prince from Protestant influence, was to last for seven years. All the letters the Prince wrote to his family were read by the Saxon General, Lutzelburg, a shrewd man, but whose morals were not of the best.

The Prince, being from the first troubled by his conscience, succeeded in communicating with and asking help from the Queen of England, Anne, and Frederick IV, King of Denmark. Queen Anne invited him to come to England, the King of Denmark wrote that should he become a Catholic, he would lose all chance of the throne of Denmark.

In the same year, the Pope assured Augustus II that in the event of the Protestant princes attacking him, he, the Pope, would support him. In the meantime the Prince, accompanied by Sulkowski, who, being the same age, became his favourite, travelled incognito in Italy, under the name of the Count of Luzacia. His court, besides Sulkowski, was composed of two generals, Koss and Lutzelburg, and of Father Salerno in civilian's clothes, and of another Jesuit, a Saxon, Father Vogler. The secretary was also a Jesuit, whose name was Kopper, who also wore the garments of a civilian and travelled under the name of Weddernoy. Consequently the influence on the Prince was constant and as it went on several years was difficult to resist. From Venice they went to Bologna, where the Prince was received solemnly by the officials of the Pope. Here Father Salerno succeeded in converting the Prince. The confession of the faith was made in strictest secrecy, before Cardinal Cassoni. Later both Albani and Salerno were rewarded with the hats of Cardinals.

The conversion remained a secret for a long time, and as the Saxon states requested that the Prince might return, Augustus, not wishing to irritate them, ordered that the proposed journey to Rome be abandoned. In 1713 the Prince was returning home, when he was told to stay for some time at Düsseldorf at the court of the Elector Palatine, a very zealous Catholic; later he went on to the court of Louis XIV, who had been advised by the Pope of his conversion. There was a rumour of a plot made by his Protestant relations about the conversion of the Prince, but the affair remains in obscurity. They feared continually that the Prince might never become a Protestant again.

In Paris the Prince was very well received, as one can see from the letters of the old Princess of Orleans; they found him very agreeable although he spoke but little, a habit that remained with him through life.

From France they took the Prince not to England as the original project was, but through Lyons and Marseilles again to Venice, where the *signoria* did everything to amuse him. Masquerades, regattas, comedies, balls succeeded each other.

By the advice of Pope Clement XI, it was decided to marry the Prince to a Catholic princess; for this purpose they began to search Venice through

Father Salerno; the Count von Harkenberg and the Prince Eugene helped so much that a Princess was promised. They took the Prince to Vienna; he could not take one step without his father's permission.

The conversion was still secret, although the reason for sparing the sensibility of the queen-mother ceased, for she died. In October of 1717, on a certain morning, the Count von Lutzelburg ordered the whole court to be ready at ten o'clock in the anteroom of the Prince. About eleven o'clock, the carriage of the papal nuncio drew up in front of the palace and Monsignor Spinoli alighted from it and was conducted to the Prince. Shortly after that there came a little man with a casket under his arm and the Count von Lutzelburg said to the courtiers that in the Prince's room something was going on, and that the Protestants could look at it or not. The door opened, the nuncio was reading, and the Prince, not being well and lying in bed, listened with great piety. After the Mass the nuncio left and the Prince said to his Protestant courtiers:

'Gentlemen, now you know what I am, and I beg of you to follow me.'

To this General Kospoth answered:

'We have not yet had time to realise it, it is difficult to decide at once.'

The Prince said:

'You are right, one must first of all become good Christians, then Catholics.'

The secret was unveiled; the following Sunday the Prince went to the Jesuit church and took the Communion. There was great joy in Rome over this success.

Saxony was again assured that the Protestant religion should be respected, but it was easy to foresee that efforts would be made towards conversions. They kept the Prince seven months in Vienna, Augustus furnished plenty of money for a splendid court and balls; and there he was married, in 1719, to the Archduchess Maria Josephine.

During the whole of that time Sulkowski was continually with the Prince. He returned with the court to Dresden where the Emperor's daughter was received with the greatest honours. Sulkowski by habit and necessity shared in all the amusements of the Prince, his hunting parties, theatres and art. During his travels with the Prince in Germany, France and Italy, he saw a great deal and educated himself; he learned to know the world, and what was more important, Frederick's likes and dislikes. He was able to take advantage of them, by pleasing him, to rule him, and he felt that he was so necessary to him that nobody could overthrow him. The Prince was very familiar with him, and the critical times made their relations still closer. The friends that Sulkowski made in various courts strengthened him still more, for he knew that in case of emergency he could count on them.

Therefore he neither feared Brühl's competition nor anybody else's. Through his wife, nèe Hëin Jettingen, he was sure of having the Princess on his side.

He was less humble than Brühl, but a more consummate courtier, more daring, in a word he was a 'cavalier' as they said in those times, of the best sort. Tall and polished, Sulkowski had not the ability necessary for a prime minister, but he was proud and very ambitious. Less familiar with the affairs of state than Brühl, who for a long time worked in Augustus' private office, he was sure of the help of a man from whom he expected assistance. Consequently he determined to become a ruler, being persuaded that he would be able to hold the position. Sulkowski's way of living was more modest than Brühl's, for he was not fond of luxury. Sulkowski's court was not very numerous, the servants not very refined, the carriages not very elegant.

The portfolio was about to be handed to him, when one morning, before he went to see the Prince, he sent for his man. Sulkowski was reading a French book, waiting, when the councillor Ludovici, whom he had sent for, entered, out of breath. Ludovici held the same position with Sulkowski that Henniche did with Brühl: he was his factotum, principal clerk in his office and adviser.

One glance at the man was sufficient to indicate who he was. His face bore no special characteristic, but it could change and assume any expression that was necessary. His whole face was covered with wrinkles; his eyes were black, and his mouth moved so quickly that it was impossible to describe its shape; while in motion it made Ludovici unpleasing. It was necessary to be accustomed to him in order to tolerate him. Fortunately for Sulkowski he was accustomed to him, and by his own dignified manner he could control Ludovici's impatience. Having entered he leaned on the chair nearest to hand and awaited the new minister's orders.

Sulkowski seemed to be thinking whether or not he would make a confidant of the councillor, and his thoughtful attitude excited the latter's curiosity.

'It is very unpleasant,' he said at length rising and looking out of the window, 'that living in the court, and having the confidence of the Elector as I have, I must yet resort to certain precautions.'

Ludovici smiled, lowered his eyes, but did not dare to interrupt.

'I can say frankly,' continued Sulkowski, 'that I am not afraid of anybody, but in the meanwhile I must not trust anybody.'

'Excellent! Beautiful!' said Ludovici, 'we must trust no one. A very intelligent man once said to me that one must treat one's friends in such a way as though we expected that tomorrow they would become our foes.'

'The question is not that they might become my foes, but that they shall not harm me; but I must know about their plans and movements.'

'Excellent! Beautiful!' Ludovici repeated.

'Until now this was not necessary, today it seems to me unavoidable.'

'Excellent! Beautiful!' Ludovici repeated. 'Yes! we must have men who will keep their eyes open on everything.'

'Yes, even on people in high positions,' said Sulkowski emphatically.

Ludovici looked and being uncertain that he rightly caught the meaning of the words, waited. He did not know how high his suspicions would reach.

Sulkowski was unwilling to explain himself better.

'I cannot,' he said with some hesitation, 'look into all the official doings of my colleagues.'

'Official doings!' said Ludovici, laughing, 'that is a trifle; their private doings are more important to your Excellency.'

'Consequently I should like to have—'

'Excellent, beautiful—a little report,' rejoined Ludovici, 'every day, regularly. Written or verbal?'

They both hesitated.

'Verbal will do,' said Sulkowski, 'you might bring it to me in person, after getting the necessary material.'

'Yes, truly, yes. I—and I can assure your Excellency, that you cannot have a more faithful servant.'

Here he bowed very respectfully and then raised his head.

'I would take the liberty of making some suggestions,' Ludovici said softly. 'The foreign resident ministers should be carefully watched, for what else are they than official spies of their countries? I do not exclude even the Count von Wallenstein although he is the master of ceremonies. And then the Prussian Waldburg, the Marquise de Monte, the resident minister Woodward, the Count Weisbach, and the Baron Zulich.'

'Ah! my dear Ludovici, very often the foreign countries are not as dangerous as home intrigues.'

'Excellent, beautiful,' Ludovici said. 'Yes! Yes! Yes! Nobody respects the minister Brühl more than I do.'

At that moment Sulkowski looked at Ludovici, the councillor at him, laughed, raised his hand, turned his head aside, and became silent. Thus they understood each other.

'He is my friend,' said Sulkowski, 'a man whose great talents I appreciate.'

'Talents—great, unusual, enormous, fearful,' Ludovici affirmed with animation. 'Oh, yes!'

'You must know that the late King recommended him very strongly to the Prince, that he is going to marry the Countess Kolowrath, that the Princess thinks much of him. Notwithstanding all that, you would be wrong in interpreting my thoughts if you suppose that I distrust him, that I fear him—'

'Yes, but it is better to be cautious, and it is necessary to watch—through him flows the river of silver and gold.'

Sulkowski changed the subject of conversation and said:

'They complain to me that Watzdorf has too ready a tongue.'

'The younger one,' Ludovici interrupted, 'yes, yes unbridled, but it is a mill that grinds away its own stones; his talk will harm himself alone, and then he cannot help being angry, because—'

He did not finish, for a loud noise was heard in the ante-room. Sulkowski listened, Ludovici became silent, and his face and manner changed; from a courtier he became a dignified official. Pushing, interrupted by a woman's laughter, was heard. Evidently someone was trying to enter by force.

Sulkowski gave Ludovici to understand that the interview was over for the present and advanced towards the door, through which there appeared a lady dressed very strangely.

Figures such as she presented are seen only on screens or made of china. Over-dressed and very plain, thin, sallow, smelling of *l'eau de la reine d'Hongrie*, wearing a large wig, the little woman rushed in looking sweetly at Sulkowski with her small eyes.

The moment that this unwelcome guest took the room by storm, Ludovici bowed humbly, left the room, and the new-comer looked at him and said:

'Ah! ce cher comte! You see, you ungrateful, before you could learn that I was in Dresden, as soon as I had kissed the hand of my august pupil, I came to see you. *N'est ce pas joli de via part?'*

Sulkowski bowed and wanted to kiss her hand, but she struck him with her fan and said:

'Let that be—I am old, it would not be seemly; but let me sit somewhere.'

She looked round and sat on the nearest chair.

'I must breathe; I wanted to talk to you privately.'

Sulkowski stood before her ready to listen.

'Well, we have lost our great magnificent Augustus.'

She sighed, so did Sulkowski.

'It's a pity that he died, but between ourselves, he lived long enough, he abused his life a great deal—I cannot speak about that: *des horreurs!* What will become now of you, poor orphans? The Prince? He is inconsolable in his grief? True? Yes? I came from my court with condolences to my august and dearest pupil.'

She bent a little and leaned on the arm of the chair, raising the fan to her mouth.

'What news? My dear Count, what news? I already know that you have been appointed to a position due to you. We are all glad of it, for we know that our court can count on you.'

Sulkowski bowed.

From those words it was easy to guess that the new-comer was sent by the Austrian court. She was a famous teacher of the Archduchess Josephine, Fräulein Kling, whom they used to send where a man would attract too much attention. Fräulein Kling was one of the most able diplomats in the service of the Austrian court.

'I suppose you already know about everything.'

'Dear Count, I don't know anything; I know only that the Kürfurst loves you, that Brühl is going to help you. But pray, tell me, who is this Brühl?'

Sulkowski became thoughtful.

'He is a friend of mine!' he answered at length.

'Now I understand. You know that the Princess promised him the Countess Kolowrath's hand and that the girl, as it seems, does not fancy him very much. Was Brühl not madly in love with the Countess Moszynski?'

All this was said so quickly, that it gave Sulkowski no time to think over his answer.

'Yes,' said he shortly, 'it seems that he is going to marry.'

'But he is a Lutheran?'

'He is going to be converted to Catholicism.'

'It is to be hoped not in the same way as the late magnificent and great Augustus II, who used to put rosaries round the necks of his favourite hounds.'

Sulkowski was silent.

'What more? I have not yet seen the Prince—has he changed? Has he become sadder? I pity him! Mourning—he will not have an opera for a long time. And what about Faustina? Is she superseded by someone else?'

'The Prince wishes to keep everything as it was during his late father's life. Nobody could supersede Faustina.'

'But she is old.'

'She charms with her voice alone.'

Fräulein covered her face with her fan and moved her head.

'It is a very delicate question,' she said softly, 'for me as a woman, but I am inquisitive, I must know. My dear Count, tell me, is he still faithful to his wife? I love her so much, my dear, august pupil!'

The Count retreated.

'It is beyond my doubt,' said he with animation. 'The Princess does not leave him for a moment; she accompanies him to the hunting parties, to Hubertsburg and Diannenburg.'

'In order that he may become sooner tired of her,' whispered the lady. 'That's unwise—I am always afraid of that passion which must be in his blood.'

She looked at the Count, who shook his head.

'The Prince is so pious,' said he.

Fräulein Kling covered her smile with her fan. The windows of the room in which they were sitting looked on the square. Although they spoke quite loudly, some laughter and shouting became so overpowering, that Sulkowski, frowning, could not help turning towards the window to see what was going on in the street.

In those times street noises and shouting of the mob were very rare. If anything of the kind happened the cause for it was nearly always an official one. In this case, one could see through the windows crowds of people in the street, in the windows and doors of the opposite houses. Amongst the crowd, moving like a wave, a strange procession advanced.

Fräulein Kling, very curious, sprang from her chair and rushed to the window, and, having pushed aside the curtain, she and Sulkowski looked into the street.

The crowd passed under the windows, rushing after a man dressed in dark clothes and sitting on a donkey, his face turned toward the ass's tail. The donkey was led by a man dressed in red. It was painful to look at the unfortunate culprit, an elderly man, bent and crushed by shame. From the window one could see his pale face with the painful expression of a punished man, who, judging by his dress, belonged to the better class. His pockets were full of papers sticking out; his clothes were unbuttoned and threadbare. A kind of stupor evidently followed the humiliation, for he mechanically clasped the donkey in order not to fall, he did not look at what was going on around him, though men armed with halberds surrounded him, while the always merciless crowd threw mud and small stones at him. His dress and face was covered with dirt. The men laughed, the children rushed, screamed and thoughtlessly tortured the unfortunate man.

'What is it?' cried Fräulein Kling. 'What is going on? I don't understand!'

'Oh! nothing!' said Sulkowski indifferently, 'a very simple thing. It cannot be permitted that any scribbler can dare to criticise the people belonging to the upper classes, and speak about them disrespectfully.'

'Naturally,' answered Fräulein Kling, 'one cannot permit them to attack the most sacred things.'

'That man,' said Sulkowski, 'is an editor of some paper called a gazette, or news; his name is Erell. We noticed that he took too many liberties. At length he said something very outrageous in the *Dresden Merkwürdigkeiten* and they ordered him to be put on such a donkey as he is himself.'

'*Et c'est juste!*' cried Fräulein Kling. 'One must be severe with such people. I should like to see the same in Vienna, that we might catch those who take the liberty of speaking about our secrets in Hamburg and the Hague.'

They looked through the window on the shouting crowd. Erell, an old man, evidently exhausted, swayed to the right and to the left and seemed likely to fall from the donkey. At the bend in the street he disappeared and Fräulein Kling returned to her arm-chair; Sulkowski took another, and they began to talk. The host however answered her questions cautiously and coolly.

'My dear Count,' the lady at length added, 'you must understand that my court is anxious that the Kurfürst and his consort should be surrounded by people with sound common sense. It is true, that officially you have accepted the Pragmatic Sanction, but—someone might easily tempt you. My court trusts you, my dear Count, and you can count on it, for we know how to be grateful.'

'I consider myself the most faithful servant of His Imperial Majesty,' said Sulkowski: Fräulein Kling rose, looked in a mirror, smiled and curtseyed. Sulkowski offered her his arm and conducted her downstairs, to the court *post-chaise* waiting at the door, which was lifted by two porters in yellow livery, who carried off the smiling lady.

Soon after the events described, one day after dinner, which was served in those days before two in the Castle, Brühl entered his house.

On his face, usually serene, one could see traces of irritation. He glanced at the clock and hastened to his dressing-room. Four lackeys here waited for his Excellency, the fifth was Henniche standing at the door; his face was very sour.

Brühl having noticed him, asked:

'What do you want?'

'A very important affair,' said Henniche.

'I have no time just now,' said Brühl impatiently. 'I am still more pressed than your Excellency,' muttered the factotum.

Seeing that he would not be able to get rid of him, Brühl came to him and waited to hear what he had to say. But the councillor shook his head, signifying that he could not speak before witnesses. Brühl took him into the next room, locked the door, and said:

'Speak quickly.'

Henniche put his bony hand into one of his pockets, took from it something shining, and handed it to Brühl.

It was a medal as large as a thaler. Brühl took it to the window, for the day was dark, and examined it: one side of it represented a throne with a man in a sitting posture, dressed in a morning gown and holding a pipe; it was easy to guess that it represented the young Kurfürst; three men, two of them in pages' costumes, the third one in livery, supported the throne. On the other side could be read the following verse relating to Brühl, Sulkowski and Henniche:

Wir sind unserer drei
Zwei Pagen und ein Lakai.

Brühl threw the medal on the floor; Henniche stooped and picked it up from under the sofa where it had rolled. Brühl was angry and thoughtful.

'What does your Excellency say to that?' said Henniche.

'What? Give me the man who did it, and you shall see,' cried Brühl.

'It was stamped in Holland,' said Henniche, 'and we cannot get at them there. But it came from Saxony, for in Holland nobody cares that I was a lackey and both your Excellencies were pages. It came from Saxony!'

'Then we must find the man who did it,' cried Brühl. 'Don't spare money, but find him.'

Henniche shrugged his shoulders.

'Give me that medal,' said Brühl. 'Where did you get it from?'

'Someone put it on my desk. I have no doubt you will find one also.'

'I shall send the culprit to Königstein,' cried Brühl. 'We made Erell ride on a donkey, but this one will be safer in a dungeon.'

'In the first place we must find him,' muttered Henniche. 'I will attend to that.'

'We must buy out the medal and destroy it and you will find the culprit. One can do a great deal with a couple of thousand thalers. Send some intelligent man to Holland.'

'I shall go myself,' said Henniche, 'and I shall find him. He would not be a man who, having done such a witty thing, did not boast about it to anybody. We shall get him.'

Brühl was in a hurry, so he nodded and went out. Henniche left the room also.

The minister, still gloomier now, washed his face, dressed carefully, matching his sword, snuff-box, wig and hat to his suit. The carriage waited at the door. As soon as he got in, the equipage rolled towards the suburb of Wilsdurf. At the entrance to it, he stopped the carriage, put on a light cloak, told the coachman to return, waited till the carriage was at a certain distance, looked round carefully, and seeing only common people he advanced and turned towards a large garden; he followed a path till he came to a gate of which he had the key; he looked once more round, opened the door and entered a small garden at the end of which could be seen a modest country house surrounded by lilac bushes. The birds chirped in the bushes—everything else was quiet.

Brühl, with bent head and thoughtful, walked slowly along the path bordered with trees. The noise of an opening window startled him. In the window appeared a very beautiful lady who seemed to expect him. He caught sight of her and his face brightened. He took off his hat and saluted her, putting his left hand on his heart.

Those who knew the perfect splendour of the unrivalled beauty of the Countess Cosel, then locked up in a solitary castle, would recognise in the lady standing at the window some likeness to that unfortunate woman. She was not as beautiful as her mother, not having her regular features, but she inherited her dignified and majestic mien and the power of her glance.

The lady standing at the window was the Countess Moszynski, whose husband was preparing in Warsaw for the election of the Prince. She preferred to remain in Dresden.

When Brühl reached the threshold she came to meet him. The interior of the house was more luxurious than one would have expected from its modest exterior. It was ornamented with mirrors, luxurious furniture and full of the scent of flowers. In the first large, quiet room, there was a table set for two people, shining with silver, china and cut glass.

'So late—' whispered the Countess, whose hand Brühl kissed.

'Yes,' answered the minister, looking at his watch set with diamonds, 'but I was prevented by an important and unpleasant incident.'

'Unpleasant? What was it?'

'Let us not speak about it today. I should like to forget it.'

'But I would like to know it.'

'My dear Countess, you shall learn it in time,' said Brühl, sitting opposite her. 'It is no wonder that a man who has reached my position by degrees has enemies in those who remain behind him, and who avenge their inferiority by calumnies.'

The Countess listened attentively, made a trifling movement with her hand, and said:

'Calumnies! And you are so weak that you pay attention to them, that they hurt you? I should have my doubts about you, my dear Henry, if you are so weak. The one who wishes to play a great part in the world, must pay no heed to the hissing of spectators. It does not amount to anything. If you feel hurt by such trifles, you will never rise high. One must be superior to such things.'

'A vile insult,' rejoined Brühl.

'What do you care about the barking of a dog behind a hedge?'

'It irritates me.'

'Be ashamed of yourself.'

'You do not know what there is in question.'

Having said this Brühl took the medal from his pocket and showed it to the Countess. She looked at both sides, read the inscription, smiled, shrugged her shoulders, and wanted to throw it through the window, but Brühl stopped her.

'I need it,' said he.

'What for?'

'I must find out who did it. The joke came from Saxony. If we don't punish the man who did it—'

'In the first place you must find him,' said the Countess, 'and then you had better think it over, if by taking revenge you would not be giving too great an importance to some childish folly.'

'They are too daring,' cried Brühl. 'We were obliged to make Erell ride a donkey through the town, and it would be necessary to send the man who ordered this medal to be struck, to Königstein.'

The Countess shrugged her shoulders contemptuously.

'Believe me, it would be better to leave vengeance to Sulkowski,' she said. 'As long as you share the responsibility of state affairs with him, see that everything painful falls on him; you take that which is agreeable. But I hope that you will not be long in partnership with him,' she added.

'I don't know how long it will last,' said Brühl. 'As far as I can see, we must wait till he makes some mistake through being too confident about his own powers.'

'You are right, and that will come soon. Sulkowski is very proud and too conceited; he thinks that he can do anything he likes with the Prince. One must give him a chance to turn a summersault. In the meantime *il tirera les marrons du feu.*'

The Countess laughed, Brühl remained gloomy.

An intelligent-looking servant, wearing high-heeled shoes and dressed like Liotard's famous 'Chocolate girl,' brought in a silver soup tureen. She smiled to Brühl as she put the dish on the table and disappeared.

The *tête à tête* dinner was animated by a lively conversation. The Countess asked about Fräulein Kling, about her mission, even about Brühl's coming marriage.

'I don't think that you will cease to love me,' she said sighing, 'the girl does not love you, and you are indifferent towards her; you marry to win favour with the Princess and the old Countess Kolowrath; I know that and therefore I keep quiet.'

'You are right,' said Brühl, 'I have not a second heart, and the one I had, I gave to you. I marry because it is necessary, as it is necessary also for me to share government affairs with Sulkowski.'

'Try to become indispensable to the Prince: amuse him, hunt with him, leave him as little as possible. If I am not mistaken, Sulkowski will wish to take it easy, to play the part of the *grand seigneur,* you must become indispensable to the King,—I call him king already, for I am certain that he will be elected. He must have somebody always near him, he is weak, and likes the faces he is most accustomed to. You must remember all this.'

'Dear Countess!' said Brühl, taking hold of her hand, 'be my guide, my Egeria, my Providence, and I shall be sure of my future.'

At that moment voices were heard at the gate. The servant rushed in frightened. The Countess rose frowning, angry.

'What is it?' she cried.

'Some one—I don't know, somebody from the court, with a letter or invitation, asks to be admitted.'

'Here? But who could have told him that I was here? I don't receive anyone here.'

Hardly had she pronounced the last words, when amongst the trees in the garden appeared a man in a chamberlain's dress. The gardener tried to bar his way but the chamberlain, paying no heed to him, advanced slowly. Brühl bent forward, looked through the window, recognised Watzdorf and at a signal from the Countess withdrew to the next room, closing the door behind him. The Countess ordered the servant to remove the second plate from the table, which was done in the twinkling of an eye, but the second glass was forgotten. The Countess sat at the table, looking with uneasiness towards the garden: she frowned and trembled with anger. In the meanwhile Watzdorf came to the house and seeing the Countess through the window, said to the gardener:

'I told you that the Countess was here, I knew it.' Saying this he bowed with an ironical smile, looking impudently round as if expecting to see someone else.

The Countess assumed a very severe expression when he entered.

'What are you doing here?' she asked threateningly.

'I beg a thousand pardons! I am the most awkward of men and the most unfortunate of chamberlains. The Prince gave me a letter for you. I went to your palace but could not find you there. The Prince's letter is very urgent. I was obliged to try and find you, and I came here.'

'I am not surprised that you tracked me like a hound,' hissed the Countess, 'but I don't like to be the game.'

Watzdorf appeared to be delighted at her anger. He glanced at the chair on which hung a napkin left, by Brühl. The Countess noticed when he smiled at this discovery. She did not grow confused; but was angry in the highest degree.

'Where is that letter?' she asked.

Watzdorf smiled ironically and began to search his pockets, muttering in the meanwhile impertinently:

'Well, this house is charmingly situated for two.'

He took out several things and among them as if by accident the medal, then he added:

'Just imagine the daring of these agitators! Who could have expected anything like this?'

He put the medal on the table and searched further in his pockets. The Countess took the medal and looked at it, pretending that she had not seen it before: then she said indifferently, replacing it on the table:

'A very poor joke indeed! It does not hurt anybody.'

Watzdorf looked at her.

'It might suggest something to the Prince.'

'What?' asked the Countess.

'That he might find other props,' said Watzdorf.

'Whom? You, Frosch and Horch?'

'Countess, you are malicious.'

'With you one might become mad. Where is that letter?'

'I am in despair! It seems that I have lost it.'

'Running after me for the purpose of amusing me,' muttered the Countess, 'to disturb me when I wish to be alone.'

'Alone!' Watzdorf repeated, smiling ironically and looking at the chair with the napkin.

'I understand you,' the Countess burst out. 'Did the Count Moszynski tell you to spy on me?'

At that moment the rustling of a silk dress was heard, and a lady who a few minutes previously had entered the room and slipped behind a Chinese screen, came slowly to the centre of the room.

Watzdorf was struck dumb with amazement. There was something so unusual in the apparition that even the Countess trembled.

The lady was tall and not young; her gaze was piercing; her mien majestic; her face beautiful notwithstanding her age; she was dressed so strangely that one might have thought she was mad. She wore a large gown, bordered with galoons. The girdle worn on the dress underneath was golden with black cabalistic signs; on her black hair she wore a kind of turban with a band made of parchment inscribed with Hebrew letters, the ends of the band hanging over her shoulders.

She looked piercingly at the intruder, frowned contemptuously, and said severely:

'What do you wish for here? Did you come to spy on my daughter and her mother in order to entertain the Prince by telling him that you have seen the old Cosel? You son of "the pagan and buffoon from Mansfeld," do you intend to annoy me also? Get out! Let us alone!'

She pointed to the door. Watzdorf, confused, retreated. His eyes shone angrily—he went out. Cosel followed him with her eyes, then she turned to her daughter.

It was not her day for her visit from Stolpen, and this time the Countess Moszynski did not expect her. Thinking that Brühl when he saw Watzdorf go out would return, she grew confused. The Countess Cosel sat on the chair previously occupied by Brühl. After having driven off the intruder she became almost absent-minded as she struck the table with her white and still beautiful hand and gazed round the room.

'I came unexpectedly,' she said at length, not looking at her daughter, 'but you permitted me to receive people here whom I wished to see. I asked the minister to come here.'

Moszynski's face expressed surprise.

'Don't be afraid; I expect him only towards evening,' added Cosel. 'But who was here with you? Why did he hide?'

Moszynski was silent, not knowing what to answer: her mother looked at her silently with a kind of pity.

'I understand,' said she with a disdainful smile. 'Some court intrigue. New master, new servants; you must try not to fall on that slippery ice.'

What Moszynski was afraid of happened at that moment. Brühl appeared at the door, and having perceived the woman whom he had never seen before but guessed who she was, became dumb with astonishment and did not know what to do.

Moszynski blushed, then grew pale. Cosel looked at the man, trying as it seemed to guess his character.

'Then it is he?' said she smiling. 'Who is he?'

'The minister Brühl,' her daughter answered.

'Everything new now! Brühl! I don't remember. Come nearer,' she said to Brühl, 'don't be afraid. You see before you a priestess of a new faith. Have you heard of me? I am the widow of Augustus the Strong. I was his wife. You see the Countess Cosel, famous throughout the world both for her success and her misfortunes. At my feet lay the rulers of the world, I commanded millions. Augustus loved nobody but me.'

She spoke quietly; her daughter did not dare to interrupt her; Brühl stood silent, and leaning a little forward seemed to listen attentively.

'You have chanced to see the queen who has come from another world— she was dead, buried, but she is still living in order to convert unbelievers to the true faith of the one God who appeared to Moses in a burning bush.'

The Countess Moszynski trembled and by her furtive looks seemed to beseech her mother to be silent.

Perchance Cosel understood that look, for she rose and said:

'I am going to rest, I shall not interrupt your councils any more. Cosel's daughter ought to rule over Saxony—I understand—'

Having said this she moved majestically towards the same door by which Brühl had entered, and through which she disappeared.

By the other door the servant appeared with a dish.

'I am going,' whispered Brühl, taking his hat. 'It is an unlucky day, but I am glad that that malicious Watzdorf did not see me here.'

'He had a medal,' said the Countess, 'he was delighted with it: I see that he is your bitter foe. What have you done to him?'

'Nothing, except that I was too polite to him.'

'He is a poisonous snake, I know him,' said the Countess.

'He is a buffoon like his father,' Brühl said contemptuously, 'but if he gets in my way—'

'That inscription on the medal, does it not sound like some of his sneers?'

Brühl looked at the Countess; her suspicion seemed to be probable.

'I shall give orders that he is to be watched,' he said shortly. 'If it is as you think, he is not long for this world.'

Having said this he kissed the Countess's hand, took his mantle, thrown into a dark corner near the door and therefore not observed by Watzdorf, and went out.

He returned by the same path by which he came full of hope for a long and free conversation; now he was thinking how he could return home without being noticed.

He passed the gate neglecting to keep a look-out and he needed all his presence of mind in order not to betray his emotion, when he perceived Watzdorf standing opposite and saluting him with an ironical smile.

Brühl returned the salute with perfect ease and amiability.

'You here!' Brühl exclaimed. 'How glad I am!'

'It is I who can call myself happy,' said Watzdorf, 'for I never expected to meet your Excellency under the apple trees. If I remember well, the fruit of an apple tree is called forbidden.'

'Yes,' said Brühl laughing. 'But I did not come for forbidden fruit. The Countess Cosel wished to see me, for she has a request to make to the Prince.'

There was so much probability in it that Watzdorf became confused.

'And you, chamberlain, what are you doing in the country?' asked Brühl.

'I was searching for happiness which I cannot find elsewhere,' Watzdorf muttered.

'Under the apple trees?'

'One might find it more easily there than at court.'

'I see you do not like court life?'

'I have no talent for it,' answered Watzdorf walking beside Brühl.

'But you have wit, a sharp tool, with which you need not be afraid of anything.'

'Yes, it's a good tool for making enemies,' said Watzdorf.

They walked in silence for a while. Watzdorf appearing to think over something.

'I have not yet had the opportunity to present my congratulations to your Excellency,' said he.

'What?' asked Brühl.

'They say that the most able minister is going to marry the most beautiful young lady in the court.'

There was so much passion in his voice, that it struck Brühl suddenly that Watzdorf might be the man whom the beautiful Frances loved. It was only a supposition, or rather a presentiment. Brühl trembled. 'If that is so, then the author of the medal and the beloved of my future wife must be put in a safe place,' he thought.

But nothing was yet proved. They looked at each other smiling, but with hatred in their hearts. The more Brühl hated anyone the more sweet he was towards him: it was not in vain that he had been brought up in the school of Augustus the Strong.

'Your Excellency neglects the Prince,' said Watzdorf. 'The Count Sulkowski is too busy, and Frosch and Horch and Padre Guarini do not suffice for him.'

Brühl smiled as sweetly as he could.

'You are right, I should like to compete even with Frosch and Horch to amuse our gracious Prince, but I have no time, for I must try to conquer the heart of the young lady of whom you have just made mention.'

'That is not necessary,' said Watzdorf, 'the one who shall have her hand, and the rest—does not need her heart. It might be left to someone else. Your Excellency has an excellent example of this in the Count Moszynski, who does not care for his wife's heart.'

Brühl blushed; he stopped, still smiling, but he was out of patience with this preaching man.

'My dear sir,' he said, 'let us speak frankly: have I done you any wrong that you should prick me, or is it only a habit of yours to bite everybody?'

'Both,' answered Watzdorf, 'but I did not expect that such a giant as your Excellency would feel the pricking of such a small fly as I am.'

'I feel no pain,' said Brühl, 'but it tickles me. Would is not be better to make a friend of me?'

Watzdorf laughed.

'Ministers have no friends,' he said, 'it is written in the most elementary catechism of politicians.'

Here Watzdorf saluted and turned into a side street.

It was something like a declaration of war. Brühl was struck dumb with astonishment.

'He declares war? He must be crazy! Why such a dislike towards me? I must find out!'

He went swiftly homeward. As soon as he entered his house, he went to Henniche's office. Henniche was a little surprised at seeing him.

'Give orders that Chamberlain Watzdorf is to be watched,' said Brühl. 'But as Watzdorf is very cunning you must choose a man more cunning than he. Bribe Watzdorf's servants and search his papers.'

'Watzdorf?' repeated Henniche surprised. 'Have you any reason to suspect him?'

'Yes.'

'Must he be sacrificed?'

Brühl was thoughtful for a while.

'We shall see,' he said, 'I don't like to make enemies, but if it is necessary—'

'Is he in the way?'

'I don't like him.'

'One can always find something against him.'

'Yes, find it then, and have it in store,' muttered Brühl. 'I always tried to be amiable. I must show now that I can be threatening.'

Henniche looked at him ironically—Brühl left the room without having noticed it.

Watzdorf, who at the turn of the road separated from Brühl, walked swiftly at first, then slowly, wandering without any aim. His face was gloomy, for he felt that in satisfying his own irritation he had committed a grave mistake which he would redeem very dearly. He was too angry with Brühl to be able to control himself.

Watzdorf although brought up at the court and accustomed to look at its perversity, which might corrupt him also, was a man to be feared for his honesty and integrity. All who surrounded him shocked him. The air which he breathed seemed to him infected and he was disgusted with it.

His love for Frances Kolowrath also contributed to make him hate the world, which had corrupted the beautiful girl. He saw all her faults: coquettishness, levity, pride, egotism and lack of heart, but notwithstanding that, he loved her madly, weeping over her and himself. All her drawbacks he attributed to her education, to the court and its customs, the air which she breathed.

He was in despair.—-All noticed lately that Watzdorf had grown gloomy and irritable to a degree. If he could he would avenge her on somebody, and as Brühl was Frances's fiancé, on him he concentrated his whole anger.

The courtiers, his former friends, avoided Watzdorf: some of them spoke frankly, that he was smelling like a corpse.

Having nothing else to do he went almost mechanically towards Faustina's house. The first part of the mourning was over and there were already whispers of an opera. Sulkowski and Brühl knowing how fond the Prince was of music and of Faustina, were inclined to persuade him to have a performance.

Although Hasse was the husband of the diva they did not live together. *Il divino Sassone,* as the Italians called him, occupied a separate house. Faustina's house was luxuriously furnished. She gave the orders for each performance, and received those who applied for appointments at the theatre.

Watzdorf asked the lackey if his mistress was at home, and received an answer in the affirmative. When announced, and entering the drawing-room, he found the beautiful Italian standing in the centre of the room; while Padre Guarini, dressed in civilian's clothes was walking to and fro. His face was smiling while Faustina was red with anger.

Guarini, seeing Watzdorf, said to him, pointing to the singer:

'Look what this woman is doing with me, the most peaceful man in the world. *Furioso diavolo! Furioso!* If she was singing instead of shrieking—'

Faustina turned to Watzdorf.

'Be my witness,' she shrieked, 'he wishes to make a puppet of me that I may not have my own will. Tomorrow his protégé would ruin my theatre. No, he must be dismissed!'

'Why?' said Guarini quietly. 'Because the beautiful youth does not admire you? Because he prefers the blue eyes of the Frenchwoman to yours?'

Faustina clapped her hands.

'Do you hear him, that abominable *prete?*' cried she. 'Do I need his homage? Have I not enough of that? I am disgusted with it!'

'Yes, as if woman had ever enough of it,' laughed Guarini.

'But about whom, is this question?' asked Watzdorf.

'*Un poverino!*' the Jesuit answered, 'whom that pitiless woman wished to drive from the theatre.'

'*Un assassino! Un traditore! Una spia!*' cried Faustina.

Watzdorf, although feeling sad, was amused by this quarrel between a priest and an actress.

'I shall reconcile you,' said he, 'wait!'

They both looked at him, for the reconciliation was a doubtful one.

'Let the culprit go,' said Watzdorf, 'and in his place, as a good actor is necessary, put one of the ministers. There are no better actors than they! And as Faustina would not quarrel with a minister, there will be peace.'

Guarini nodded, Faustina became silent, and threw herself on a sofa. The Jesuit took the chamberlain by the arm and led him to the window.

'*Carissimo!*' he said sweetly, 'it is still very far to hot weather, and you seem already to be sun-struck.'

'No, I am not mad yet,' said Watzdorf, 'I cannot guarantee, however, that I shall not become mad soon.'

'What is the matter with you? Confess!'

'Shall Faustina's knee be a confessional?'

'What a heathen!' laughed the Jesuit, 'What is the matter with you? Tell me!'

'The world seems to me stupid, that's all!'

'*Carissimo! Perdona*,' said the Jesuit. 'But it seems to me that you are stupid, if you say such things. I shall give you some advice. When you have an excess of bad humour, go into the forest; there you may swear as much as you like, shout as much as you like, and then return to town quieted. You know that in old times they used that remedy for those who could not hold their tongues.'

Watzdorf listened indifferently.

'I pity you,' added Guarini.

'If you knew how I pity you all,' Watzdorf sighed. 'But who could say whose pity is the better?'

'Then let us leave it,' said the Jesuit taking his hat. He came to Faustina and bowed to her humbly.

'Once more I pray your Excellency for the *poverino*, don't dismiss him for my sake.'

'You can do what you please without me,' answered Faustina, 'but should you force me to sing with him, I give you my word that I shall slap his face in public.'

Guarini inclined his head, bowed, and went to the Prince with his report.

It was the hour of rest which Frederick enjoyed after doing nothing the whole day. The hour in which he smoked his pipe, enjoyed the tricks of Frosch and Horch, and the company of Brühl and Sulkowski, for no one else could see him then.

Guarini entered whenever he liked. He was the more amiable companion. The Prince was fond of laughing, and Guarini made him laugh: when he wanted to be silent, Guarini was silent: when asked a question, he answered mirthfully, never contradicting.

Brühl was alone in the room with the Kurfürst. He stood at the master's chair and whispered something. The Prince listened attentively and nodded.

'Father, do you hear what Brühl says?' said the Prince to the Jesuit as he entered.

Guarini came nearer.

'Speak on,' said Frederick.

Brühl began to talk, looking significantly at Guarini.

'He is ironical, and for a long time has been too biting and too bitter.'

'Oh! That's too bad!' the Prince whispered.

'About whom is this question?' asked the Jesuit.

'I have dared to call his Royal Highness's attention to Chamberlain Watzdorf.'

Guarini recalled his meeting with the man.

'The fact is,' he said, 'that I also find him strange.'

'And at the court it is contagious,' Brühl added. The Prince sighed, evidently already bored, and did not answer.

'Where is that fool Frosch?' he said suddenly. 'I am sure he is already asleep in some corner.'

The Jesuit ran to the door and made a sign. Frosch and Horch rushed into the room so precipitously that Horch fell down and Frosch jumped on his back. The Prince began to laugh heartily.

The humiliated Horch tried to avenge himself on his adversary, rose, thinking that he could shake him off, but the cautious little man slipped down and hid behind a chair.

Frederick's eyes followed them—he was anxious to see the result of the contest. Behind the chair both fools, squealing, began to fight. Frederick laughed and forgot all about what he had heard that day. It would be difficult to say how long this would have lasted if Guarini had not whispered to the Prince that it was time to go to the chapel for prayers; the Prince becoming suddenly grave went with the Jesuit to the chapel, where the Princess was already awaiting them.

One day towards evening both the great ministers were sitting in Sulkowski's house: they were silent and seemed to try to penetrate each other's thoughts. Through the open window came the joyful chirping of the birds and the rumbling of carriages.

The faces of the two rivals to a close observer bore a striking difference. One who looked at Brühl at a moment when he thought he was not observed, would have seen under that sweet smile a cold perversity, the depths of which were frightening. In his eyes could be seen the keenness and cunning of a society man who guesses and understands everything, who penetrates the springs of social movements and does not hesitate to take hold of them, if he can do so safely, and provided they can be turned to his own advantage.

Sulkowski was a proud petty noble, who having become a lord, thought that he was so sure of his high position, that he believed everything was subservient to him. He treated Brühl as *malum necessarium* and looked down upon him with that superiority, sure of itself, which shuts its eyes to peril. He was not lacking in ideas, but he was lazy and disliked every effort.

Looking on them it was easy to guess the result of so unequal a fight, for never did a beautiful face conceal more falsehood than that of Brühl, who, when he knew that he was watched, could assume an innocent, childlike expression.

Two men of such calibre, placed in opposition, could not help fighting, but they did not fight yet; on the contrary they seemed to be the best of friends. Some instinct made Sulkowski feel that Brühl was his antagonist, but he laughed at the idea. Brühl was perfectly aware that he would not be able to rule absolutely over the Prince, until he overthrew Sulkowski, who furnished arms against himself. Although he could dissimulate and wait, Sulkowski sometimes avowed to himself, that he disliked the omnipotence of the Jesuit at the court, and that the Princess's influence also stood in his way.

He did not make Brühl his confidant, but he did not exercise sufficient caution and permitted him to guess. While Brühl and Guarini were the best of friends Sulkowski kept aloof from him. He was very respectful towards the Princess, but did not try to win her particular favour. Sometimes he would say something that would have passed muster under the rule of Augustus, but was unadvisable with so severe a Princess.

Father Guarini, knowing that the Prince was fond of him, bowed to him but kept his distance.

He very seldom met Brühl alone, as one of them was obliged to be always with the Prince, to keep him amused.

Evidently they had said all they had to say to each other, for Sulkowski was silent, and Brühl did not interrupt him, but he did not leave him, plainly wishing to say something further before he left.

After a long silence, the Count said:

'All that must remain *entre nous*. The house of Hapsburg is near an end, the glory of the Saxon family should begin. I know well, that we gave up all right of inheritance, that we accepted the *Pragmatic Sanction*, but with the death of the Emperor, things must take another turn for us. We should, at least, take Bohemia, even Silesia, recompensing Prussia elsewhere. I told you that I made a plan. I told Ludovici to make a copy of it.'

'I should like to have it and to think it over,' said Brühl. 'The plan is good and worthy of you and most important for the future of Saxony. I need hardly say that it will give me great pleasure to assist in its realisation. You have in me the most zealous helper and servant. Tell Ludovici to make a copy for me.'

'I do not wish,' said Sulkowski flattered by his approval, 'that this plan for the division of Austria be seen twice by Ludovici. I shall make a copy of it myself.'

Brühl smiled very sweetly.

'It would be a great favour,' he said, 'the means of realising such a wonderful project must be thought over beforehand. One could find in Berlin—'

'Ah!' said Sulkowski smiling, 'there is no doubt that it will be well received there: I rest assured that Prussia is our best friend.'

'I agree with you,' said Brühl, 'the question is only that they might not wish too much.'

'But it's not yet time to treat about it.'

'But it is to prepare the way for the strategy we are going to use.'

After saying this, Brühl rose and observed carelessly:

'I am almost certain that that medal was stamped by someone from Dresden, and I have my suspicions as to who did it.'

Sulkowski turned to him.

'Who could be that daring man?'

'Who could be, if not a courtier, who is confident that his position will protect him? A man of small importance would not dare, for he would know that it would bring him in contact with the executioner and the pillory.'

'Yes, but as he attacked our august lord, he might meet with something worse, because we could not overlook that.'

'I think likewise!' said Brühl. 'They are already too daring and the good-heartedness of our Prince and your magnanimity give them still more courage. Have you noticed how daring Watzdorf junior is?'

Sulkowski looked at Brühl with pity.

'You don't like Watzdorf,' he said. 'He is a buffoon like his father, but not dangerous.'

'Excuse me,' said Brühl with animation. 'The one who trifles with everything, will not respect anything. He will harm me, and you, my dear Count, and at length, our gracious lord.'

'He would not dare.'

Then taking hold of Brühl's button, he said confidentially:

'Tell me frankly, why do you dislike him?'

'He annoys me,' said Brühl, 'by his jokes.'

'I think you imagine,' Sulkowski continued, 'that he is in love with Frances Kolowrath.'

'I should not mind that, because it would prove his good taste,' said Brühl apparently with indifference, although he was irritated.

'But he annoys the Countess Moszynski for whom I have the greatest regard.'

'Ah!' exclaimed Sulkowski laughing.

'The Countess could defend herself,' Brühl said.

'She could ask the Prince to punish the man, but the worst of it is that he slanders us all, without any exception.'

'What? Me also?' asked Sulkowski.

'I could prove it to you.'

'It would be too daring!' said Sulkowski. 'Take my word for it. I think that he ordered that medal to be struck—' said Brühl.

'It is only a suspicion, my dear Brühl.'

'Perhaps it is more than a suspicion,' said Brühl.

'I am certain that he personally gave away four such medals.'

'To whom?'

'To the people belonging to the court. Where does he get so many of them? And why such zeal in distributing a medal which I buy out and destroy?'

'But are you certain of it?'

'Henniche will furnish you with the names of the people.'

'That alters the question,' Sulkowski said. 'It is a fact, and although I explain it by his animosity towards you, it hurts me also.'

'To be quite certain,' Brühl remarked, 'I must tell you frankly, that I ordered secret search to be made in his rooms. A number of those medals were found, which left no doubt that he was the author of them and you must punish him for that. In your high position you might be indifferent,' Brühl continued with well-played animation, 'but for such a small man as I am—'

Sulkowski frowned.

'I never could suspect that Watzdorf would be capable of such villainy.'

'You shall have proofs of it, but, in that case, I shall not act without you; only I beg of you to punish him. To Königstein—'

Sulkowski became thoughtful.

'I would pity him,' he said, 'but if he is guilty—'

'I shall not ask the Prince to do that—you must act. I am your servant, your assistant. I am nobody, and I don't wish to be anybody by myself: my warmest wish is to remain Sulkowski's right hand.'

Sulkowski took his hand and said with his usual pride:

'I wish to have you for my friend, only my friend, my dear Brühl, and for my part, I shall serve you as a friend. I need you, and I can be useful to you.'

They shook hands; Brühl played admirably the part of being moved.

'Listen, Brühl, I speak as a friend; many people know that Watzdorf is in love with Frances; if you wish to get rid of him for that reason, believe me they will accuse you and not me.'

Brühl simulated surprise also admirably.

'My dear Count,' he said with animation, 'I am not jealous at all, but I can be for my lord's and your honour. Today they attack us as well as the throne, tomorrow they will attack our gracious lord alone. We must prevent that.'

'You are right,' said Sulkowski coolly, 'but we must prove that he is guilty.'

'Naturally,' said Brühl, going towards the door.

'Au revoir!'

Yes, at the shooting,' said Brühl. 'The Prince, needs some distraction, and we must furnish it—He is passionately fond of shooting—It is such an innocent amusement.'

Brühl hastened, for it was time to go to the park where targets were placed, and the court was going there. They did not wish to shoot in the castle grounds in order to preserve the appearance of mourning.

In the park, situated near Dresden, the court often found enjoyment. Beautiful avenues of linden trees, enormous beech trees and oaks, a great number of statues, and a lake, made that spot one of the most charming round Dresden. It was situated only about half an hour from the capital. The park in which there was an amphitheatre was surrounded by a densely wooded forest. The scent of freshly opened buds and the quiet made the place charming.

The targets were placed in the amphitheatre. Father Guarini, not satisfied with the preparations made by the huntsmen, and knowing Frederick's character, wanted to prepare some surprise for him and was busy all the morning. Not far from the amphitheatre a shanty was erected, at which a guard was placed with orders not to allow anybody in, for it contained Father Guarini's secret. Three times the Jesuit came with some boxes, and every time he, and several men who helped him, remained there quite a long time. The Jesuit's face beamed with satisfaction when he came for the last time. Evidently he had got everything ready, for, when the rumbling of carriages were heard, the Jesuit putting his hands behind his back, walked quietly down the avenue leading to the amphitheatre. The royal carriages, preceded by the runners, with lackeys in front and rear, cavaliers on horseback, and beautiful ladies, arrived one after another. The Prince was accompanied by his consort who never would leave him, especially when there were ladies in the party. The Countess Kolowrath with her daughter, ladies-in-waiting, chamberlains, pages, followed the Prince. Sulkowski and Brühl in elegant hunting costumes walked beside him.

The rifles were ready, the huntsmen in charge and the pages were to hand them. As Frederick got ready to shoot, Father Guarini appeared in the right-hand alley. He pretended to be very much surprised to see the court: he approached the Prince humbly, and exclaimed:

'Ah! Your Highness, what do I see? Shooting at the target—what a splendid amusement!'

'Is it not?' said Frederick laughing, 'but you shoot only at souls.'

'And not very fortunately either—I miss very often,' rejoined the Jesuit sighing. 'Here the competition will be splendid. But where are the prizes.'

'What prizes?' the Prince asked, a little surprised.

'Your Highness must pardon me,' answered Guarini, 'but to put it plainly, those who prove the best marksmen ought to get some souvenir for their skill.'

'I had not thought of that,' the Prince replied, looking round as if searching for someone.

'If it is permitted me,' said Guarini bowing, 'I will offer five prizes. I cannot give much, for I am poor, but for the amusement of my beloved lord, I deposit my modest gift at his feet.'

The Prince's eyes brightened.

'What? What?' he asked.

'It is my secret!' said the Padre, 'I cannot disclose it until the right time.'

He pointed to the shanty.

'My prizes are there. There are five of them for the five best shots.'

It looked like some funny joke, for Father Guarini was always most anxious to amuse the Prince; very often his jokes were not very new or very elegant, but he always succeeded in making Frederick laugh.

'You make me anxious to see your prizes,' said Frederick.

'The only condition I would make, is that your Highness does not compete. There is no doubt that nobody here shoots better, but I have not prepared a prize worthy of your royal hand. Consequently—'

The eloquence in his eyes ended the sentence.

Frederick began to shoot first. Being used to a rifle since he was a mere boy, it was true that very few people could compete with him, and directly he took hold of a rifle he became so absorbed in the sport that he paid no attention to anything else.

The targets were so arranged that if the ball struck the centre, a white and green—Saxon colours—little flag sprang out: a yellow and black flag—colours of Dresden—marked the first circle beyond the centre; and a black flag marked the further circles.

When Frederick began to shoot and hit the centre with one ball after another, he was applauded by the whole court. After having shot a great many times, the others shot by turns: Sulkowski, Brühl, the envoys of foreign courts, the old General Bandissin, the Count Wackerbarth-Salmour, the Count Los, the Baron Shonberg, the Count Gersdorf and the rest. Every shot was marked. The Prince seemed to wait impatiently for the distribution of Father Guarini's prizes.

It happened that after counting all the marks, old Bandissin won the first prize. The Prince rose from his chair, gazing after Guarini, who told a lackey to bring out the first prize from the shanty.

Curiosity was at its height. The door opened, and two lackeys in court livery—yellow tail coats with blue facings—brought out a large basket covered with a white cloth.

'General,' Guarini said seriously, 'it is not my fault that you do not receive a prize more suitable to your age, but it so pleased the Fates, and nobody can avoid his destiny.'

They opened the basket and took from it an enormous goose, but not in its natural attire. A clever artist had made a very amusing thing of it. On its wings a silk dress, such as was then worn by fashionable ladies, had been put; on its feet there were slippers, while its head was ornamented with a wig and feathers.

The apparition of the frightened bird was received with a burst of laughter, as it began to scream and wanted to fly away; but its wings were entangled in the dress, its feet in the shoes; so it opened its beak as if crying for help and rolled among the spectators.

The Prince laughed till the tears came; all laughed, even the stern Princess.

'The second prize!' cried Frederick.

'Your Majesty,' said Guarini, 'The first prize is called *Angelo o l'amorosal.*'

'Who takes the second prize?' the Prince asked.

The second prize was won by Sulkowski, who was disgusted with Guarini's joke.

The second basket was brought out—and from it jumped a monkey dressed as a clown; the monkey was not less frightened than the goose, but notwithstanding the clothing, it began to run away and having reached the first tree climbed up it.

The Prince seized a rifle and fired: the monkey screaming, hanging bleeding on the branch, fell to the ground.

The third prize, destined for Brühl, was an enormous hare, dressed as *Crispino*. The Prince killed the hare also. He was much excited and happy; his hands trembled, his eyes shone, he laughed.

The fourth prize was a rabbit dressed as *Scaramuzzia*. It was also killed by the Prince.

The last prize was a very amusing one, and it was spared: it was an enormous turkey clad as *Dottore*, with a tail coat, wig, waistcoat and everything that belonged to its official costume. Its comical gravity saved its life.

They all laughed heartily.

The Prince thanked Guarini and made him a longer speech than usual. He assured the Jesuit that not only would he never forget that excellent farce, but that he should order it to be repeated.

They shot till dark: the evening was quiet and warm, the air sweetly scented and the landscape charming; nobody wished to return to town; the court dispersed, forming small groups.

It happened that the Chamberlain Watzdorf stood by the side of the beautiful Frances Kolowrath. Her mother noticed it and tried to separate them, but she did not succeed. Not wishing to draw more attention to them than was proper, she was obliged to leave them alone.

Watzdorf did not neglect to take advantage of his opportunity. Usually ironical, that evening he was sad and depressed. As there was nobody near them he could speak to the girl.

'I am grateful to fate,' said he, 'for the opportunity it gives me of seeing you today: and this happens very seldom. The opportunity is the more precious to me, as I see you for the last time.'

'What do you mean? Why for the last time?' asked the girl with uneasiness.

'I feel that over me hangs the vengeance of that minister-page. They dog my footsteps, they have bribed my servants, for many of my papers are missing. They must have taken them secretly, and if that is so, I am lost.'

'Run away!' cried the girl passionately. 'I beseech you by our love, run away. Nobody watches you just now, take the best horse, and in a couple of hours you will be in Bohemia.'

'Yes, and tomorrow the Austrians would catch me.'

'Then flee to Prussia, to Holland, to France,' said the girl wildly.

'I have no means,' answered Watzdorf, 'and what is worse the charm of life is lost to me. There is no happiness for me. Frances—do not forget me— and avenge me. You will become that man's wife, be his executioner—'

Watzdorf looked into her eyes; they shone with love.

'Should you not see me tomorrow at the court, it will mean that I am lost,' he continued. 'I have a presentiment of which I cannot get rid.'

'But what reasons have you to suspect this?'

'An hour ago I found everything upside down in my room; the lackey has disappeared. Farewell,' he said with a voice full of emotion. 'You will live, I shall die between four gloomy walls. Frances, I beseech you, drop a handkerchief for a souvenir. I shall carry it on my heart; looking at it my grief will be less painful.'

The girl dropped the handkerchief: Watzdorf stooped, picked it up, and hid it in his bosom.

'Thank you,' said he. 'One moment more, and I shall not see your eyes again. Farewell, Frances, *addio*, my sweetest!'

The girl's mother came up at that moment, and, taking advantage of the general confusion, she pulled her daughter away almost by force. Watzdorf withdrew. At a distance of a few steps from him, Sulkowski encountered Brühl, while Guarini entertained the Prince.

'One word—' said Brühl, 'my suppositions were right.'

'What suppositions?' the Count asked indifferently.

'I ordered Watzdorf's apartments to be searched and they found fifty copies of the medal and a letter from the manufacturer, who tried to justify himself because he could not execute a better facsimile of the drawing sent him. It is absolute proof that he is guilty.'

Sulkowski grew pale.

Brühl slipped a paper into his hand.

'Take this: I do not wish to do anything on my own responsibility; do what you please, but if you don't put Watzdorf in Königstein, who knows if one of us will not take his place there? Impudence can do much—Count, do what you please, but I wash my hands of it.—I would not condescend to a search to avenge myself—but the Prince is attacked—It's *crimen læsae majestatis* and for that death is the penalty.'

Having said this Brühl stepped aside quickly; his face assumed its usual sweet smile. He perceived the Countess Moszynski and he turned towards her, bowing in a most ceremonious and respectful way.

Frances Kolowrath followed her mother; she was silent and proud; she gazed several times after Watzdorf and paid not the slightest attention to what was going on around her.

While she was so deeply thoughtful Brühl came to her, bowed respectfully and smiled sweetly. The proud girl's eyes shone; she drew herself up and looked at the minister contemptuously.

'Don't you think,' Brühl said, 'that we succeeded in amusing the Prince?'

'Yes, and you proved a good marksman,' answered the girl. 'I don't doubt that you could shoot just as well at people—'

Brühl looked sharply at her.

'I am not very skilful,' he said coolly, 'but if I were obliged to defend His Majesty, I don't doubt I should shoot well. I noticed that you enjoyed your conversation with the Chamberlain Watzdorf.'

'Yes,' said the girl, 'Watzdorf is very witty, he shoots with words as you do with balls.'

'That is a very dangerous weapon. If one does not know how to handle it,' said Brühl, 'one might shoot oneself.'

The girl's mother interrupted this unpleasant conversation, Frances' look closed it. She wished to intercede with Brühl, but pride closed her mouth: besides she was not certain that Watzdorf did not exaggerate his peril.

The Princess had already left with her ladies in waiting, the Prince still remained. Sulkowski tried to come near him, and the Prince expressing his desire to walk some little distance, the favourite seized the opportunity and walked at his side. Brühl accompanied the Countess Kolowrath.

Sulkowski did not wish to postpone the affair, for he was afraid that Watzdorf might fly if it were delayed.

'It's a very unpleasant duty,' said Sulkowski, 'to be obliged to spoil your majesty's humour after such pleasant amusement.'

Having listened to this, Frederick became gloomy, and looked askance at his minister, who continued:

'The matter is pressing; Brühl and I and even your Majesty are exposed to the ridicule of the whole of Europe: I did not speak before, wishing to spare your Majesty's feelings.—In Holland an abominable medal has been struck—'

Frederick stopped; his face grew as pale as his father's used to do when extremely angry, and he lost control of himself.

'I did not wish to mention it, until we had found the culprit,' Sulkowski wound up. 'I and Brühl would forgive the offence to ourselves, but we cannot forgive the insult to your Majesty.'

'But who? Who?' asked Frederick.

'The man whose whole family including himself, owes everything to your Majesty's father. It is unheard of gratitude and daring—'

'Who? Who?' exclaimed Frederick,

'The Chamberlain Watzdorf.'

'Have you proofs?'

'I have a letter found in his rooms and several medals.'

'I don't wish to see them,' the Prince said extending his arm, 'nor him either; away, away—'

'Shall we let him go unpunished?' Sulkowski asked. 'It cannot be. He will carry his calumnies and spread them in other countries.'

'The Chamberlain Watzdorf? Watzdorf junior?' repeated Frederick. 'But what do you propose?' Saying this he wiped the perspiration from his forehead.

'Königstein,' said Sulkowski shortly.

There was a moment of silence. The Prince walked slowly, with bowed head. It was the first offence that he was obliged to punish.

'Where is Brühl?' he asked.

'Brühl left it to me,' answered the Count.

'Watzdorf! Königstein!' repeated Frederick sighing. Then stopping he turned to Sulkowski and said:—I don't wish to hear any more about it; do what you please.'

Sulkowski turned to Guarini, who walked behind them, and signed to him to approach, for he was the best man to amuse the Prince. The Padre ran as quickly as he could, guessing that he was needed.

'I am in despair!' cried he, 'my goose *Angelo o l'amorosal* is lost, flew away, seeing that Bandissin did not care for it; I am sure it will commit suicide in the forest. I rushed after it and was unfortunate to take three ladies for my goose; they will never forgive me this.'

The Prince's gloomy face brightened up; his white teeth appeared from beneath tightened lips. He looked at the Jesuit as if wishing to find the necessary cheeriness in the bright smiling face, remembering the Italian *puleinello*.

Guarini having guessed that something must have saddened the good lord, did his best to counteract its bad influence.

And in proportion as the Italian's jokes came out, the Prince seemed to forget all else and smiled. But the merry Father was obliged to renew his efforts to disperse the returning cloud, and he did not stop his joking until he heard the loud, hearty laughter, which announced that the Prince had forgotten about the sorrows of this world.

The next day the Chamberlain Watzdorf disappeared; he was the first victim of that reign. A few days later they began to whisper that Watzdorf had been escorted to Königstein. The Prince never mentioned his name; Sulkowski and Brühl did not wish to know anything about the affair.

Fear fell on the court and on the secret enemies of the two ministers.

In *The Historical Mercury*, a newspaper published in Paris, there appeared the following paragraph:

'Those who were familiar with the playful and satirical mind of that young nobleman, who was mixed up in certain affairs after the death of Augustus the Strong, and who showed his cutting wit, will not be astonished at the sad lot which befel him.'

Watzdorf never again appeared in this world. He died in Königstein after fourteen years of seclusion, killed by longing and solitude.

A year after the preceding events, the palace occupied by Brühl was profusely illuminated. Nowhere was greater magnificence displayed during festivities than in Dresden, nowhere more enjoyment than in the capital of Saxony, where the tradition of luxury had been left by Augustus the Strong. From the court the luxury spread amongst those who surrounded the Prince, and on those who came in contact with them, even extending to rich burghers. The banks in those times gave balls for the court; everyone who furnished opportunity for enjoyment and could do something unusual in the way of entertaining, was welcomed.

Fireworks, illuminations, flowers, music, pictures were employed whenever there was opportunity for displaying them.

Brühl was one of the greatest spendthrifts among the *nouveaux riches*; he astounded even those whom nothing could surprise. The illumination of his palace surpassed everything of the kind ever seen in Dresden. A great crowd gazed from a respectful distance at the house of such a grandee; the palace shone with multi-coloured lanterns and wreaths of flowers. Over the *porte-cochère*, on a shield, from which two garlands of pink and white flowers hung down were the letters F and H lovingly blent. A little lower were placed two transparent shields with heraldic hieroglyphics unintelligible to the crowd. The courtiers explained that these were the coats of arms of the newly married couple.

The crowd had been standing for a long time when from the palace came a carriage preceded by runners and postillions on horseback. The carriage contained the mother, and the newly-married couple, coming to their home after the reception at the court. The beautiful young wife was about to enter the house for the first time.

Although no other guests were expected, on both sides of the stairs up to the first floor stood numerous lackeys wearing magnificent scarlet livery; on the first floor stood butlers and the minister's pages.

The house was furnished with princely magnificence; china, silver, bronzes, rugs and thousands of *bibelots* ornamented it. Brühl explained this luxury by saying that he wished to do honour to his lord; he declared that he spent his last penny in order to contribute to the magnificence of the house of Saxony. When the carriage stopped in front of the house, the Countess, assisted by her son-in-law, alighted first and went upstairs. Brühl offered his arm to his wife but she pretended not to see his movement and walked independently beside him. Her beautiful face was sad, stern and proud. There was not the slightest trace of joy on her gloomy features. She looked with indifference on the luxury of the house, as though she did not care to see it; she walked like a victim, who knows that she cannot change her fate and does not expect any happiness. She evidently had had time to grow cold, to think the matter over, to become familiar with her situation, for her face was chilly as a piece of marble. If there was grief within her, it had become chronic, slowly devouring.

The Countess Kolowrath stopped in the drawing-room and turned to look after the married couple. Frances came to her and was silent. On her other side Brühl, wearing a blue and gold velvet dress, stood smiling sweetly at his mother-in-law.

The Countess kissed her daughter silently on the forehead, and although the life of the court had hardened her, tears appeared in her eyes, while the newly married lady remained indifferent.

'Be happy,' the mother whispered. 'I bless you. Be happy!' and she pressed her hands to her eyes to hide her emotion. Brühl seized the other hand and kissed it.

'You need not be left alone,' the mother continued in a broken voice. 'It was my duty to accompany you here and to give you my blessing; but I don't wish to intrude upon you; I myself need rest after such emotion.'

She turned to Brühl.

'I commend you to your wife,' she said, 'be kind to her, love her. Frances will become accustomed to you; be happy! The happiness of this world is fragile and unstable—one must try to make life sweet and not embitter it. Frances, I hope that you will be good to him—'

She covered her eyes, as though some thought had prevented her from finishing what she had had in her mind.

Once more she bent over her daughter's forehead and kissed it. The son-in-law graciously offered his arm and conducted her downstairs to the court-carriage waiting for her, which she entered and hid herself from the gaze of the crowd.

The young bride remained alone for a time and when Brühl returned and wished to take hold of her arm, she looked at him surprised as if she had forgotten where she was and that she had become his wife.

'For God's sake,' the minister whispered, 'let us look happy at least before strangers. On the stage of life, we are all actors'—it was his favourite saying—'let us play our part well.'

Having said this he offered her his arm and conducted her through the row of lighted rooms, to her apartment. Everything she looked at was so magnificent, that to anyone but her it would have been a succession of surprises. She walked not looking and not seeing. At length they came to her dressing-room, situated in front of the chamber, in which two alabaster lamps were throwing a pale, mysterious light.

The young lady, seeing the open door before her, stopped; looked round for a chair, sat on one standing near the dressing-table, and became thoughtful.

They were alone; only the murmuring of the crowd admiring the illuminations was heard.

'Madam,' said Brühl sweetly, 'you are in your own house, and your most obedient servant stands before you.'

He wished to kneel; Frances rose suddenly, sighed, as if throwing off a burden, and said with a voice in which there was sadness:

'I have had enough of this comedy, played the whole day, and it is not necessary for us to continue it. We must be sincere and frank; let us be so from the first day. We have contracted, not matrimony, not a union of hearts, but a bargain; let us try to make it advantageous to us both.'

Speaking thus and not looking at her husband, she began to take off her wreath and veil. There was no emotion in her voice.

'If you do not wish anyone to overhear our conversation,' she added, 'be so kind as to assure yourself that nobody listens at the door.'

'I am sure of that, for I have given orders,' said Brühl, 'and usually my orders are executed.'

Frances took some perfume from a bottle standing on the dressing-table and put it on her temples.

'I cannot be happy,' she continued while undressing, 'as other women are; the man whom I loved, I don't conceal that, is in a dark prison; you love another woman, therefore we are indifferent to each other: although nobody told me what kind of sacrifice I am destined for, I understand it all the same. But I wish to enjoy life and I shall enjoy it—I must have all its pleasures. The poison must be sweetened; that I deserve. I like luxury and I shall have it; I must have distraction in order not to cry; I must have noise in order not to hear the voice of my heart: I must have all that.—You are a stranger to me, I am a stranger to you.—We may be good friends, if you try to deserve my friendship. Who knows, I may take a fancy and be good to you for a few days, but I will not be anybody's slave—even—'

She turned to Brühl who stood silent and embarrassed.

'Do you understand me?'

The minister remained silent.

'Nobody said a word about it to me,' she continued. 'I guessed it with the instinct of a woman; I know to what I am destined.—'

'Madam,' Brühl interrupted, 'there are things about which one must not speak; to betray them means—'

'You don't need to tell me that, I know everything. I can reveal to you, what you think is a secret. Augustus II wished to be famous by his amours, his pious son would not wish to be suspected of it. Therefore everything must be arranged in such a way that nobody can see or hear.'

She laughed ironically.

'I expect, if I give you power, favour, that I must have something in return, and I demand that my fancies shall be respected; and it is quite sure I shall have fancies. I am anxious to know life, I am thirsty for it; I must become intoxicated in order to forget my pain. Do you think,' said she with animation, 'that I shall ever forget about that unfortunate man? I see the walls, between which he is shut, the dark room, hard bed, the face of his jailer, and himself looking through a small window. But in that man dwells a strong spirit, which may keep him alive till the door of the prison is opened. Is it true that your other victim, the poor Hoym, has hanged himself in the prison?'

Brühl looked at the floor.

'Yes,' he said drily, 'it is no great loss; I shall not cry for him.'

'Nor I either,' rejoined Frances, 'but I shall never forget the other man. You understand that the hand that has done this, although I was bound to it in church,—cannot touch mine. We are and shall remain strangers.'

She smiled ironically and continued:

'You became a Catholic, although this is also a secret. It commends you to me! What tact and policy! The king of Poland must have a Catholic for his minister in Poland—Brühl there is Catholic; the Kurfürst of Saxony must have a Protestant minister in Saxony: Brühl here will be a zealous Lutheran. If Zinzendorf became King of the Moravian Brothers I am sure you would belong to the Herrnhut community—*C'est parfait! C'est délicieux!*'

'Madam,' said Brühl with emotion in his voice, 'unknowingly you wound me very severely. I am a Christian and a pious one; denomination to me is a secondary thing, by the Gospel, our Saviour's love—'

He raised his eyes.

'It is a part of your rôle; I understand,' said Frances. 'Then let us leave it, I should like to rest and be alone.'

She looked into his eyes.

'But what would the servants say? What would the people say if you dismiss me like that? It cannot be!'

'It cannot be otherwise!' Frances exclaimed. 'You can spend the night here on the sofa or in an armchair, I will lock myself in the bedroom.'

Brühl looked at her uneasily.

'Then permit me to go and change my clothes and to return here. Nobody will know what our mutual relations are, but nobody must guess it.'

'I understand that! It must be a secret and we must appear the most loving couple. Our platonic marriage will be very amusing. The men will envy you, the women will envy me; you are not bad-looking for the women; the king is better looking than you, but then he is a king! I prefer to be the mistress of the King secretly, than the wife of his minister openly.'

She began to laugh sarcastically.

'I can imagine how his Majesty will be afraid to look at me in the presence of his consort—'

'Madam,' said Brühl wringing his hands, 'the walls have ears.'

Frances shrugged her shoulders.

'You know,' whispered Brühl, 'that should there be even the slightest suspicion, we are both lost.'

'Especially I,' the woman rejoined, 'as I should have to remain with you *en tête à tête*, without any hope of consolation, and that would poison my life.—Consequently I shall be silent.'

Brühl slipped out of the room. The rooms through which he passed were still illuminated; he walked slowly and at the other end of the house entered his dressing-room. Two lackeys waited for him knowing that he would come to undress.

A morning attire lay on the table; it consisted of a gorgeous *robe de chambre* made of blue Lyons satin with bright flowers, snow white linen, and light silk slippers.

As orders were given to extinguish the lights, the lackey took a silver candelabra and lighted Brühl to his chamber. At the door the minister dismissed him with a nod and entered.

There was no one in the dressing-room, the door leading to the bed-chamber was locked.

Brühl looked through the window, the street was already empty. The illuminations were out; a night lamp burned at a corner; a clock in the town struck midnight. Over the black houses, standing in half shadow, the moon stood surrounded by fleecy clouds.

The night was warm, quiet.

In the chamber there was not the slightest movement.

The husband of the beautiful Frances walked several times to and fro looking for a place to rest. He was obliged to content himself with a small sofa and a chair instead of a bed. He lay down, smiled sardonically, thinking about the future, then began to doze.

He dreamed of gold, diamonds, lace, of princely luxury, but not of a human face and heart; then about white clouds with his own monogram, over which there shone the coronet of a Count.

When he opened his eyes, it was already daylight. He ran down from his improvised and uncomfortable bed, and went quickly to his apartment.

First he looked at a clock and was surprised to find that it was already six o'clock, at which hour he usually began his work. When he entered his study he saw Father Guarini standing in the centre and smiling sweetly.

The Jesuit put out his hand to him; Brühl, confused and blushing slightly, kissed it. Before they spoke their eyes met. Then Guarini said mysteriously:

'Ministers cannot sleep long even the first night after their wedding, especially when they have as powerful enemies as you have.'

'With you, Father, and with the Princess's protection, I need not be afraid,' said Brühl.

'It is always necessary to be cautious,' whispered Guarini, 'kings do not rule for ever, my dear Brühl.

'But you, Fathers,' said Brühl also in a whisper, 'rule, and shall rule over the King, and his conscience.'

'My dear friend, I am not immortal, I am already old, and I feel that it will soon be all over with me.'

They were silent for some time. Guarini walked to and fro, with his hands behind his back.

'The Princess and I have prepared the Prince von Lichtenstein,' said he, 'but it goes very slowly. We shall not hasten with that campaign, we must wait until I and circumstances have prepared our lord. At present Sulkowski is first with him. Sulkowski is everything. On your side you have the memory of his father; try to have something more—'

He became silent.

'Piano, piano, pianissimo!' whispered the Jesuit. 'One must know how to talk to our lord. *Al canto si conosce l'ucello, ed al parlar il cervello.'*

Next he began to whisper in Brühl's ear, then having glanced at the clock he took his hat and rushed out.

There was a rap at the other door.

The yellow, contorted face of Henniche appeared through the half-opened door, and then the whole man appeared. Under his arm he had a pile of papers.

First he glanced at Brühl's face consulting it as if it were a barometer to tell his humour.

'Your Excellency,' he said, 'in the first place, my congratulations.'

'Business before all,' the minister interrupted, 'we need money, money, and always money for the court, for our affairs in Poland, for the King, for me, for you, not to mention Sulkowski.'

'They whisper,' said Henniche. 'The noblemen are angry, the townsmen grumble and appeal to their privileges, to *immunitates*.'

'Who?' asked Brühl.

'Almost all of them.'

'But who is at their head? Who speaks most?'

'Many of them.'

'Send the Swiss guard, seize a few of them and send them to Pleissen-burg. There they will keep quiet.'

'But whom shall I choose?'

'I should doubt your acuteness if you do not understand. Do not reach so high as to touch some partisan of Sulkowski's. Do not reach too low, for it would be useless. Do not take a man who has relations at the court—'

'But the reason?' asked the ex-lackey.

Brühl laughed.

'Must I give you a reason? A word spoken too loud, *crimen laesae majestatis*. You should understand if you are not a blockhead.'

'I understand,' said Henniche sighing.

Brühl began to walk to and fro.

'You must tell Globig to carry out my orders. During the last hunting-party a petition was nearly handed to the Prince. A nobleman hid behind a bush. A few hours before a hunting-party, or a ride, or a walk, the roads should be inspected and guards posted. Nobody should be allowed to approach the Prince—'

'I cannot do everything by myself. There are Loss, Hammer, Globig and others.'

'You must supervise them.'

The conversation changed into a confidential whispering, but it did not last long. Brühl yawned, Henniche understood and went out. Chocolate was brought. Brühl swallowed it quickly, drank some water, and rang the bell for a lackey to help him to dress. In the dressing-room everything was ready, and the changing of clothes did not take long. The *porte-chaise* with porters stood at the door. It was nine o'clock when the minister ordered them to carry him to the house occupied by the Austrian envoy, the Prince Venceslas von Lichtenstein. The house stood in the Old Market Square and the journey was not a long one. This hour Brühl usually spent with the King, but today he took advantage of his wedding and went to see the Prince von Lichtenstein. Brühl did not forget that that morning it was essential he should appear to everybody the happiest man in the world; therefore although he was tired, his face beamed with joy.

The Prince von Lichtenstein, a lord, and, in the full meaning of the word, a courtier of one of the oldest ruling houses in Europe, was a man well fitted for his position. He was tall, good-looking; his features were regular, his mien was lordly; he was affable and polite; in his eyes one could see intelligence and diplomatic cunning. Although Brühl was only a petty nobleman, but now, as prime minister of a Prince related to the reigning house of Austria, and as husband of the Countess Kolowrath, almost equal to Lichtenstein, he was clever enough not to show it and he greeted the envoy with respect.

They entered the study. The Prince asked Brühl to be seated, and he himself took a chair opposite him.

'I return,' Brühl said 'to our conversation of yesterday.'

'My dear Brühl, I assure you that you may expect every assistance from my court; title, wealth, protection, but we must go hand in hand—you understand.'

Brühl put out his hand immediately.

'Yes,' he said, 'we must go hand in hand. But nobody must see our hands—the greatest secrecy must be observed, otherwise everything would come to nought. I should be overthrown and with me the man who serves you faithfully.'

'Do you doubt?' asked the Prince? 'My word is as good as that of the Emperor.'

'I am satisfied with your word,' said Brühl.

'Is it the case, that Sulkowski has some plans?' the Prince asked.

'There is no doubt about that.'

'But nothing definite.'

'On the contrary, the plan is written.'

'Have you seen it?'

Brühl smiled and did not answer.

'Could you get it?' asked the Prince.

Brühl's smile became still more significant. The Prince bent towards him and seized both his hands.

'If you give me that plan in writing—'

He hesitated for a moment.

'It would mean much the same as giving you my head,' said Brühl.

'But I hope you could trust me with your head,' the Prince rejoined.

'Certainly,' said Brühl, 'but once the plan is in your hands there could be no further alteration, one of us must fall, and you know how attached the Prince is to him.'

Lichtenstein rose from his seat.

'But we have on our side the Princess, Father Guarini, you, Father Volger and Faustina,' he said eagerly.

Brühl smiled. 'Sulkowski has on his side the Prince's favour and heart.'

'Yes, it is true, that weak people are stubborn, said the Prince, 'but acting on them slowly and intelligently one can always influence them. Never too suddenly, for their feebleness, which they feel, makes them stubborn; one must act on them in such a way as to make them believe that they act by themselves.'

'Sulkowski was the Prince's playmate in boyhood, he trusts him in matters in which he would trust nobody else.'

'I do not deny that the work is difficult, but I do not think it impossible,' answered Lichtenstein. 'But that plan? Have you seen it? Have you read it?'

Brühl checked the Prince's impatience by a cool business question.

'Prince, permit me to speak first about the conditions.'

'With the greatest pleasure.'

'I am very sorry, for I respect Sulkowski for other reasons,' said Brühl; 'he is attached to the Prince, he is faithful to him; he thinks he could make Saxony powerful; but if his influence increases, his ambition may lead him on wrong roads. Sulkowski does not appreciate our saintly Princess; Sulkowski does not respect the clergy.'

'My dear Brühl,' interrupted the Prince, 'I know him as well as you do, if not better; he does not stand on ceremony when he is with me; I knew him in Vienna, where he was with the Prince.'

'We must overthrow Sulkowski.' said Brühl emphatically. 'I ask for nothing more, but this must be done for the King's and the country's good. Then I shall remain alone, and in me you will have the most faithful servant.'

'But that plan? That plan?' repeated Lichtenstein. 'Give it to me and I consent to everything.'

Brühl put his hand carelessly into his side pocket; seeing this, Lichtenstein drew nearer.

Brühl took out a paper and held it before the Prince's eyes. But at the moment when the paper was about to pass into Lichtenstein's hands, there was a rap at the door, and a lackey, appearing on the threshold, announced:

'The Count Sulkowski.'

In the twinkling of an eye the paper disappeared into a pocket and Brühl, sitting comfortably back in his chair, was taking snuff from a gold snuff box.

Sulkowski, standing in the doorway, looked at Brühl and Lichtenstein, but more especially at his competitor who put out his hand to him and smiled sweetly.

'What an early bird you are!' said Sulkowski. 'The very next day after your wedding you visit ambassadors in the morning. I thought you were still at your lady's feet.'

'Duties before all,' Brühl answered. 'I was told that the Prince was going to Vienna, and I came to take leave of him.'

'Prince, are you going to Vienna?' asked Sulkowski surprised. 'I did not know anything about it.'

Lichtenstein seemed a little embarrassed.

'I do not know yet—perchance—' he stammered after a pause. 'I said something about it yesterday at the court, and I see that Brühl, who knows about everything, has learned it.'

The two antagonists were still to all appearances the best of friends, although, on both sides there had begun a secret conflict. That same morning Sulkowski spoke to Ludovici about Brühl's marriage.

Ludovici was more suspicious than the Count.

'Count,' said he, 'that marriage ought to make us careful. Brühl has married not the Countess Kolowrath alone, but with her he has married the Austrian Court, Father Guarini and the Princess. Brühl is sweet as honey, but he overthrew Fleury, Manteufel, Wackerbarth and Hoym; he put Watzdorf into Königstein; I do not trust Brühl.'

Sulkowski began to laugh.

'My dear Ludovici,' he said proudly, 'remember who they were, and who I am! He will not be able to overthrow me were he helped by Guarini and all the Austrians. I shall drive off Guarini and all the Jesuits. I shall give other courtiers to the Princess. With regard to Hoym and Watzdorf, you are mistaken, I sent them away, not he.'

'That is to say he did it by means of your Excellency's hands; *is facit, cui prodest;* I remember that when I studied law. Watzdorf was in love with his present wife.'

'You must not try to teach me anything about court affairs,' said Sulkowski, 'I know what I am about, and none of you know how strong my influence is with the Prince.'

'I do not doubt that,' Ludovici said bowing.

Sulkowski however remembered that conversation. Although he did not betray his thoughts even to his confidant, Ludovici, the Count had distrusted Brühl for some time. It was a suspicious circumstance to him that Brühl was continually with Frederick, remaining for hours with him together with the two fools and Guarini, and accompanied him everywhere, so that the Prince grew accustomed to his face. Several times already he had asked after Brühl when he had been absent longer than usual. Little by little his presence became indispensable.

Sulkowski did not even dream that this could menace him, but he did not wish for any rivals; he was jealous, and alone must be the object of the Prince's favour.

'Brühl must be got rid of,' he said to himself. 'I shall easily find an excuse. I must prepare the Prince.'

The same day after dinner, when the Prince retired as usual to his apartment, put on his *robe de chambre*, sat in a chair and began to smoke a pipe, Sulkowski entered followed by a man carrying a case; he took it from the servant in the ante-room and brought it to the Prince's room.

The Prince during his travels in Italy had taken a fancy to certain masterpieces of Italian art. Wishing to imitate his father, and having inherited his love of music, hunting, luxury, theatres, and even for Leipzig fairs, he also inherited his love of art. He was passionately fond of pictures, he would purchase as many as he could get hold of to increase the collection started by Augustus II.

The best way to please him was either to tell him of some good picture, or present him with one. Usually cold and phlegmatic Augustus' successor would become quite another man at the sight of a good picture; his eyes would shine as they did on hearing Faustina's voice. It seemed almost that thought circulated more quickly through his brain, and, usually silent, he would talk and exclaim.

Even in his saddest mood, at the mention of a picture or an opera, his face would brighten up. Sulkowski, no less than others, was aware of this weak point in his lord.

Augustus III began to blow out the first whiffs of smoke when Sulkowski appeared on the threshold with the case. He looked round him, drew himself up, put out his hand, without a word. Evidently he guessed the contents of the case, personally brought by his favourite.

The King's eyes brightened.—As he disliked talking he urged Sulkowski by gestures only to be quick and disclose what he had brought.

'Your Majesty,' the Count said in a whisper, 'this is certainly a masterpiece, but—'

'But what?' muttered the King frowning.

'But,' the minister said, 'the subject is a little too mythological and if by accident her Majesty should come—'

The King became gloomy and less insistent; his face was stern and he moved his head significantly.

Sulkowski put the case in a corner; Frederick's eyes followed it. 'And who painted it?' he asked.

'The divine Titian Vecello,' said Sulkowski. 'It is not very large, but a true masterpiece.'

On hearing the name the King bowed as though greeting Titian himself, and whispered:

'*Gran maestro!*'

Sulkowski turned the conversation. The King looked at him as though he did not understand, became thoughtful and said to himself:

'*Troppo mitologico!* H'm!'

After a while when the minister spoke of hunting he said, 'What does it represent?'

The Count made a gesture with his hand.

'A very improper scene,' he said.

'Fie 'Hide it! If the Queen should come in, or Father Guarini—fie!'

Notwithstanding his apparent disapproval, his gaze turned constantly to the case.

'I think it would be best to take it away,' said Sulkowski, going towards the case.

The King frowned.

'But just tell me what it represents.'

'Mars and Venus at the moment when Vulcan catches them *in flagrante* and puts a net round them.'

The King shut his eyes and waved his hand.

'Fie! Fie!' he exclaimed. Sulkowski put the case under his arm.

'But to see it for the sake of art,' said the King, 'is only an ordinary sin. I shall confess it to Father Guarini—three *paters* and all is over—'

He stretched out his arm, Sulkowski smiled, opened the case, lifted the cover, and moved the picture towards the King. The pipe fell from his hands.

It was indeed a small masterpiece. The woman it represented was the same belle who sat for Titian's Venus and Diana; a marvellously beautiful woman, but in very fact in a very mythological position.

The King looked at it furtively, evidently ashamed of his curiosity; he blushed, but continued to gaze at the picture. He repeated, *'un gran maestro!'* His eyes shone. He paid no attention to Sulkowski and began to whisper:

'Venus is very beautiful. Classical forms! What a charming, what a lovely *favola!'*

Suddenly overcome with shame, he looked round, pushed aside the picture, spat, made the sign of the cross, and said severely:

'Away with it! I do not wish to lose my soul. Why do you show me such things?'

'But what about the painting, your Majesty?'

'It is a masterpiece, but away with it!' Sulkowski shut the case and was about to carry it away, when the King stopped him.

'Wait—it is better that no one else should be scandalised by it; put it there in the corner; then we shall see—we shall burn it.'

'Burn such a masterpiece?'

The King became thoughtful and continued to smoke the pipe. The minister put the case behind the sofa and returned to the King. Still under the influence of the picture Augustus III continually murmured: *'Diavolo incarnato!'* and he shrugged his shoulders, 'but the picture is admirable. If Mars were not there, and if one could change Venus into repenting Magdalene, I would hang it in my room.'

'Your Majesty, there is no indecency in works of art, one admires only the picture of a master.'

The King was silent.

'I must confess to Father Guarini,' he said presently.

'I am sure that the Padre himself,' said Sulkowski, 'would look at this masterpiece, and not think of confession.'

'*Siete un birbante!*' muttered the King. '*Tace! basta!*'

Thus the conversation about Titian's Venus ended, and as Brühl was not there the King asked after him. Sulkowski sighed. Augustus III glanced at him.

'I see,' said Sulkowski, 'that Brühl supersedes me in your Majesty's favour, and the sight hurts an old and faithful servant like myself. For that alone I could dislike him.'

The King cleared his throat significantly.

'He is a useful man, but has many drawbacks,' continued Sulkowski. 'I am afraid of him. He is mixed up with everything, he takes hold of everything—he squanders the money—is fond of luxury—'

'Oh! Oh! Oh!' muttered the King, shaking his head.

'It is true, your Majesty.'

Sulkowski became silent and looked sad. The King pitied him.

'Sulkowski,' he said, 'don't be afraid, there is plenty of room for both of you, and you will always stand first with me.'

After these words, which were quite an effort for the silent Augustus III, Sulkowski kissed his hand. The King embraced him.

'You are my true friend, but I need Brühl.'

This time Sulkowski did not press the matter further, but made up his mind to pursue the same subject on some future occasion, and allow it to act slowly on the King; he noticed however, that Augustus III was growing accustomed to Brühl, and of this he was afraid.

The King smoked his pipe contentedly, sitting up straight in his chair, blinking his eyes and thinking, as he was wont to do when at peace with all the world. There was a soft rap at the door. It announced that some privileged person, one who was permitted to enter the King's room without being previously announced, was coming. It was Father Guarini. He entered quietly and smiling; the King greeted him with a friendly nod, and continued to smoke his pipe and blink his eyes. Sulkowski, silent, stood near him.

The Jesuit's eyes, searching round the room, were quick to notice the case behind the sofa. He went towards it as though wishing to inspect something with which he was not familiar. The King seeing his movement, blushed and looked reproachfully at Sulkowski, who rushed to the priest and whispered something to him; Augustus III evidently wishing to be beforehand with his excuse muttered to Guarini,

'I did not wish to look at it—it is mythology.'

'Eh!' answered the Padre laughing, 'mythology might be dangerous for your Majesty, but not for an old man like me.'

Sulkowski tried to stop the priest, but the Padre insisted, while the King was embarrassed, and he frowned at Sulkowski. Guarini had no wish to give in, and repeated, 'I must see it.'

Sulkowski's position became unpleasant, for through this picture he had now compromised the King, who always wished to be regarded as a man of severe morals.

'Sentile!' said Guarini to Sulkowski, 'if you do not show me the picture, I might think that you have brought something very ugly into the palace, and that you are endeavouring to serve two gods at the same time,—ruling the country and being fond of art,—one of these two you must do badly, for the saying is—chi due lepri caccia, una non piglia e l'altra lascia.'

Sulkowski's conscience pricked him, and he went towards the case followed by the Jesuit. The King inclined his head towards the window. They lifted the cover; Guarini clapped his hands.

'A masterpiece!' he exclaimed, 'miraviglia! But why do you say that the picture is immoral? On the contrary! The culprits are punished. Vulcan catches them, and he, according to sensus paganorum, represents God's justice. As to Venus, the poor thing is not dressed, ma—'

The Jesuit waved his hand. The King looked at him relieved and happy at this explanation, and cried to Sulkowski: 'Bring it here! Show it to me!'

The minister brought the picture. The King was looking at Venus with evident admiration, when there happened what they dreaded most. While all were bent over Venus, the door leading from the Queen's apartment opened and Queen Josephine, like an avenging angel, proudly entered the room.

In the twinkling of an eye the cover was replaced, Father Guarini retreated towards the window, the King looked up to the ceiling, and Sulkowski tried to conceal the case. But nothing can escape a jealous and suspicious woman. The Queen Josephine guessed everything, blushed, frowned and moved towards the King who slowly rose to greet her.

'We are to have an opera today,' he said, 'Faustina will sing.'

'Very well,' the Queen answered, looking at Sulkowski, 'but I see that you have some other entertainment here. What is it that the Count so carefully conceals?'

The Queen painted herself and was fond of art, and by the shape of the case easily guessed its contents. The King, knowing her strict and exaggerated modesty, grew confused.

'An interesting picture,' the King said, 'but a little too mythological!'

Josephine blushed, grew angry, and looked at Sulkowski.

'I am also fond of art,' she said, 'but not that art which panders to vulgar, sensual propensities; the best painting cannot redeem a wicked thought.'

Understanding the nature of the picture the Queen could not insist on seeing it, and perchance imagined it worse than it was.

Sulkowski guessed that she was angry with him for showing a lewd picture to the King. It was a fact, that the Queen suspected the courtiers of inducing the King to indulge in such amours as his father had, and she considered that to show Augustus III lewd pictures would be one of the means of corrupting him.

Father Guarini changed the subject of conversation, protected Sulkowski, saved the King from embarrassment, and began to talk about the quarrels of Italian actors, whom he continually had to reconcile.

The Queen remained deep in thought and gloomy; she did not know how to conceal her thoughts. The King knew that she would scold him severely for being too familiar with Sulkowski; he sighed and longed for the opera, where, in his musical ecstasies, he might forget the sorrows that were unavoidable in private life, even though he occupied a throne where he could sit half the day smoking a pipe in a *robe de chambre* and smiling at the fancies of a slow imagination.

Sulkowski and Guarini slipped out, leaving the consorts alone, which was the best way of putting the Queen into a better frame of mind.

One of the greatest enjoyments of the court of Saxony during the reign of both Augustus's was the opera, one of the best of those times in Europe and in some respect perhaps even superior to the most famous theatres and orchestras.

Excellent as was the selection of singers in Augustus the Strong's times, the opera was in no way inferior during the reign of his son, who was also fond of music. While listening to the music he was exempt from talking, which he disliked, and permitted to plunge into reverie, in which he spent almost his whole life.

The French singers of the King, at the head of whom was Louis André, numbered about twenty and with them from time to time sang Germans, such as the tenor Gotzel, and Italians such as Annibal.

The court orchestra under the famous Hasse, Faustina's husband in name, was composed of fifty members; besides this there was also a Polish orchestra for chamber music, conducted by Schultze, which consisted of seventeen members. The King would take it to Warsaw when staying there a long time.

Operas and French comedies were performed by turns, for which purpose there were eleven actors and sixteen actresses, and in order to vary the performance there was a French ballet composed of sixty people under the direction of M. Faxier.

Enormous sums of money were spent to maintain so large a company. When they were going to give Hasse's opera 'Egio,' for which Metastasio wrote the libretto on the triumph of Caesar, conqueror of barbarism, there were on the stage a hundred horses, the whole Roman senate, knights, lictors, pretorian guards, heavy and light cavalry, infantry; and the booty was represented by gold and silver lent from the king's treasury for use on the stage. The spectators were amazed, the members of the orchestra were stupefied, and it is a fact that the drummer made a hole in the drum from sheer astonishment. There were two hundred and fifty people on the stage; the opera house was lighted with eight thousand wax candles and the manager was brought specially from Paris; his name was Servadoni. Some of the performances cost as much as 100,000 thalers.

Faustina Bordoni, still beautiful in figure and fascinating in voice, made a great impression on Augustus III. The same opera would be repeated again and again for months and the enthusiastic and dreamy king never tired of the same songs, which would lull him charmingly in the land of dreams.

About that time, besides Faustina, who ruled absolutely behind the stage, appeared the so-called Faustina the second, Teresa Abbuzzi Todeschi, not younger, but perhaps more beautiful, and equally daring. It was said that Brühl was her patron.

That day, after being performed many times, 'Cleophile' was again to be repeated. The King was already in his box, the theatre was full, the hour arrived—but the curtain did not rise.

This was most unusual. But *la diva* Faustina was a privileged person; they waited patiently.

In the mean while a storm was raging behind the stage. Faustina would not sing with Teresa—Teresa swore that she would not appear on the stage with Faustina.

Nobody knew why they were so angry. They both quarrelled madly, but though their tongues were let loose, they did not reveal the cause of their wrath.

A third singer, called Piloja, stood aside, listening to the stream of coarse street language, and smiled as though the spectator of a comedy.

The voices from behind the stage reached the hall, and Sulkowski sent a page to learn what the trouble was. The page returned, having learned no more than that it would require Neptune with a three-pronged fork to pacify the excited waves. Sulkowski whispered to the King and a page was despatched for Father Guarini who alone could unravel the mystery.

In the meanwhile Faustina and Teresa stood opposite to each other as though ready for a fight, both were ready dressed for the stage and neither paid any attention to the fact that their anger ruined the colours with which their faces were painted.

The duel might have been fought, had not Father Guarini rushed in like *Deus ex machina*. Seeing him both women became silent. The Padre looked at them, then took Faustina aside. He seemed to be scolding her tenderly.

A wave of expectation followed the dispute. The orchestra began to tune their instruments. Faustina went immediately to the mirror, which was a good sign, and Guarini began to talk to Teresa, threatening her with a finger laid on his big nose. Teresa was nearly crying. They whispered for a while, then the Padre cried:

'*Pace!* If you are stubborn, *mia cara*, you might *cader dalla papella nelle brage*. Hasten. The overture should commence. The King is waiting.'

At that moment Brühl came behind the stage; he looked at Faustina, nodded to her, then at Teresa, to whom he made some sign, and while the orchestra was playing, all took their places.

Father Guarini nodded to Brühl, and they both went through narrow passages in which the managers were omnipotent, making storms, thunderbolts, ruling over heavens and gods, into a small room behind the stage, in which a dressing table and women's clothing indicated that it was the dressing room of one of these ladies, who not long ago quarrelled so passionately, and who were now singing a most harmonious duet.

Guarini and Brühl were both tired and silent, they sat beside each other, looking into each other's faces; the Jesuit began to smile.

'Here,' he said, 'nobody can see or hear us, it is the hiding place of that viper Teresa, here we are safe. Let us talk.'

He clasped Brühl's knee.

Brühl bent to the Jesuit's ear.

'Lichtenstein has the plan; go with him to Vienna.'

'*Va bene*,' said Guarini. 'I prepared the Queen. I am certain that Sulkowski threatens that he will drive us from the court, that he will separate the King from the Queen, and that he will give him somebody else.'

The Jesuit laughed and shrugged his shoulders.

'He thought of it a little too late!'

Brühl's face became gloomy.

'One must know how to act with the King,' said Guarini. 'It is not his fault that he inherited his father's passions and that he must fight against them. The Bible calls it visiting the sins of the fathers upon the children. The Great Augustus in giving him life gave him also a passionate disposition. He will not be able to control it, therefore we must at least guard it from scandal, shield his sins and make them secret, and not allow them to be suspected. If we required from him absolute purity of life, there would be outbursts of this passion. *Cosa fatta capo ha.* What is done is well done. Sulkowski calculated badly, poor thing; the place is taken, the transaction is closed and although the King loves him he will not betray his secret to him. We are the masters of the situation; and I rejoice, for I know that I save a soul—the sin I take on myself.'

They began to whisper.

'Sulkowski,' said Brühl, 'is wearied; the King made him a general, and he cannot become famous by knightly deeds during the peace. He mentioned that he would like to make a military excursion on the Rhine or into Hungary. Did the King himself suggest that idea to him? During that time—'

Guarini muttered that he understood and approved the idea.

'I will tell the King that Sulkowski needs rest, and everything shall be done.'

The Italian made some quick gestures like a magician's pass before Brühl's eyes, rose and continued:

'Go to the King, applaud Faustina in order to please him; do not prevent Sulkowski from being near the King. I have good reason to believe that he is going to criticise the singer; the King will be annoyed, and it will be useful.'

He laughed, made a movement with his head, opened the door, and having stepped out into the dark labyrinth of passages behind the stage, disappeared.

Brühl presently appeared in the King's box.

The opera house was profusely illuminated. The court, as splendid as in Augustus II's time, was gathered there. The Polish nobles, clad in their rich national costumes, shining with precious stones, occupied the first places. The King looked towards them with a friendly smile. Among the ladies one could see the most brilliant stars of the court; the richly dressed Countess Moszynski, proud Frau Brühl, quiet Countess Sulkowski, the wives of the envoys, the Queen's ladies-in-waiting, everybody who had access to the court.

The King turned towards the stage every time the beautiful Faustina came upon it, and listening to her voice, closed his eyes as if he dreamed of angels. Sometimes he would applaud *la diva*, and then everybody clapped their hands.

The King very seldom looked towards the beautiful ladies and when he did glance their way, his eyes immediately returned to Faustina.

His admiration for her was justified by her voice.

Frau Brühl, luxuriously dressed, was sitting opposite the King, looking thoughtful. Her great challenging beauty attracted everyone's attention; the King alone remained unconscious of it, or did not wish to see her, and had not Augustus III been a simple-minded man, one might have suspected that he wished to hide something.

Beside Frau Brühl, sat, modestly dressed, the Countess Sulkowski, formerly the Queen's lady-in-waiting, née von Stein Jettigen. Her beautiful face had not the irresistible charm so attractive in Frau Brühl. With the Countess Sulkowski was a young girl. Nobody knew her. But being with the Countess as well as by her face and dress, one could guess that she belonged to a distinguished family.

The beautiful women of those times, more than any other, were remarkable for their ample, round figures. Small and frail girls found no admirers. Those famous favourites of Augustus II's were almost all bold riders, fond of hunting, of rifles and horses, looking like silvan goddesses, not frightened to meet a wild beast.

The unknown young girl, sitting with the Countess Sulkowski, was one of those beauties and looked like a flower blossoming on a strong stem. Pink and white, built like Diana, black-eyed and black-haired, she looked about her boldly and proudly. But in that daring manner there was yet a childlike innocence of any experience of the world. Her eyes looked at everything with childlike enthusiasm and boldness.

A black dress with some scarlet ribbons and a few jewels enhanced her wonderful beauty; all eyes were turned inquisitively towards her, and their owners asked feverishly:

'Who is she?'

Frau Brühl also looked at her neighbour.

The Countess Moszynski did not take her eyes off her, and the young men went in search of the Countess Sulkowski's servants in order to learn something from them; but they learned nothing more than that the young lady was the Countess' relation, and that she came from Vienna.

In the meanwhile Sulkowski, having noticed that Brühl went to his wife, bent to the King's ear and whispered:

'Your Majesty, works of art are worthy of admiration, but the work of the Creator also deserves attention. Although the Countess Stein is my wife's relation, I venture to draw your Majesty's attention to her extraordinary beauty. Neither Titian nor Paul Veronese ever created anything like her.'

On hearing this, the King turned, as though frightened, to his minister, looked at him reproachfully and in surprise, and plunged into further admiration of Faustina's voice and charms. Sulkowski withdrew. He knew the King so well that he was certain that, struggle with himself as he might, he would play the same comedy as he did with Titian's Venus. He was right in his supposition. The King with great caution, pretending that he looked elsewhere, directed his eyes to the beautiful Countess Stein. Then as though alarmed by her loveliness, he turned his eyes back to the stage. Some time elapsed and the King looked again at her. Augustus III's head still turned towards the stage, but his half-closed eyes gazed on that shining star.

As he looked round the King's eyes met Frau Brühl's, whose white finger lay against her little nose as if she were threatening him.

At that moment the King began to clap his hands applauding the singer, and everybody followed his example. A keen observer would have seen how Faustina frowned at the King; how Frau Brühl looked at him impatiently, how Moszynski eyed her husband, and how Brühl smiled maliciously.

At last the grand *finale* resounded with the power of all the voices; the opera was ended. The ladies rose and with them the beautiful Countess Stein, the star of that evening; her graceful figure appeared then in all its splendour. The King dared not look again in her direction.

The court, after supper, retired before midnight. Brühl having received the King's orders went home; Sulkowski remained. Frosch and Horch slept in the corners. Augustus III donned a *robe de chambre* and smoked a pipe in his own apartment, for the smell of tobacco was forbidden in the rooms which he shared in common with the Queen. All those who smoked had separate rooms for the purpose; the ladies, feeling an aversion to the fumes, would not suffer smoking in theirs.

'I don't know' Sulkowski said, 'whether your Majesty deigned to look at Adelaida Stein, but I venture to insist that she is unusually beautiful. If our lord the King, Augustus the Strong, of blessed memory, were alive, I am sure he would admire her extremely.'

The King turned, looked at Sulkowski, but said not a word. Sulkowski laughed, took the King's hand and kissed it.

'I am your Majesty's old servant,' continued he, 'and I admire my lord's virtue. Your Majesty lives like a model nobleman, although kings have some privileges. During the performance today I noticed with what admiration the women looked towards your Majesty. Adelaida Stein told my wife that she never saw a better-looking man than your Majesty.'

He became silent. The King played with his china pipe and did not look at him, pretending that he heard not the tempter.

'Faustina sang like a nightingale,' said the King, changing the drift of the conversation.

'But Faustina looks well only on the stage. If I am not mistaken she is nearly forty and Italian women grow old quickly; Adelaida Stein is lovely.'

Augustus III, instead of answering, shrugged his shoulders.

'May it be permitted me to express my admiration? Your Majesty might be a saint, and yet not a happy man. The court is not a monastery.'

Augustus III listened, looking at the ceiling.

'Would your Majesty permit my wife to present her relation at court?' asked Sulkowski not abashed at the King's silence.

'Ask the Queen,' impatiently said the King.

'Adelaida Stein is an orphan: her only relation is my wife. We should like to do something for her future. If she were to win your Majesty's favour, here in the court, she might find a husband, and I know that she would like to stay here.'

Again he was silent, waiting for a word in reply. The King's reticence led him into an error: he thought he must be more explicit. Therefore he continued:

'If your Majesty should care for Adelaida Stein, nobody would guess your fancy.'

He looked at the King, whose face grew pale, his hands trembled and his eyes fell. Sulkowski became frightened and ceased speaking. Augustus III rose.

'Sulkowski,' he said in a suppressed voice. 'I do not wish to be angry with you—but you forget yourself.'

He paced up and down, his face flushed; evidently he was struggling with himself, trying to prevent his anger from bursting forth.

Never had his favourite seen him so angry with him. He was alarmed and kneeling on one knee put out his hand for the King's hand. Augustus III hesitated, but at length he gave it to him.

'Not a word more; everything is forgotten. Stein must leave Dresden at once.'

Thus saying, he turned away.

'Tomorrow,' the King said after a moment of silence, 'send hounds and huntsmen to Hubertsburg. I have not hunted for a long time. Brühl and you shall come with me—the Queen also. I wish to hunt for three days. First day reindeer, the second *par force*, the third woodcock.'

Sulkowski bowed.

'I shall give orders at once.'

'Yes, have everything ready—we start in the morning.'

And having dismissed Sulkowski with a nod of his head, Augustus directed his steps towards the Queen's apartment. The minister followed him, and silently asked for the King's hand. Augustus III seemed to have already forgotten all that had happened, gave it willingly, and smiled as carelessly and cordially as usual.

The next and the following days they hunted in Hubertsburg and the forests by which it was surrounded. The King was in a good humour, which was the case every time the hunt was successful. Brühl and Sulkowski accompanied him. The first day the Queen mentioned that she had heard from Padre Guarini, who loved Sulkowski, that the Count would like to make a military excursion on the Rhine and into Hungary. It was attributed to his desire to get military experience in order to be better able to serve Saxony. The King listened to his consort and shook his head.

'He is already a good general,' he said, 'I cannot get along without him.'

The Queen did not insist. The third day they returned to Dresden and the same day the King ordered arrangements to be made for target practice in the courtyard of the castle. His usual companions tried their skill against his, but Brühl, although he shot well, took great care not to shoot better than the King.

Having rested for one day, the King went to hunt in Klappendorf. The following day he hunted reindeer in Grossenhayn, then in Stanchitz, and passed the night in Moritzburg.

Then he returned to Dresden, for Faustina was going to sing. The ladies occupied the same places; Augustus III looked at Faustina alone. Only when he perceived General Bandissin turning towards him, did he look round.

Countess Sulkowski occupied her box by herself. The King breathed more freely. He made some remark to the General and when the singing began, turning his eyes towards the stage, he glanced at Frau Brühl, who, sad and thoughtful and more beautiful than ever, was looking with contempt as if the whole world was a matter of indifference to her.

The King's birthday, the seventh of October, was celebrated at Huberts-burg Castle. Augustus III was very strict about maintaining the etiquette of the court, introduced by the Queen. The whole court was gorgeously dressed at eight o'clock in the morning, waiting in the large hall for the King, whose custom it was at this hour to attend Mass. All the men wore orange-yellow uniforms, but as they were going to hunt immediately after breakfast, they wore jack-boots. Emerging from the chapel, the King and Queen, and everybody from the court who wished to please them, repaired to the so-called Rubenstein Cross. From there the hunt started, and the King rode after reindeer which had been brought to the spot for the purpose. Sulkowski, Brühl, the old General Bandissin and all the men belonging to the court accompanied the King, who was in an excellent humour. In the morning the Queen had prepared a surprise and presented him with her own portrait painted by herself. Having kissed the hand of the august artist, the King ordered the precious picture to be hung in his room. Sulkowski brought from Giustinian's in Venice a very beautiful picture by Palma Veccio, and deposited it at the King's feet. Brühl brought him a picture painted by Rembrandt. Pictures always pleased the King well. Those which he liked, he would order to be hung in his room and would gaze at them in silence, and only when tired of looking at them would he order them to be hung in the new gallery.

They killed three reindeer that day and the King became still more good-humoured, he did not speak more, but he smiled, winked his eyes, raised his head, and his face beamed with satisfaction. He smiled several times to Sulkowski, as if wishing to smooth over any impression that he was still angry after that unfortunate evening.

The hunt was over early and they went to Hubertsburg, where dinner awaited them. During the hunt the Queen was present, and although her gloomy face betrayed that she was tired, she made an effort to smile and be agreeable to everybody. Even Sulkowski got a few kind words from her.

As soon as dinner was over they started for Dresden, where an opera, three ballets between the acts, the smiles of Faustina and a cantata composed by Hasse specially for the day, awaited the King. At five o'clock, the curtain rose in the theatre, lighted magnificently and filled with the court beautifully dressed, and Faustina, dressed more carefully than ever, came forth staring at the King's box.

The new King was beaming with joy, quite happy because his life flowed smoothly, not disturbed by anything. He never asked the Fates for more, neither for fame, nor conquests; all he cared for was perfect quiet, during which he could eat, laughing at Frosch and Horch, then smoke a pipe, look at good pictures, listen to Padre Guarini's chatter, enjoy Faustina's singing and go to bed, with no misgivings for the next day.

In his quiet life there was however a dark secret. No one knew the King better than Sulkowski, but even from him was hidden one of the corners of his character, in which was hiding a passion ashamed to show itself to the world and the people.

Father Guarini alone, as a confessor, knew how strong that passion was, and he alone could entirely subdue the King. Following his directions Brühl assisted by his mother-in-law and his wife took the impregnable stronghold and was master of it before Sulkowski made the attempt. When he took that unfortunate step it was already too late. The place was taken, another was already in possession, even his best friend Brühl, who pretended that he knew nothing and that he did not wish to know anything, never betraying the secret even by the slightest allusion, and was more powerful than Sulkowski who never even suspected that there could be anyone more essential to the King than himself.

After the attempt with Adelaida Stein, he felt still stronger, thinking that his failure was the best proof that no one could dominate the King by means of a woman. While he felt so assured he stood on the edge of a precipice which he did not see.

Faustina made a great effort that day and sang marvellously. The King raising his eyes was in ecstasies. It seemed that he was looking only at her, although a sharp eye could have detected that from time to time he glanced towards Brühl's wife.

Frau Brühl was charming that day. Everybody was astounded that Brühl could afford to pay for all the luxury with which she was surrounded. Frau

Brühl evidently wished to be the greatest beauty of that evening and she had put on a gold and white dress in which she looked like a virgin. A very becoming head-dress, with a stream of diamonds, white lace on satin, diamond earrings, that shone like two big stars, made her the queen of the evening.

The Countess Moszynski with her severely beautiful features, reminding many of Cosel, was beautiful but in no way did she rival Frau Brühl. All eyes looked at her, she did not look at anybody. Leaning on one arm, she turned towards the stage, but her eyes fixed on one spot were sad.

Brühl was envied, at which he smiled. Dressed as gorgeously as his wife, looking fresh and young, he seemed rather to be a dissipated lazy man, than the most hard-working of ministers to whom the fate of the state was entrusted.

After the first act, a French ballet followed, conducted by Monsieur Favier, with the famous solo dancer Desmoyers, Mademoiselles Rottier and Vauriaville, who were dressed as ideal peasants.

After the opera the elite of the court were invited to a supper, as was the custom in the time of Augustus the Strong.

The enormous hall of the castle was illuminated with thousands of candles; the table was set for eighty people; there was a separate table for the King and Queen. According to the etiquette of the Austrian court only cardinals were invited to the King's table.

The King was in an excellent humour that night; the Queen was gloomy, uneasy, and sad as usual. The beautiful women, who softened her cold and majestic bearing by their charms, saddened and irritated her, although the King gave her no reason to be jealous: on the contrary he was most attentive to his consort and did not gaze at any of the ladies present.

The supper was served very ceremoniously. The dishes were brought in with great pomp, and every toast was announced by trumpet and drums. After ten o'clock all left the table in excellent humour; the King accompanied by Sulkowski and Brühl went to his apartment. Passing the row of ladies Augustus III affected not to see any of them, but when he passed Brühl's wife he exchanged with her a significant look.

Sulkowski did not see anything, neither did he guess anything. Taking advantage of the King's good humour he decided to speak to him confidentially and try to overthrow Brühl. Augustus was equally kind to them both.

They entered the room where the lackeys were in readiness to undress the King and to give him his much-preferred *robe de chambre*. Both ministers waited till the lackeys were dismissed, when Sulkowski whispered something to the King, smiled and pointed to Brühl. The minister noticed the movement and came near; Sulkowski began to whisper to him. It was evident that Brühl did not like what he said, he looked at the King, hesitated a little as though he regretted leaving them together, then he bowed submissively and left the room.

When the door was closed, Augustus III smiled and sitting in a chair, said laconically as was his custom:

'There are only you and Brühl.'

Sulkowski did not like the sound of the rival name, but he was obliged to put up with it.

The pictures presented to the King that day stood before him, and he looked at them with evident delight. Sulkowski tried to guess the King's thoughts.

'Yes,' said he after a while, 'Brühl is excellent for many reasons; he is modest, intelligent, never contradicts me. I do what I please with him. I am very satisfied with him.'

The King only nodded. Perhaps it may have seemed to him strange that Sulkowski should speak in that patronising way about Brühl, but he did not show it.

The minister walked to and fro as if he were in his own room.

'I have not the slightest reason, as I said,' continued Sulkowski, 'to be dissatisfied with Brühl; he is intelligent and capable, but has some faults—'

The King looked at him sharply; Sulkowski finished imperturbably.

'He is a spendthrift, he will cost us too much.'

Having said this the Count stopped before the King, as if waiting for some reply. The King cleared his throat, raised his eyes and was silent.

'He is a good man—' he whispered at length, seeing that the Count waited for his answer.

He finished by stroking the arm of his chair and looking at the pictures.

'If my gracious lord will permit me to express my thoughts—' Sulkowski continued.

Augustus nodded affirmatively. The minister bent a little and said in a whisper:

'Not now, for we need Brühl, but later on we could get along with small officials and thus save a great deal of money, for it would be very difficult to teach him economy. Although I fear no rivalry, because I am sure of the heart of my gracious lord, why should we make Brühl unhappy by letting his ambition grow? The Emperor would give the Kolowraths some estate in Bohemia, if your Majesty were to ask him. They could not retire there—'

Sulkowski looked to see what impression his suggestion had on the King, but he was gazing so intently at the pictures that he seemed not to hear.

The Count added—'Later, later!' but Augustus glancing at him replied neither in the negative nor affirmative and got rid of him by silence.

After a time he rose to look at the pictures, walked several times across the room and yawned, which was the sign that he wished to retire. Sulkowski, not at all satisfied with the result of his proposal, kissed the King's hand and left the room.

While this was going on in the castle, Brühl, sent away on some pretext, gave orders that he was to be carried home. In front of him there was another *porte-chaise* which he recognised as his wife's. They both alighted almost at the same moment. Brühl, who seldom met his wife, offered her his arm. She was about to refuse it but upon reflection accepted it, smiling ironically, and not saying a word she went upstairs with him.

On the stairs Brühl did not speak, but when they reached the first floor, although the lady wished to withdraw her arm, he did not allow her to do so and escorted her to her apartment. They found themselves again in the same room in which the first night after their wedding they held that interesting conversation.

From that moment they had met only for a moment and in the presence of witnesses. In the mornings the mother would be with her daughter, would take her to her house and keep her there under some pretext.

Brühl's duty was only to satisfy all his wife's fancies, which he already willingly performed; for the rest they lived as strangers, meeting only when obliged, and getting as little in each other's way as possible. Brühl was patient and polite. Sometimes he would meet his wife's inquisitive glance which she withdrew as soon as he noticed it.

Frances changed a great deal: she grew still bolder and more fanciful, she learned how to command her household, and required that her will should be obeyed in the twinkling of an eye: sometimes she was unnaturally merry, sometimes mercilessly ironical, sometimes coquettish with strangers, so much so as even to arouse jealousy in such an indifferent husband as Brühl seemed to be; she grew more beautiful every day. Although he was in love with the Countess Moszynski and although it was suspected that he had relations with Abbuzzi, being yet a young man he could not be indifferent to his wife's charms, which seemed to mock his passionate looks.

When they entered the dressing room Frau Brühl withdrew her arm and, going to the dressing table, put down her gloves. She expected that her husband would leave her and was surprised to see him standing between a table and a chair.

Her look seemed to say: 'You are still here?' Brühl's enigmatical smile seemed to answer: 'Yes, madam, I am waiting.'

'Have you anything to tell me?' asked she.

'Will you not permit me to sit down and rest, and look on your beauty?'

Frances turned and laughed, shrugging her white shoulders; then she turned again towards the mirror not without a certain coquettish movement, which Brühl noticed.

'Will you not agree that my position is a very peculiar one?'

'Mine is also peculiar; but neither you nor I need be surprised at that.'

'You made me hope, that sometimes—you might have a fancy even for your husband.'

'Yes! It may be that I said that, I do not remember,' she answered carelessly, 'but it is certain that I have not that fancy yet. Go and play cards with Moszynski or amuse yourself with Abbuzzi, and let me alone. You worry me.'

'I ask you only for a moment's conversation.'

'Let us talk then but about something else.'

'About the King?' said Brühl.

'I do not know if that will be permitted,' answered Frances laughing.

'Between ourselves—we have no sentiments, only a common interest.'

'You are right; then?'

'How is the King disposed towards Sulkowski?' asked Brühl.

There was a long silence. Could one have seen within the woman's heart, one would have noticed that the question hurt her. She knew that this man did not care much for her, and because of some strange caprice she wanted to please him, in order to enjoy tormenting him. An indifferent question hurt her but she did not betray it.

'Ah!' she exclaimed. 'You wish me to be sincere? Sulkowski, you and even the King, you worry me horribly! What do I care about your ambitions and your quarrels? I wish to enjoy life! The King is a doll without life!'

'For God's sake!' exclaimed Brühl, wringing his hands.

'Nobody is listening to us,' said she indifferently. 'You told me to amuse myself with the doll, or rather you gave me to understand that he might play with me, but you can't expect me to be in love with him. You know the King best. Good-looking, kind, incapable of anything doubtful, passionate without sentiment, attached without courage to show it, pious and superstitious, lascivious, timid, thoughtless, tiresome—dreadfully so.'

'Madam,' Brühl cried, 'were all that true you should not say it, and I should not listen to it.'

'Then let us yawn,' the woman answered and she opened her mouth: then she threw herself on the sofa as if she were tired, her head hanging down, her arms fallen along her body; in that melancholy and coquettish position she was charming. Brühl looked and sighed.

'You asked me about Sulkowski,' said Frances slowly. The minister nodded.

'Who can guess what that doll the King thinks? Has he a heart? Is he capable of love? Can he love anybody sufficiently to become attached? He is fond of Sulkowski as he is of his two fools, I know nothing more.'

'But if we are to rule, I through you,' said Brühl, 'we must get rid of him.'

'And send him to Königstein as you did Watzdorf?' the woman rejoined frowning.

The name fell as a stone between them; the minister grew confused.

'I give you my word, that it was not I, but Sulkowski, who sent Watzdorf to Königstein.'

'The word of a diplomatist?'

'No, of an honest man,' said Brühl, putting his hand on his breast. 'You could not say that I got rid of him on account of jealousy. Till now I have had no right to be jealous—'

'What do you mean by till now? Do you expect to have the right?'

'It seems to me,' said Brühl gallantly, 'if not today then tomorrow you may tire of this, who knows? Perchance you might deign to look at your servant.'

'It seems to me that you will have to wait a long time for that,' the woman whispered.

'I shall be patient,' said Brühl.

'*Croyez et buvez de l'eau,*' rejoined the woman.

Brühl shivered but said coolly:

'You ought to help me to overthrow Sulkowski.'

'Yes, mother told me the same, implying that he might introduce Adelaida Stein or some other woman to the King. What do I care for that?'

'But are you not fond of diamonds, dresses, luxury, high living?' Brühl asked.

They looked into each other's eyes.

'Very well then,' she said, 'we shall overthrow Sulkowski, it will be a revenge for Watzdorf; it will be a distraction. We shall overthrow that boaster.'

'But you must act carefully, slowly, you must—'

He wanted to explain to her at length, when Frances rose, as if lacking in patience.

'You think I need some instruction?' she said laughing. 'And what am I a woman for? You think it necessary to teach me cunning, how to pour the poison by drops, how to whisper traitorous words? How to answer suspicions with a double-meaning word? Ah! my dear sir, I was brought up at court. I looked at you ministers, my mother was my teacher, who, while still in the cradle, taught me how to lie, how to love falsehood!'

And she laughed strangely, almost desperately.

'Be assured, I shall overthrow him, and when I choose, you also—'

Suddenly she became silent, she put a handkerchief to her eyes, and went slowly to her chamber. She locked the door behind her; Brühl remained alone.

In a narrow street near the wall of the old city, not far from the river Elbe, stood a small house in a garden surrounded with a wall. One could easily see that it had been recently erected, and care had been taken to make it handsomer than the other houses. On the walls the architect had suspended stone flowers, round the windows were placed ornaments, graceful curves took the place of straight lines, thus making the building very fantastic.

On the gate stood two vases brought from Italy in order to remind one of that country. On one side of the house a verandah also reminded one of the Italian *pergole*. The front of the house turned towards the river Elbe. Young trees already gave some shadow, and two old linden trees, which remained from byegone times, spread their branches widely.

One autumn evening a woman was sitting on the balcony. She was the personification of wistful longing. She was young, beautiful, but sad as night; her black eyebrows were contracted, in her dark eyes shone tears; she put her elbows on her knees, leaned her head on her hands, and looked into the distance.

It was easy to recognise in her an Italian, for such a beautiful form nature grants only to her elect children, growing in air filled with the scent of orange blossoms. On the half-open red lips, between which could be seen her white teeth, there lingered a song. Her thoughts interrupted it, the voice stopped, and after a while flowed on again like a dream, then died away in silence, changing into a sigh.

She was alone, her thoughts concentrated on herself, turned into stone by longing, wearied of life. The song flowed from habit, the tears flowed from the heart.

Dressed as if she were in her own country, she could dream about the warm Italian autumn, for the day was warm. She wore a light dress, slipping from her shoulders, her black hair was loose, her arms were bare. It was difficult to guess her age—the first years of youth had hardly passed and it was followed by those in which one longs after youth and looks forward to the future, though fearing the latter in the meanwhile. Her eyes were already familiar with tears and the mouth seemed no more to yearn after kisses, for she was already familiar with their sweetness. Her body was near the dreary river Elbe under the sky of the North, but her thoughts were far beyond the mountains and seas.

To the left the sun was setting in an orange-yellow sky and she turned her eyes in that direction. Just then steps were heard in the narrow street. The dreamy woman heard them and awoke from her dreams. She became frightened and listened. Someone knocked at the gate. Afraid, she wrapped herself in her gown, gathered up her dishevelled hair and disappeared into the house.

Another knock was heard at the gate. An old grey-haired man, wearing only a shirt and a cotton cape opened the door and looked out. At the gate stood a good-looking man, who, without asking permission, walked through. The old man muttered something, closed the door and followed him.

The new-comer asked the old man in Italian whether Teresa was at home and received from him an answer in the affirmative. He went quickly towards the house, the door of which stood open. The entrance hall was empty; he went upstairs and knocked at the door; an old, poorly dressed woman opened it and let him in.

The guest entered and found only the stool upon which the Italian was sitting a short time ago. The door leading to the balcony was open. The view from here was so charming that he stopped, looked at it and grew meditative.

The rustling of a dress was heard behind him, and the same woman whom we saw on the balcony advanced slowly. She now wore a voluminous black dress and her hair was negligently tied. Her face bore the same expression of weariness.

She nodded as her guest turned to greet her. They spoke in Italian.

'What is the matter with you?' the stranger asked.

'I am not well! I am dying from longing,' answered the Italian sadly. 'I cannot live here!'

'Where does such despair come from?'

'From the air!' the woman cried, throwing herself on a sofa.

The man sat opposite her on a chair.

'From the air!' she repeated, 'I cannot breathe here! I cannot live here! I must die here!'

'But what is the matter?'

'You see——'

'Then again that longing?'

'It has never left me.'

'I am sure Faustina has done something again,' said the visitor. It was Brühl, as one could guess.

'Faustina?' she said looking at him angrily. 'You think and talk only of her!'

'Why do you not eclipse Faustina? Why do you not try to please the King? She is older——'

'She is a witch as old as the world—' interrupted Teresa. 'An abominable comedian. But with that King——'

'Pray, speak with respect about him!'

Teresa's mouth twitched.

'I will give you some advice,' said Brühl, 'when you sing, always turn towards the King, look at him, smile to him, be coquettish. If he applaud you, you are first.'

'But in the meanwhile that old Faustina is first. The King is ruled by habit, and has no taste. She has a coarse voice and grey hair. But it does not matter, she is a *diva*, and we *compars!*'

'Teresa, listen,' said Brühl, 'do not despair, it shall be changed, Faustina shall return home, you shall remain.'

'I would prefer the contrary,' Teresa muttered.

'I have not time today to talk that matter over with you,' said Brühl. 'At any minute I expect Padre Guarini to rap at the door. Tell old Beppo to let him in. I could not see him elsewhere and I told him to come here. Give him something sweet, but not your lips which are the sweetest, and leave us alone.'

Teresa listened with indifference; then as though forced to obey, she rose and moved slowly towards the door calling her old woman, to whom she whispered a few words. Brühl paced up and down the room.

Teresa turned, looked at him and went to the sofa, but a muffled knock at the door forced her to rise again to welcome the Jesuit.

A swift step was heard on the stairs and the long face of the Padre, smiling kindly, appeared in the doorway. He noticed Teresa as she put in order the things scattered about the room.

'Let that be,' he exclaimed. 'I am not a guest, but one of the family. I feel so happy to be with my countrymen.'

Brühl came over to Guarini.

'What news?' he asked. 'Is he going away?'

'Yes,' said the Padre laughing. 'The King himself told him to go and rest after working so hard. Do you understand? Very cleverly done. I never expected the Queen to be so cunning. She said to the King, "I know that you will be longing after Sulkowski, that we shall not be able to find a substitute for him, but he is killing himself with hard work. He is made for the active life of a soldier, let him go and smell some powder, and return refreshed." The King kissed her hand, thanking her for her sympathy for his favourite, and he said: "I shall tell Sulkowski today to go and travel, and pay his expenses." We must not stint the money! Let him go! Let him go!' exclaimed Guarini.

Brühl accompanied him.

'Let him go!'

'He shall stay a few months,' the Padre continued, 'we shall have plenty of time in which to prepare the King's mind to dismiss him.'

Brühl's face brightened.

'During that time you know what you have to do,' added Guarini. 'You must not act against him; that would be dangerous. Leave that to me and the Queen. Sulkowski hurt many by his pride; as soon as they realise that his good luck may forsake him, they will help us. You must remain his friend till the end.'

'That was my idea also,' said Brühl, 'even I shall protest against his departure, arguing that I shall not be able to do everything without Sulkowski.'

'Very well,' said Guarini. '*Al nemico il ponte d'oro chi fuge*—when the King asks for money, give it lavishly.'

'Even to the last thaler,' said Brühl, rubbing his hands; then recollecting that he must show his gratitude, he kissed the priest's hand.

'*Lontano dagli occhi, lontano dal cuore,*' muttered the Padre. 'The King will get accustomed to you.'

They both walked to and fro, the Padre was pondering.

'He leaves his wife, she will communicate with him,' he said quietly.

'We must have some people round her.'

'One would do,' said Guarini, 'but it seems that she is not so easy to deal with, and it is difficult to find a man for such a function.'

They began to whisper.

'*A goccia a goccia si cava la pietra*—' added the Padre.

Teresa entered from the other room; she was better dressed out of respect to the priest; she brought some fruit which she placed on the table.

The priest clapped her on the shoulder in the Italian fashion, she kissed his hand. He took several medals from his pocket, and gave Teresa one for herself, and two for her mother and the old Beppo, for which she kissed his hand again.

The dusk was already falling when Brühl and the Padre left the room in which Teresa remained, as sad as before. The old mother came to keep her company, but they both longed so wistfully after their own sun-bathed country that they could not speak.

They had not yet lighted the lamp in order not to attract the mosquitoes, when there was again a rap at the door. Teresa did not rise although she was curious to know who was there: who could bring her any consolation?

They could hear a conversation being carried on in Italian with Beppo on the stairs; it was a woman's voice. Teresa sprang from her seat, her mother also rose. In the dusk they perceived on the threshold a tall, well-dressed and good-looking woman, and Teresa to her great surprise recognised her antagonist Faustina.

The stage queen looked round the room and seemed to be thinking what to say.

Teresa stood silent.

'Do you see, I come to you, I!' Faustina said laughing. 'I waited in vain for you to come to me, and I came to make peace! My dear Teresa, we are Italians, both from that beautiful country, where the oranges blossom, and instead of making our life sweet, we poison it. Give me your hand and let us be friends.'

Teresa hesitated, then she began to cry and threw herself on Faustina's neck.

'I never was your foe!' she exclaimed. 'I have not taken a lover from you, I never spoke ill of you.'

'Let us forget about the past!' Faustina rejoined. 'Let us not speak of it, let us be friends. Our life is bitter enough, poisoned by others; we need not help them.'

Faustina sighed.

'I come to you, for I pity you; but what is the use of good advice and of kind words? They are too late, nobody can stop that which is to be.'

She became silent; Teresa's mother left the room; the two women seated themselves.

'The people mar our happiness,' said Faustina, 'and we must swallow our tears. It is not our world—and at their court one must walk as cautiously as on ice, in order not to slip or fall. Fortunately I have the King, and he will be faithful to my voice. He is a good creature, who goes to his box as a horse to his stable, and I furnish him with his food of songs.'

She laughed and bent and kissed Teresa's forehead.

'I pity you, you are in that man's hands.'

Teresa looked timidly round and said:

'I am afraid of my own mother.'

'And I am not afraid of anybody,' said Faustina. 'But tell me do you know him?'

Teresa shivered.

'He is a dreadful man!' Faustina said. 'He is sweet, kind, but his laughter hisses like that of a serpent; he smiles but he has no heart. And so pious, so modest—'

Faustina shook herself and continued:

'I have come to tell you, that soon he will rule absolutely over us all, and then woe to any of us if we resist him. *Poverina!*'

Teresa was silent. Faustina continued:

'Perhaps he is good to you, but if you could hear complaints, as I do everyday, about his oppression, you would hate him.'

'My dear Faustina,' Teresa at last replied, 'I am glad you came to see me. I am so miserable! I dream continually of the Adriatic sea: it seems to me that I sit on the threshold of our cottage—*lucciole* fly in the air, Andrea plays the guitar—the song resounds, the wind brings the scent of flowers. I wake up, listen: the wind rustles, but it brings snow, and the strange tongue resounds and the people laugh and their irony wounds and their love humiliates.'

Teresa covered her face with her hands.

'*Cara mia,*' said Faustina kissing her, 'therefore let us not tease each other but help each other on this thorny path.'

And she put out her hand whispering:

'Be careful of that man, for he is dreadful, and may the Madonna take care of you.'

Teresa rose and accompanied her to the door.

'*Addio!*' she said. 'May God reward you for your good heart; you came when I was sad—I am happier now that we are friends.'

Thus they separated and the thoughtful Faustina, whose *porte-chaise* was waiting in front of the house, told the men to carry her home. She was obliged to pass the castle. The dusk was not yet as dark in the street as it was in the houses and one could recognise people's faces. Faustina looking distractedly in front of her recognised, in a porte-chaise passing hers, Sulkowski's pale face and black moustache.

She rapped at the window and cried:

'*Fermate!*'

Sulkowski leaned out. Both *porte-chaises* stopped so that their windows were opposite each other and their occupants could converse.

Faustina dropped the glass; the minister, a little surprised, looked at her.

'I must have a word with your Excellency,' she said in Italian.

'Beautiful *diva!'* said the Count, 'if it is a question of some quarrel, Padre Guarini is for that; if about some favour, our gracious King never refuses you anything, but I have no time to listen to you!'

'Count! the question is not about myself, not about a favour, but about you and the King,' said Faustina boldly.

'I am at your service and I listen to you,' said the Count smiling.

'Ah! if you would also believe me!'

The Count was silent and tried to control his impatience.

'Count,' said Faustina, 'is it true that you are going away, that you leave the place to your foes?'

Sulkowski laughed.

'I have no foes,' he said quietly, 'and were I so fortunate as to have them, (for I should consider it an honour to gain enemies by serving the King), I should not be afraid of them.'

'Do not mistrust me,' rejoined Faustina. 'But from behind the stage one sees the world well and one knows people better than in the drawing-room. Count, I am a friend of yours, for you love the King and you wish for the welfare of this country which I consider my second fatherland. You wish that others also loved the King but they think only of themselves and do not care about the country at all.'

Sulkowski frowned.

'But who? Who?'

'Are you blind then?' Faustina exclaimed. 'Do you not see anything? Have I to open your eyes? The Queen is jealous of the King's favours to-wards you, the almighty Padre Guarini is your foe and Brühl your rival. They made a plot secretly, they send you away in order to take from you the King's heart. And you do not see it! That man will take your place!'

Saying this she wrung her hands; Sulkowski listened; his pale face flushed.

'My dear Signora,' he said, 'these are dreams and visions. I am going, but I myself asked for leave of absence; I have no enemies and I am sure of the King's heart. Be assured it is gossip, flying round the court like mosquitoes about the marshes. Believe me, I am not blind and it is difficult to fool me and still more difficult to get rid of me.'

He began to laugh. He wished to withdraw when Faustina exclaimed:

'Count, is it possible that you are so blind? Your noble character does not admit of treachery which everybody sees.'

'Because all that has no sense. Brühl would not dare, even had he such allies as the Queen and the venerable Padre.'

Faustina lowered her head and said slowly:

'Therefore that which is destined is unavoidable. *Chi a la morte è destinato, muore santo o disperato. Addio, signor conte* and may Providence guide you and bring you back. Do not stay long away. You may recollect Faustina's warning, but it will be too late.'

The Count took hold of her hand.

'Beautiful and good-hearted signora,' he said, 'I am very grateful to you, for that which you have done is the proof of a good heart. I know how to appreciate it. But things are not as bad as you imagine. I can call the King my best friend; I trust him and shall not be disappointed! Be easy about me!'

Faustina said nothing more; the Count saluted her.

But he changed his plans and ordered his men to bear him to Brühl's palace.

It was a time at which he had a good chance of finding him at home. He did not need to ask to be admitted, for before the almighty Sulkowski all doors were thrown open.

Brühl was at home.

Sulkowski rushed upstairs and did not notice that a page preceded him through another door to tell his master about the visitor.

Brühl was with Henniche whom he dismissed, and before Sulkowski, who was obliged to pass through several drawing-rooms, reached his study, he fell on his knees before a crucifix and began to pray.

The easy manner in which he assumed that position proved that it was not for the first time that he found it advisable that a visitor should come upon him unexpectedly praying.

The contemporary writers assure us that Brühl was very often found praying.

Sulkowski entered the room without knocking at the door and stood there in surprise; it was the first time he had seen Brühl praying and he could hardly believe his own eyes; he stood motionless, while Brühl with his back turned, as though he had not heard the door open, knelt, sighing. At length he beat upon his breast, bending his head as low as a beggar in front of a church asking for alms.

Sulkowski could not have suspected that all this was a comedy, for he entered unannounced and in the dusk the *porte-chaise* could not have been noticed.

The farce lasted quite a long time, and every time Brühl lifted his hand Sulkowski could see a rosary-round his wrist. At length the Count coughed slightly.

Brühl started as if frightened, and having perceived Sulkowski covered his eyes:

'Ah! dear Count! You must excuse me—I am ashamed—but sometimes one needs to pray—so much time do we give to the pleasures of life and it is only right that some should be given to prayer—'

'It is I that must beg your pardon,' said Sulkowski advancing slowly, 'and I am edified by your piety. Forgive me that I have interrupted you.'

'I was just finishing,' Brühl said pointing to the sofa.

Two candles were burning on the table.

'A man who prays like that,' thought Sulkowski, 'cannot be bad and perverse; it is impossible.'

A heavy weight fell from his breast. He looked at Brühl who seemed to be still in pious ecstasies.

'Well,' said Sulkowski, seating himself comfortably on the sofa, 'you know that I am going away.'

Brühl's face became melancholy.

'You must do as you please,' he said slowly, 'as for me I neither approve your voyage, nor do I advise it. Speaking frankly, I was against it and I am still. In the first place nobody can be a substitute for you with the King. I can and I must be frank with you. The Queen is a saint, but she is a woman. If you go her influence will increase and the King will fall under her and Guarini's influence. You know that I am a good Catholic but I should dislike to see the King's mind too much under the influence of the priests. Our gracious lord hearkens too much to them already and hurts the feelings of his Saxon subjects.'

Sulkowski listened very attentively.

'My dear Brühl,' he said, 'you are right and I endorse your opinion. All that you say is true. You blame me for going away, but I am a soldier. The King made me commander of his army. I expect a war and I persuaded the King that war is inevitable, that Saxony must take advantage of the situation of Austria. That is the reason why I wish to acquire military experience; I go, but not to satisfy my fancy—'

'I would prefer that you stayed,' Brühl rejoined,

'And do you know what they say?' asked Sulkowski.

Brühl's face expressed surprise.

'It is very curious,' said Sulkowski slowly. 'They warn me not to go, for you and Guarini have made a plot against me, to send me away purposely, in order to overthrow me.'

Brühl wrung his hands, sprang from his chair and said angrily:

'Show me that slanderer! They dare to say that against me! I and Father Guarini! I who fear him as a pestilence! I would dare to attack you whom the King calls friend! It is stupid and ridiculous!'

'Calm yourself,' said Sulkowski laughing. 'I told you this to show you how stupid people are. I hope you do not think that I distrust or fear you.'

And he added after a while:

'It is possible that a foolish man might make such an attempt, but it would cost him dear; I am sure of the King's favour, he has no secrets from me.'

He shrugged his shoulders contemptuously.

'In that case,' Brühl rejoined, 'I shall still more insist that you remain.'

'Excuse me, but exactly for the same reason I must go, in order to prove to the idiots that I am not afraid of anybody.'

Brühl waved his hand.

'I am sure it came from Berlin, where the gossip about Saxony originated,' he said.

'I am going to Prague tomorrow,' said Sulkowski, for I must look at Prague from a strategical point of view, as we are going to take it. Can I take leave of your wife?'

Brühl rang the bell. The lackey entered.

'Is your mistress at home?'

'Yes, your Excellency.'

'Announce the Count Sulkowski and me.'

The lackey left the room; there was silence; then he returned and said:

'My lady is ready to receive your Excellencies.'

Sulkowski rose from the sofa and went to the drawing-room; Brühl followed him, smiling notwithstanding the emotions he had just experienced.

In the drawing-room Brühl's beautiful wife was waiting for them. She had just returned from the Queen's *cercle*, which was usually held from four to six o'clock. She was dressed and radiant in her beauty which astonished more than attracted. There was something wild in her eyes, something cruel in her mouth, those who looked at her became uneasy. It was the reflection of the disquiet raging in her soul.

She looked at Sulkowski.

'I have come to take leave of you.' said Sulkowski with indifference, bowing slightly. 'I am sure you know I am going away. I am sorry to leave such a charming court, but there are duties—'

'Ah, yes,' said the beautiful Frances, 'I heard at her Majesty's *cercle* that you are leaving us. I was very much surprised.'

'Did your husband not tell you about it?' asked Sulkowski.

'My husband!' said Frau Brühl, making a funny face, 'he is so busy that sometimes I do not see him for a month. I have to learn his whereabouts from other people.'

'You ought to scold him for it.'

'Why?' said Frances ironically. 'He is free and I am free also. Can there be anything more agreeable in matrimony? We have not time to be saturated with each other and we are happy.'

She looked scornfully at her husband, who took it as mirthfully as he could and laughed in the most natural way.

'Does the countess remain?' the lady asked.

'Unfortunately, I must leave her!' rejoined Sulkowski. 'Although I should like her to accompany me on the campaign.'

'Then you think of fighting?'

'Yes! Pray wish me good luck that I may bring you a Turk's head.'

'I do not wish for that,' she said maliciously. 'Bring back your own head safe, that will suffice. With a wreath of laurels on it, it would look very well on a medal.'

Her own allusion to a medal recalled Watzdorf to her memory and made her eyes burn with fire.

'I wish you good luck,' she said, making a curtsey. Her eyes said something else.

Sulkowski bowed carelessly. The hostess turned towards her apartment. The host took Sulkowski by the arm, and whispering something confidentially, led him back to his study.

One winter evening, several months after Sulkowski's departure, Father Guarini entered the King's room. It was the hour which Augustus III was accustomed either to spend in the Queen's apartment, or in the opera, or shooting at a target.

That day Augustus III remained closeted in his room. Twice a chamberlain came to tell him that the Queen was waiting for him, but he sent him away. It was a sign that the King was in a very bad humour. So they told Father Guarini about it and he rushed to the rescue. He alone could improve his temper. The old priest entered smiling as usual.

The King looked at him gloomily and turned away his head.

Notwithstanding that, the Padre sat on a stool and said:

'May I ask your Majesty what makes my lord so sad? His faithful servant is sorry.'

Augustus III moved his head, muttered something and took a pipe.

'It would relieve your Majesty,' continued the Jesuit, 'if your Majesty would tell me.'

'A trifle,' said the King.

'Then it is not worth while to be sad about,' rejoined the Padre.

'A trifle!' the King repeated, and having risen, he walked to and fro, sighing, as was his custom when angry.

Guarini watched him attentively.

'It is bad,' he said, 'that your Majesty, working so hard, does not try to find some amusement. Distraction is necessary to a man. St John in Patmos had a tame partridge.'

'Partridge!' the King repeated thoughtfully. 'I prefer hunting for woodcock.'

He resumed his walk, sighing.

'We must have either an opera, or hunting, or pictures.'

Augustus III waved his hand.

'Where is Brühl?' asked the Padre.

'Ah! Brühl! Only Brühl! But he is busy, poor man, let him rest. Brühl is a good man.'

'Excellent!' affirmed Guarini. 'But it is not with him that your Majesty is angry?'

'The idea! Brühl—capital fellow, Brühl!' said the King, but lowered his head.

'Well, I do not suppose that your Majesty is craving for Sulkowski.'

The King stopped suddenly, and Guarini recognised that he had discovered the cause of the King's bad humour.

'Yes, Sulkowski,' said the King, 'just imagine, Josephine does not like him. How can anyone help liking Sulkowski? Tell me that.'

Guarini became silent. The question was straight but he did not answer it.

The King repeated:

'Father, how can one help liking Sulkowski?'

The Jesuit thought for a long time. The moment was decisive, it was necessary that the attack should be skilful, and he thought how to do it.

'Your Majesty,' said he, 'personally I have nothing against Sulkowski. As a Catholic he is indifferent, that is true. Then it seems to me that he does not show sufficient respect to our saintly Queen.'

'Oh! Oh!' broke in the King.

'At least people think so,' said Guarini imperturbably. 'It is certain that your Majesty's favour made him very proud.'

As the King listened he grew gloomier.

'Your Majesty,' said Guarini with ardour, 'we are alone, nobody but God hears us. Pray tell me, as on confession, did Sulkowski never lead the King into temptation?'

At this Augustus III blushed, turned his back and continued to perambulate the room. His silence was an answer in the affirmative. Guarini laughed.

'Is it not too daring? I can understand that a servant and friend might sometimes like to take something on his own conscience for his master's sake, but he might at least wait until a sign is given him to act so.'

The King went on with his walk.

'The Queen has a presentiment,' said the Padre. 'And no wonder! But *satis* of this. It is well known that he has some plans against Austria, against the house from which we have our Queen, and against our promises—'

Augustus sat in an arm-chair as if he were tired and looked at the priest.

'His worse fault is his pride which makes him believe that he can do anything he likes with the King. There are people who have heard him say so. A little humiliation would do him good, for it is not well that people should say he rules over Saxony and not our gracious King.'

'Eh! Eh!' said the King, 'who says so? Whoever it is, hang him!'

'Those who heard Sulkowski boast.'

'Boast! That is bad!' rejoined the King. 'I shall scold him for that!'

Guarini saw that the King was already tired of the subject, and he tried to find something to amuse him, certain that the seed would take root and grow.

At that moment a chamberlain entered again and announced that the Queen was waiting for the King to have some music.

'Let us go!' said Augustus III sighing.

Guarini bowed and they went. The lackeys preceded them with candelabras.

The Queen's apartments were furnished according to Josephine's taste. There was no luxury, but in the severity one could trace the majesty of the emperor's palace.

The pictures were all religious. Instead of *bibelots* there were plenty of relics and crosses. The court was composed of elderly ladies and so chosen that their beauty would not prove distracting to the King.

That day, John George Pisendel, the most famous violinist of those times, was going to give a concert in the court music hall. Besides him Pantaleon Heberstreit was going to play on an instrument invented by himself and called a *clavicembolo*. Buffardia and Quanz were to play the flute.

The Queen, already a little annoyed, walked to and fro waiting for her consort. When he entered she came up to him and tried to read his humour in his face and she understood that he was displeased. Music was the best remedy.

As soon as the King sat down and Buffardia began to play the flute, the clouds dispersed and the forehead became serene. The Queen remained behind the King for a moment and made a sign to Guarini. The Jesuit had only time to whisper:

'Poca roba—Sulkowski.'

The Queen hastened her pace and reached her chair beside that of the King. The orchestra struck up an overture and the King listened to it with great attention.

During the concert it was evident that the Queen was thinking about something more important than the music. Pisendel in vain did his best, the Queen did not seem to hear him. Brühl's wife was also present at the concert; she was sitting beside her mother; the minister stood behind the King and looked as modest as if he were not prime minister and also the only minister.

Padre Guarini passing by him, whispered:

'The war has begun, the enemy defends himself, we must concentrate all our forces, be on your guard.'

Brühl stood quiet as though he had not heard anything. Buffardia and Quanz played a duet. The King closed his eyes and enjoyed the music. Anyone seeing the scornful looks of Brühl's wife directed at the King, would have been surprised and frightened at the contempt with which she dared to look at him.

Behind her chair stood the minister's retinue who were admitted to the concert, and among them might have been seen a young man looking so much like Watzdorf that he might have been taken for his ghost. Frau Brühl's eyes often wandered in that direction, rested on the beautiful face of the youth and tried to meet his eyes; their glance met and the youth blushed.

After the concert supper was announced, with a separate table for their Majesties. The King had such a famous appetite that he seemed to forget about everything else: but after supper he asked Brühl to follow him to his apartment.

The greater part of the court dispersed; the ladies remained for evening prayers, for there was a custom that on certain days they recited prayers conducted by Father Guarini.

That day the spiritual *exercitia* took place in the Queen's little chapel and then only was the rest of the court dismissed.

Guarini was also going when the Queen called him.

'Father, how was it? The King—'

'Began to talk about Sulkowski of his own accord. He is very sorry that there are people who are against Sulkowski. As I was asked I could not be silent and I began the war.'

'But what? what?' the Queen asked inquisitively. 'I said as much as I could without wearying the King,' said Guarini. 'I told him everything I had in my heart.'

'And the King?'

'He listened in silence.'

'Do you think it will make any impression on him?'

'Undoubtedly, but we must repeat the attacks. Sulkowski will return, we must press the matter, he must find the King cool; otherwise the old friendship would assert itself, he would take his old place and nobody would be able to move him from it. We must not ask too much; we cannot ask to be allowed to act with him as with Hoym. One cannot prove much against him. It would do if he were dismissed.'

'But you know how fond the King is of him,' said the Queen, 'would he not take advantage of that? A godless man as he is would be ready to use any means. Did you ever see him in a church? And you know that he never observes Lent.'

The Queen shivered and became silent for a moment.

'I shall not give in,' she added, 'you must act also. Brühl cannot.'

'I will act, only at the last moment,' said Guarini, 'and very carefully. For good work one must use all possible means. God will help us. When does he return?'

'His wife expects him every day; he wrote to the King that he would be back this week. We must hasten,' said the Queen.

Guarini bowed humbly and went out.

The next day in the morning, Brühl was in the King's room. His duties were not fatiguing but tiresome. Usually Augustus was silent; one was obliged to stand looking at him and to bow when he smiled or cleared his throat.

Brühl had additional trouble in watching the King so closely that no one could unexpectedly approach him; at all audiences, without any exception, Brühl was present. If the King was going to Mass the way was cleared of all persons who did not belong to the court. Nobody could approach him without the minister's permission or in his absence. It seemed that Augustus III, who above all things was fond of quiet and afraid of surprises, was glad of this, for he never tried to get free and was grateful to his guardians.

After the Mass and audiences, during which the silent King did not waste many words, Brühl remained with him alone.

He could guess that the King wished to converse about something, for he walked uneasily about, stopped opposite him, blinked his eyes, smiled sadly, but could not begin the conversation. At length he stopped, put his hands on the minister's shoulders and asked:

'Brühl, what do you think of Sulkowski?'

Although Brühl was prepared, he could not answer at once and dropped his eyes.

'Sire,' he answered, 'I am sure I think the same as your Majesty.'

'And do you know what I think of him?'

'I do not know, but I am my lord's faithful servant and thus I retain those whom he likes as friends, and as foes those whom the King dislikes.'

The King's face brightened.

'Brühl! I love you!' he exclaimed.

The minister bent to kiss his lord's hand.

'Brühl, I love you very much,' added Augustus, 'and that is why I ask your advice. Listen, they frighten me about him——'

He looked into Brühl's eyes solemnly.

'Speak frankly——'

'I have nothing against Sulkowski, but my lord's favour, which makes me humble, arouses great pride in him; it may be that he boasted that he can do anything, not only in the state affairs, but also with your Majesty.'

'H'm! You say it may be! Yes, it may be!' said the King. 'Between ourselves, he knows nothing of music, and does not understand much about pictures: he is satisfied when the subject is nude! What a Venus he brought here once, and what trouble I had with the Queen about it! She ordered the picture to be burnt. Well, it is true also, that he takes too many liberties——'

Augustus III, not finishing his sentence, looked out of the window, became dreamy and yawned.

'What do you think,' he asked 'is it an authentic Ribera, sent yesterday from Venice?'

Brühl shrugged his shoulders.

'I am of your Majesty's opinion.'

'It might be Ribera.'

'Yes, it might be Ribera,' Brühl repeated.

'But it might be *il Erote*——'

'There is no doubt that it looks like *Frate*——'

'Brühl, you are an expert.'

'I learn from your Majesty.'

Augustus well-satisfied came to Brühl and whispered to him.

'The Queen wishes me to send him away, for somebody told her that he induced me to have some amours——'

'Nobody could suspect your Majesty of that!' cried Brühl. 'Everybody knows your virtuous life.'

'I shall never give cause to be suspected,' the King whispered. 'Never, never! I prefer——'

He could not finish. Brühl whispered.

'Nobody, not a soul could suspect your Majesty.'

'It must be so,' whispered Augustus. 'Do you think that he knows something? Does he suspect me? He?'

'I am sure he does not know anything yet, but if he is here continually, spying—he could—who could foresee——'

The King, alarmed, drew himself up.

'If it is so, then I must dismiss him: yes, yes, it will be better. You shall take his place with me.'

Brühl again kissed his lord's hand. Augustus was still sad, he sighed, his eyes filled with tears—it distressed him to part with his friend.

'Brühl,' said he, 'it is decided; the Queen wishes it to be so, Guarini advises it, you have nothing against it; but tell me, how can it be done? How?'

The minister drooped his head and assumed an embarrassed mien. The King looked at him awaiting his decision.

'Your Majesty,' said Brühl raising his head, 'there are good reasons for disgrace, but I would not advise you to be severe with him; it will suffice to dismiss him, and not to let him see his lord's face. Banishment from the court is the worst of punishments.'

'Yes,' the King muttered, 'but I shall leave him a small pension.'

He looked at Brühl who nodded in the affirmative.

'Then banishment,' Augustus added, 'and I leave the execution of it to you. Do what you please, but save me any annoyance. Let him go——'

Augustus having shunted his trouble on to somebody else's shoulders, was already serene again.

'Brühl,' he said, 'announce to the Queen that I should like to see her; the Queen either prays or paints; if she paints I can see her.'

Brühl went out; five minutes later, the King, preceded by a chamberlain, went to his consort's apartments. He found her painting. A young artist stood respectfully behind her. The august artist was painting a head of Christ. The fact was that very little was done by her, for the artist, when the Queen was absent, corrected and improved that which was badly done; but the next day the Queen thought it was her own work and was satisfied with herself. That way the picture progressed; when it was finished it was said that it was painted by the Queen and the court admired her talent.

When the King entered, the Queen did not rise, but pointed at the work. Augustus stood behind her and admired the picture, which having been recently improved by the artist was not at all bad. The King, having complimented the Queen, made a sign to the artist to retire for a time into the next room, which he did as quickly as he could, bowing humbly.

Augustus III bent to the Queen's ear and said:

'It shall be as you wish; we shall dismiss Sulkowski; I came to tell you this.'

The Queen turned quickly and smiled at the King.

'But not a word!' said the King. 'Brühl will arrange the matter, I do not wish to trouble myself about it.'

'You do not need to,' said the Queen. 'Guarini and Brühl will do everything.'

The King did not wish to prolong the subject and began to talk about the picture.

'I congratulate you on your colouring,' he said, *très fin*, and very fresh. Listarde could not paint a better pastel; you paint beautifully—only do not permit that artist to spoil your work and do not follow any advice.'

'He only sharpens my pencils,' said the Queen.

'Beautiful head! I shall hang it in my room if you will make me a present of it,' and he smiled.

As the dinner hour had not yet arrived, the King bowed, kissed the Queen's hand and went to his apartment; on his way he nodded to the artist to go and help the Queen with her artistic effort.

The King's face beamed with satisfaction now that he had got rid of his trouble. Today he was altogether a different man from yesterday; his forehead was serene, there was a smile on his lips, he breathed more freely and could think of something else. He cared less for Sulkowski than for his disturbed peace and few unpleasant days. He was ready to sacrifice a man in order to get rid as soon as possible of any difficulty in his own life.

Brühl was waiting in the King's apartment. The King, having glanced at him, laughed and said:

'The affair is finished: after dinner, shooting at a target, in the evening a concert, tomorrow an opera.'

He drew near the minister and added:

'Nobody must mention his name; all is over.'

He thought for a moment.

'Employ anybody you wish, provided I do not know anything more about the affair.'

He became thoughtful and ended with:

'Listen Brühl, it is Ribera—'

'Yes, your Majesty, it is Ribera,' affirmed the minister.

The carnival promised to be brilliant that year. In Saxony everything was satisfactory; the noblemen, who dared murmur, were sent to Pleissenburg; in Poland quiet was assured by the last Sobieski. Faustina always sang marvellously, and there was plenty of game in the forests round Hubertsburg. Day after day, arranged in advance, passed very pleasantly.

The blessed peacefulness was disturbed by the news that Sulkowski was returning; it hastened the Queen's attack and sealed his sentence. It was not expected that the favourite would be admitted to see the King.

Henniche and his accomplices gave orders that all roads were to be watched; the guards were at the gates, private detectives watched Sulkowski's palace.

The general-minister's carriage came. His wife had intended to go towards Prague and meet him, but they were afraid of that, and the Countess Kolowrath told her that the Queen desired her to be in readiness in case she was called to the castle, and that she must not leave Dresden. The Countess was obliged to obey.

On the first of February, 1738, the Count Sulkowski arrived at Pirma, where he stopped to feed and water the horses before proceeding to Dresden. In the inn a courier sent on ahead prepared everything for the minister's reception. Nobody yet could even suspect his downfall. The whole borough, the officials, burgomasters, in gala uniforms, were awaiting, notwithstanding the intense cold, the man whom they thought to be almighty and before whom all trembled.

The courier announced the arrival of his Excellency for four o'clock; but as that day there was a heavy fall of snow, he did not arrive at the appointed hour. While all eyes were looking down the road in the direction of Prague, a cavalier wrapped in a mantle came from the direction of Dresden and stopped his tired horse before the inn. The owner of the inn called 'The Crown,' Jonas Hender, a very resolute man, having perceived the stranger, who at any other time would have been very welcome, rushed to tell him that there was no room for him.

'Excuse me, sir—we expect his Excellency the Count Sulkowski; I have no room either for you or your horse; but at the 'Palm Branch,' an inn kept by my brother-in-law, the accommodation is not bad.'

The stranger hardly listened to Jonas. He threw the reins on the horse's neck and looked towards the inn. He was a middle-aged man, as one could judge by the wrinkles round his eyes, for the rest of his face—it must have been done on account of the cold—was wrapped in a shawl and his cap was drawn over his eyes.

'Exactly,' he muttered, 'because his Excellency is going to stay here, I must find a room, because I am sent to him.'

The innkeeper bowed and took hold of the horse.

'That alters the case,' he said, 'pray come in and warm yourself. Hot wine with spices is ready, and there is nothing better than *glükwein* for the cold. The horse shall be taken to the stable.'

A groom took the tired grey horse. The innkeeper conducted the stranger to a room; he looked at him in order to guess who he was, but he failed to do so either by his dress, or his mien. The dress was an ordinary one, the speech pure but not Saxon; his manner full of assurance betrayed a courtier, but not one of great importance, since he came on horseback without a servant and he wore jack-boots.

For such a great lord as Sulkowski, every room was engaged, as his retinue was large; there remained only the innkeeper's room, into which the stranger was shown.

The room was clean and bright and a good fire was burning in the fireplace. Hender helped the stranger to take off his large mantle and the shawl, from under which there appeared the thin, bony face of an official. His eyes were piercing and his mouth twitched.

Hender looked at him, and as he was very shrewd at reading character, he said to himself:

'He is a dangerous man.'

But it was necessary to be overwhelmingly polite to such a dangerous-looking messenger from the capital. Therefore he placed a chair near the fireplace and asked the stranger, who received all civilities very indifferently, to sit down. Several times when the host ventured some remark he received no answer. He brought a glass of hot wine and handed it to the traveller, who accepted it, but did not even thank him for it.

'This must be a man of some importance,' said Hender to himself.

He became even more civil, and told his two children to keep away; at that moment a trumpet resounded, Sulkowski was coming. The innkeeper rushed out to receive him.

The stranger remained motionless, deep in thought. The minister was brought triumphantly to the room assigned to him; the servants brought the boxes, Hender returned to his room and found the stranger sitting before the fire and drinking the wine. He did not appear to hear the host, who felt it his duty to say aloud:

'His Excellency has arrived!'

The guest made a grimace; he finished his wine, shook his head, took his cap and went out.

Had Jonas Hender been acquainted with Dresden and had to do with higher officials, he would have recognised in his guest, Ludovici.

The councillor slowly opened the door and entered the room in which Sulkowski was resting.

The table was set, the servants were busy, a young aide-de-camp stood in the window, Sulkowski was lying on the sofa.

When he perceived Ludovici, he sprang up, beaming with joy.

'It is you!' he exclaimed. 'How good of you to come to meet me! I am very grateful to you, for I shall get some news; the last letters were very insignificant. How are you?'

The councillor's face was not indicative of good news. He was silent and looked askance at the aide-de-camp. Sulkowski passed to the other room and nodded to Ludovici to follow him. He was surprised at the councillor's long face. The Count was in an excellent humour. On the Rhine and in Hungary he had been well received, thanks to letters of introduction and to his position. He returned happy and still more proud, with a greater supply of self-assurance than ever.

No sooner had they entered the room than the Count begun to ask questions, to which the answers were scanty, Ludovici seeming to lack courage to speak. He looked sadly at the Count's joy, which he was about to destroy or perchance change into despair.

He let the Count speak, who laughing told him of his success, of the honours with which he had been received, of the experience he had gained. It seemed that he thought he would become as famous as Maurice de Saxe.

Ludovici looked and shook his head.

'What is the matter with you?' asked Sulkowski. 'Are you cold? Why don't you speak?'

Ludovici glanced round.

'I do not bring good news,' he said, 'that is why I do not hasten to talk.'

'Is my wife well?'

'Yes, thank God.'

'Is the King well?'

'Yes, but—'

Ludovici looked at the Count and said sadly:

'But you will find him changed. A great many things are changed. I was against your travelling.'

'What has happened?' said Sulkowski carelessly.

'The worst that could happen. Your enemies accused you; the Queen is at their head, then Guarini, and the cunning Brühl. We are lost.'

Sulkowski looked at him as at a madman, shrugged his shoulders and laughed.

'You must be dreaming.'

'I should like to dream,' said Ludovici gloomily. 'There is no time for illusions, we must try to save ourselves, if there is still time for that. I came, risking my life, to warn you. The gates are guarded, the houses are surrounded by spies: if you come to Dresden, so that they recognise you at the gate, they will not admit you to the King; such are the orders.'

'But it cannot be,' the Count cried passionately. 'It is a stupid hoax, someone has told the King some nonsense, and you believed it. There is no man in this world who could take the King's heart from me. It is impossible, it is a lie! I laugh at it! They would dare not to admit me to the King? Ludovici, you have lost your senses—'

Ludovici looked at the minister with a kind of commiseration.

Sulkowski walked to and fro, laughing to himself.

'Where did you get that stupid gossip from?' asked he.

'From the best source. I gave my word that I would not reveal the name of the person who told me and ordered me to warn you. That which I say is true.'

'But how could it come to that?' asked Sulkowski a little alarmed.

'The King is weak,' said Ludovici, 'the Queen is a stubborn woman, Father Guarini is the most cunning of men, and Brühl is master of the art of using other people to achieve his aims. Your Excellency never tried to hide his aversion to priests, and such is the result of their work. Everything is arranged. They forced your dismissal upon the King. You will be banished from the court with a small pension, so that you will not hinder Brühl from making millions. They are afraid of your influence over the King and they will not permit you to see him.'

Sulkowski frowned.

'Are you sure of it?' he asked.

'Very sure! the guards at the gate have orders not to let you in; the castle is also guarded.'

'And the King does not even wish to see me!' burst out Sulkowski.

'The King is a slave,' said Ludovici.

Sulkowski relapsed into thought.

'If you intend to go with all your retinue to Dresden,' Ludovici continued, 'you will fall into their hands. If there is any means you could use to see the King, don't hesitate to act. You have some influence, take advantage of it, but it will be a fight for life or death, with the Queen, confessor and Brühl.'

Sulkowski paced to and fro, frowning, then he asked:

'Are you sure of what you say?'

'As I live.'

'Then be it so, but—I am not afraid of them; they cannot crush me as they did Hoym and the rest. We shall see. Let us now have something to eat. I shall leave my retinue here and we shall go to Dresden on horseback. I should like to know who would dare to bar my access to the King to-morrow. We shall see! Can we not reach town without being recognised?

'We must!' answered Ludovici.

'Come then and let us eat well, that they may not guess anything here.'

Having said this he returned to the other room in which the meal was ready. They spoke very little and only of extraneous matters as they eat. Ludovici had a very good appetite, while Sulkowski seemed only to be thirsty, he drank so much.

The Count said to his aide-de-camp:

'Count, you and the horses are tired; stay over night at Pirma. I wish to take my wife by surprise and go to Dresden on horseback with the Councillor Ludovici.'

The aide-de-camp seemed to be very much surprised, for Sulkowski was fond of travelling in comfort, with much pomp and ceremony: such an *incognito* during bad weather, on the road covered with snow, in the night, seemed very strange. Sulkowski noticing his astonishment said with a smile:

'There is nothing extraordinary in my project, sometimes one must satisfy a fancy although one is not very young.'

Having said this, he took his aide-de-camp aside and gave him secret orders.

The aide-de-camp left the room at once.

Sulkowski stood silent and pensive.

Soon two saddled horses stood at the door of the inn; the minister was advised at least to take a groom, but he refused. The journey for Ludovici, who had already made it coming from Dresden and who was not accustomed to riding on horseback, was more painful than for the Count; but he did not wish to let him go alone.

Fortunately for both of them the weather improved, the snow ceased to fall. The horses were accustomed to the road on which they travelled often and followed the highway. The sun was setting, they pushed on at a smart trot, the Count ahead, the councillor behind him, both silent.

They quickly passed villages, houses and inns. The night was quite dark and the numerous lights in the distance presently announced that they were approaching Dresden. Here the road was less lonely. Several sledges passed, men on horseback and pedestrians. Against the bright sky could be seen the dark towers of the churches.

Sulkowski slackened the speed of his horse until Ludovici came up with him.

'If they guard the gate,' he said, 'we must use some precautions.'

'Your Excellency will wrap himself in the cloak and will follow me. It is true that they guard the gates, but they look for the equipages and retinue with which they expect you.'

'You said that they watch my house also?'

'Yes,' Ludovici answered.

'I must go there on foot and enter without being noticed.'

'I would not advise you to do that,' said Ludovici, 'in our times one cannot be sure of the servants, some of them might betray us.'

Sulkowski laughed bitterly.

'It is very amusing,' he said, 'who could have told me this morning that I should not be able to pass the night in safety in Dresden?'

He shrugged his shoulders.

'If my position is so dangerous,' he said proudly, after a while, 'then I do not wish to expose any one else. Take care of the horses, and I shall find a place to pass the night, and then do what I have to do.'

Thus saying he turned his horse, covered his face with the mantle, let Ludovici pass in front, bent to the saddle, and having assumed the mien of a groom, following his master, followed the councillor. They approached the gate. In very truth the guards were there, but Ludovici gave them some name and as they did not pay much attention to two men on horseback they entered the town.

A soldier rushed after Ludovici.

'Do you come from Pirma?'

'Yes,' answered Ludovici.

'Did you hear anything of the Count Sulkowski, who is expected today?'

'The inn called the Crown,' said Ludovici, 'was engaged for his Excellency, but a courier came to say that he would not be leaving Prague for two days.'

The soldiers returned, glad that they would not be obliged to watch very closely during the night and the Count with the councillor proceeded.

In the town there was still much stir as was usual during the carnival. Sulkowski dismounted near the post office, gave the horse to Ludovici, and went towards his palace.

He no longer doubted that what Ludovici had lately told him was true, and tried to enter his house unperceived. Even he hesitated whether it would not be better to pass the night elsewhere; but his pride prevented him from hiding like a culprit. The question was how to enter unnoticed by servants whom he distrusted. Not being accustomed to subterfuges he did not know how to act.

A strange feeling was aroused in him at the sight of the people, many of whom he recognised, of passing carriages, of all that merry carnival movement. Smaller officials passed him without recognition of the man wrapped in the mantle; before whom, not long since, they almost kneeled. His situation seemed to him like a dream, the danger a nightmare. He was angry that he could have believed it. He measured the position he occupied with the menace of downfall, and could not imagine it possible.

Under the influence of these thoughts he went more boldly. At about the distance of a furlong, he noticed several dark figures walking about and apparently awaiting someone. Those figures, hiding stealthily in corners, were the best proof that the house was watched. Sulkowski entered a side street, uncertain what to do. At that moment he recollected a man whom he could trust. It was Father Vogler, a Jesuit, the King's former confessor, an old man, who apparently left the court of his own will, giving way to Father Guarini.

He lived quietly, seldom showing himself in the court, and entirely engrossed in his books. Formerly the King's favourite, now almost forgotten, for he did not know how to amuse him. Father Vogler was a silent retiring man. He was Sulkowski's chaplain and confessor and had gained his esteem. Although Vogler apparently lived far from the intrigues of the court, even Guarini seemed to fear him and was very respectful towards him. Vogler did not hide his dislike of Brühl and although he said little, one could see that he disliked the court and everything that was going on there. Sulkowski remembered that Vogler had warned him before his departure that he should not stay away long, that he should not be too confident of the King's favour, and should not trust those who were apparently his best friends.

If anyone was well informed it was certainly Vogler. The Count, being obliged to steal through the old market and a much populated street leading to the castle in which the Jesuit lived, wrapped the cloak very carefully around him and walked in the shadow of the houses in order that he might not be recognised. Carriages were going towards the castle and he recognised Brühl's *porte-chaise* and smiled bitterly. The street scene with Erell led by on a donkey recurred to his mind, and it seemed to him that he had met with a similar fate to that of the editor.

The house, in which Vogler lived, belonged to the castle, and the entrance to it was from a small dark street. He knew that Vogler occupied the second floor. He passed the dark stairs, and rang the bell at the door which he found with difficulty in the darkness.

He waited long. A small boy with a candle in his hand opened the door.

'Is Father Vogler at home?'

The boy looked timidly at the stranger and hesitated as to what to answer.

'I wish to see Father Vogler on urgent business,' he said.

The boy left the door open and disappeared into the room. He returned shortly and showed the Count into a small room full of books and bookshelves, and a large table on which was an abundant supply of papers. A reading lamp was burning. From an old chair, upholstered with leather, rose a tall, thin, bent, bald-headed man. He seemed to be surprised at such a late call and turned his feeble eye on the visitor, whose face was still half covered with the mantle. Only when the boy closed the door, did Sulkowski uncover his face and head and come near Father Vogler, who seizing him by the hand cried out with astonishment.

'Hsh!' cried Sulkowski.

Vogler embraced him and made him sit down on a chair, then he went to the ante-room and gave some orders to the boy.

The Count leaned thoughtfully on the table.

'I see,' said the Jesuit, coming back, 'that you know all, although nobody here knows yet. Has anybody seen you?'

'I came here straight from my journey,' answered the Count. 'In Pirma I learned about the plot, and by your manner I see that it is true. Is it true? Then they dread—'

Vogler shrugged his shoulders.

'Yes, your good friends await you with this surprise,' he said slowly, 'they will not admit you to the King.'

'It is I who will prepare a surprise for them and see the King notwithstanding them all,' cried Sulkowski. 'They are mistaken; the King under pressure would give in in my absence, but if I get half an hour's conversation with him, I shall regain my influence and then—Then,' cried Sulkowski rising and clenching his fist, 'it will not be I that will be sent away, but those who dared to intrigue against me.'

He became silent.

Vogler wrung his hands.

'The question is where I can pass the night and wait till tomorrow, so that they may not know that I have arrived. I am sure that they will not give orders that I am not to be admitted to the court; by my right and my rank I have free access to the King at any hour. At eleven o'clock the King is alone; Brühl is not with him.'

The Jesuit listened attentively, not showing what he thought of the Count's plan.

'You have nothing to lose, you must try to win,' he said.

'Will you have the courage to let me sleep here?' asked Sulkowski with a smile of doubt.

'You are welcome; my humble dwelling is at your service. You are safe here, for nobody calls on me.'

Sulkowski's eyes shone.

'If I am able to see the King, I am sure of winning—'

'May God help you,' whispered Vogler.

The next morning Brühl heard through Henniche, that Sulkowski was not expected to arrive for two more days. In the court the whole plot had been kept in great secrecy; the Countess Sulkowski, whom the Queen always received very kindly had not the slightest suspicion. The King was in an excellent humour.

Early in the morning Brühl came to the King for his orders, and having left Guarini with him, returned to his palace. Here he changed his clothes, because the etiquette required him to do so several times during the day, and ordered his *porte-chaise* to carry him to the Countess Moszynski. He now felt at home in her house, for her husband had died a few months previously, and Brühl was certain that she was too much in love with him to marry anybody else. His relations of tender friendship with the beautiful widow were no secret. Every day he would take counsel with her, every morning the Countess Moszynski would visit him. It was known that she did what she pleased with him. Very often when they had something very urgent to communicate to the minister, for he did nothing without her advice, they would go to the Countess to find him there.

That day Brühl also went to her house as though it were his own. The Countess on seeing him said:

'Has Sulkowski arrived?'

'Not yet! I had news from Pirma; they do not expect him for two days.'

The Countess Moszynski shook her head with evident dissatisfaction.

'It is not natural,' she said, 'it is suspicious. His wife told me that at the latest she expected him last night. Somebody must have warned him.'

'Impossible! Nobody knows!'

The Countess laughed.

'Let us count up how many people know the secret,' she said, counting on her fingers. 'The Queen, the Countess Kolowrath, the King, Guarini, you, I, and to be sure, your wife. If she was not told she would guess: let us add Henniche. Have you ever heard of a secret being kept by eight persons?'

Brühl shook his head carelessly.

'Even if he had learned, it would not help him at all. The Queen wearied the King so much about Sulkowski, that for the sake of his beloved peace he must give him up.'

The subject of conversation was soon changed. Brühl, however, notwithstanding his apparent calm, was thoughtful and gloomy. Towards noon, just as he was about to take leave of the Countess, there was a rap at the door, and Henniche rushed in.

His changed face and hurried entrance into the drawing-room announced bad news. The Countess sprang from her seat. Brühl ran to him.

Henniche could not speak.

'Henniche, what is the matter? Come to your senses!' exclaimed Brühl.

'What is the matter with me? Sulkowski has been in town ever since last night, at eleven o'clock he came to the castle, and asking no permission, entered the King's room. Father Guarini, who was with the King, said that his Majesty became white as marble. The Count, as if not aware of anything wrong, greeted the King in most tender words and kneeling he said that his first step was to fall at his Majesty's feet. The King became tender and embraced him. The Count began to talk about his travels and made the King laugh—and thus he resumed his former duties. At this moment Sulkowski is with the King; everybody is alarmed in the castle: the Queen weeps, Guarini is pale—everything is lost.'

Brühl and the Countess looked at each other.

Brühl did not appear to be frightened but very much annoyed.

'Henniche, listen!' he said, 'Sulkowski cannot remain with the King for ever; I do not wish to meet him; let me know when he leaves the castle. They watched well at the gates and fulfilled my orders nicely!' added the minister drily.

He went to the Countess, kissed her hand, whispering a few words, and went out with Henniche.

The scene described by Henniche was very interesting indeed. A ghost would not have been more alarming in the castle than the sudden appearance of Sulkowski. When he entered the King's room. Augustus III was struck dumb with surprise, for the things he most disliked were reproaches and quarrels. Father Guarini, notwithstanding his usual self-composure, could not conceal his confusion. Sulkowski kneeling greeted the King with apparent joy, telling him how happy he was to look on his lord's face again. This calmed Augustus a little. Guarini noticed, however, that he only smiled, but said not a word.

The Padre's first intention was to remain to the end of the interview, but later on it occurred to his mind, that it was his duty to communicate the incident to the Queen in order that some precautions might be taken at once. In consequence, having listened to Sulkowski's narration for about an hour, he was obliged to leave the room. Sulkowski spoke merrily and quickly as though in a fever. Although he did not, even by the slightest allusion, let it be known that he knew what was going to happen to him, one could guess by his agitation and daring that he was playing his last card. The King glanced round as if he were afraid and grew more and more stiff: one moment his face grew brighter, the next it became cold.

As long as Father Guarini was in the room, the Count confined his conversation to his travels; when Guarini left the room he changed both the tone and subject.

'Your Majesty,' he said, 'I was longing to see my liege: I had a sad presentiment, although thank God, it is not realised, and your Majesty's heart is the best guarantee that it could not be realised. I have served my lord since childhood, I sacrificed my life to him, and I am ready to sacrifice the rest of my days; I was able to gain my lord's favour and confidence, my conscience does not reproach me with anything; I am not afraid of the plots of my enemies, even if I had any, and I do not believe I have them, for I have done no harm to anybody.'

The King listened with forced dignity, which did not promise well.

Sulkowski asked to be permitted once more to kiss the King's hand; Augustus gave it to him muttering, changing uneasily from one foot to the other, but not saying one intelligible word. The Count's enthusiasm increased and he spoke with growing fever.

'Sire, my lord, I believe in your heart as I believe in God. Only may the intriguers not take it from me by their calumnies!'

'Oh! Oh!' interrupted Augustus, 'there are no intrigues here.'

'Into what court are they not able to penetrate? What dress must they assume?' said Sulkowski laughing. 'Sire, I am a soldier and I speak straight. There are bad people and those who are the sweetest, the most humble, the most useful, they are the most dangerous. Sire, and my lord, I do not wish to name the others—but Brühl must be dismissed, otherwise he will get all into his own power and deprive your Majesty of his best friends, in order that he may rule absolutely.'

Thus saying he looked at the King's face, which became crimson and then pale, his eyes assumed a wild expression, the result of suppressed anger. Sulkowski, knowing well that it was necessary to conquer the outburst in order to dominate the monarch, favoured peace above all things; the anger never lasted long. Several times the King had wished to break the chain of dependence, but every time he had shirked the effort necessary to effect it. The Count had seen him several times in that state of mind and became still bolder.

'Sire,' he said, following the King, who went to the window, 'your Majesty respects the memory of his great father; may he serve as an example! He never permitted anyone to domineer over him, neither the Queen, nor favourites, nor ministers, nor priests. He ruled supreme. Your Majesty has only to wish, to command, and those who murmur will become silent; the chain shall be broken. One must have courage to live and to rule, and for that one must break all chains.'

The King listened but grew more and more frightened; he stopped up both his ears and instead of answering retreated further and further towards the window.

Sulkowski having gone so far could not retreat, and determined to strike the iron while it was hot.

'I know,' he said, that I attempt a great thing, but I do so out of love for my lord, whom I wish to see as great and as happy as his father was. Your Majesty wishes for a peaceful life, and it will come as soon as your Majesty asserts his authority. Those tutors, Guarini and Brühl, must be sent away. The Queen is a saint, let her pray for us and edify us by her virtues, and we, sire, shall go and conquer Hungary, for the Emperor Karl VI will not live long. Your Majesty will breathe more freely in the camp.'

Sulkowski laughed. The King looked sullenly about him: not a movement, not a word betrayed his thoughts.

He was evidently tired.

Happily a movement in the corridor announced the dinner. Augustus made a movement as if he wished to go. Sulkowski seized his hand and kissed it. The King blushed. At that moment the Grand Marshall of the court entered and perceived Sulkowski taking leave of the King in such a tender way, that he did not doubt that the Count had returned to his former favour.

Unfortunately the last part of that conversation was overheard by the Queen and Guarini, who stood at the door.

Sulkowski went out, assured that he would be able to change everything and that no danger threatened him. He greeted the courtiers and officials whom he met in the castle with his former pride, and after a short conversation with them, he ordered a *porte-chaise* to be brought for him and was borne home.

He was persuaded that all trouble was over and that he had conquered all obstacles. He believed in the King's heart. He received his wife with a serene face and told Ludovici to prepare all documents accusing Brühl of false accounts, showing his abuses, etc. Ludovici having received these orders went out immediately to see that they were fulfilled.

While this was going on, the King had no appetite at the commencement of his meal. His attendants knew him well and immediately used the most effectual remedy. Frosch and Horch were soon before him, looking at each other challengingly. Frosch with his hands in his pockets did not wish to look at Horch, while the latter having contorted his mouth, and half-closed his eyes, pointed at his adversary with his finger and slowly advanced towards him.

When he was near he gave him a ferocious kick. Frosch shrieked, the King looked and his face brightened. Then the two fools began to abuse each other.

'Traitor,' cried Frosch opposite Horch, 'you have not the courage to challenge such a hero as I am, for you know that I could crush you! You take me by treachery and you shall be punished for it.'

Horch pretended to be frightened, kneeled, clasped his hands and seemed to beg for mercy. But Frosch rushed upon him, but it happened that he passed over his adversary's head and found himself mounted on his shoulders. Horch had risen and holding Frosch by his feet began to race round the room with him. In the meantime Frosch pounded Horch on the back with his fist and seized him by the ears and both then rolled on the floor.

The King, having forgotten all his troubles, began to laugh; the entertainment restored his appetite and he ate voraciously.

The Queen, although it did not amuse her at all, pretended to laugh also.

In addition to this a few glasses of good wine improved the King's humour so much that Josephine did not doubt that after dinner she would be able to renew her attacks upon Sulkowski.

Brühl and Guarini were waiting in the King's apartments. The minister did not hesitate on his own responsibility to give orders that in the event of Sulkowski appearing he was to be told that the King could not receive him. The chamberlains were told to excuse themselves as best they could, but not to admit the Count.

It was a serious fight in which it was difficult to foresee who could win, because Sulkowski's speech would have made a great impression on the King but for the fact that the Queen overheard some of the Count's insinuations and his advice to the King to try and recover his independence.

After dinner, Augustus as usual hastened to his apartment to smoke his pipe and enjoy his *robe de chambre;* he was already taking leave of the Queen, not having mentioned a word about Sulkowski, when she stopped him: 'Augustus,' she said, 'I heard what Sulkowski was advising you.'

'Where? How?'

'I was at the door,' answered the Queen, 'and I am glad I was there though it was by an accident. You are as kind as an angel and a King cannot be kind. That audacious fellow offended the King's majesty, he has offended you and me; he dared to advise you to lead a bad life. Augustus, if this man remains in the court, God's punishment will descend upon us. How could you suffer—'

'Well? What?' said the King. 'It worries me. I need rest. Drive him away then.'

'Give orders!'

Augustus nodded in the affirmative. But mistrusting him the Queen sent for Guarini and told him to act immediately.

Apprehensive and confused Brühl waited for the King. Seeing him Augustus did not say a word and sat down in an arm-chair. Almost at the same moment Guarini entered laughing.

'Sire, we have at last found what we lost. Sulkowski has come back; evidently he must have come to the conclusion that it is useless to hunt after happiness. *Chi sta bene, non si muove.* Evidently he was not satisfied here, but he has come back just the same, for elsewhere must have been worse.'

Augustus began to smoke and pointed at Brühl with his pipe.

'He is at fault,' he said. 'Why did they let him in? The Queen listened—he talked nonsense—phew!'

'Sire, I am not guilty, somebody betrayed our secret,' said Brühl.

'Do what you please,' said the King with asperity. 'I do not wish to know anything. Write a warrant, I will sign it—'

'There is no reason for your Majesty to be in a bad humour and spoil your health,' Guarini said. 'Faustina is going to sing tonight with Abbuzzi, they now love each other very tenderly.'

Augustus looked round and muttered:

'Amor quel che piace!'

It was the beginning of a song which he was nearly humming.

Guarini, taking great pains to disperse the king's gloomy feelings, ordered a magnificent portrait painted by Giorgione, and recently purchased in Venice, to be brought. The King on seeing it said enthusiastically: *'A, che bello!'*

He again forgot about everything.

'What softness of the brush, what colouring, what life!' he exclaimed, delighted with the picture, and his eyes smiled.

Half-an-hour later Faustina asked for an audience on important theatre affairs, and it was granted.

All withdrew and she entertained the King for about half-an-hour with a very animated conversation; when she left, Augustus was beaming with delight as if there were neither ministers, nor state affairs, nor any sorrows in this world. The clouds were entirely dispersed.

It was not so easy a matter to calm the anxiety of the Queen and her accomplices in the plot. They knew how daring Sulkowski was, how he loved the King, how many friends he had at the court, and how, as he was familiar with the habits of the King, he could easily reach him. Consequently guards were stationed all round the Count's palace, round the opera, at the side door of the castle, at the entrance leading to the King's apartments.

Guarini did not leave the King for a moment, the Queen was watchful; Brühl and the Countess Moszynski took counsel together: Henniche, Globig, Loss, Hammer, and the whole crowd of officials employed by Brühl, scattered through the town and took up their appointed stations.

Their movements were a matter of the most perfect indifference to Sulkowski, as, sure of his victory, he drew up a report with which he proposed to overthrow his adversary. The Count was persuaded that his speech had made a deep impression on the King, and that it would counterbalance everything else.

His wife, less confident, went to pay a visit to the Queen. She was not received. Alarmed by this she insisted on obtaining a short audience and at length it was granted.

The Queen received her very coolly, but following Guarini's advice she pretended not to know anything about the affairs of the court and that she did not wish to be mixed up in anything.

The Countess Sulkowski, upon entering the room in which the Queen was reading a pious book, did not know what to say.

With a smile, she told the Queen, that she came to share her happiness with her beloved lady, that her husband had arrived. From that she passed to the rumour, that her husband's enemies wished to injure him.

'My dear Countess,' said the Queen, 'pray, let us talk about something else; I am occupied with my children, prayers and art, but I do not mix in the affairs of the court and I do not wish to know anything about them.'

Once more the Countess attempted to explain, but the Queen repeated:

'I know nothing. The King does not ask for my advice, I do not interfere with his affairs—'

After a short conversation the subject of which was a newly converted Israelite, and Lent prayers, the Countess took leave of the Queen.

It would be difficult to guess whether she believed in the Queen's ignorance about the intrigues of the court. But accustomed to trust her husband, she calmed herself and went home.

Ludovici appeared late in the evening but his manner indicated nothing good. He came to tell the Count that he found insuperable difficulties in finding documents, that the officials did not want to obey him, and that consequently it was impossible to have the papers ready for the next day.

There are people like Sulkowski, who do not wish, to see or to believe when there is danger. Neither what his wife told him, about her very cool reception by the Queen, nor what Ludovici communicated to him, took one iota from the assurance the Count had in himself or from his faith in the future.

It seemed to him that the King was so fond of him, that he could not get along without him, and he was perfectly confident. His wife, a timid and modest lady, well knowing the life of the court and the value of that which is called the King's favour, was very much afraid although she did not show it. She was aware that disgrace in Saxony, especially when it was trumped up by one's antagonists, did not end in a simple dismissal and banishment. It was usually followed by the confiscation of the estates and very often by imprisonment for life without trial. Sulkowski, in disgrace, could be threatening to his enemies through his connections with the courts of France, Austria, and Prussia; what then could be more natural than to imprison him for safety?

The Countess spent the night in fear, hiding her tears from her husband, for she did not wish to discourage him.

Her husband, on the contrary, was in high spirits, repeating to his wife what he had said to the King, and what impression it made on him. He flattered himself, that he had broken the snares which his foes had set for him; that everything would be as it was before, that he would overthrow the whole of that clique, and so surround the Queen, as to render her harmless for the future.

The next morning, the fifth of February, the Count was up very early, dressed, and, according to his old habit, went to the castle.

Had he possessed more penetration and less confidence in himself, he would easily have noticed that everyone in the court, on perceiving him, became grave; some of the courtiers drew aside and those, who could not avoid meeting him, were very cold and spoke but little. Sulkowski being privileged to see the King at any time he liked, went straight to his room, but the Baron von Lowendhal barred his way and told him very politely, that the King being very busy had given orders that no one was to be admitted, without any exception.

'But this order cannot apply to me,' said Sulkowski smiling.

'I do not know about that,' answered Lowendhal, 'perchance it may be cancelled later, but for the present you must excuse me for executing my orders.'

Sulkowski not wishing to condescend to a quarrel, sure that later he would be able to avenge such improper behaviour, saluted, turned and went off.

He determined to come again at eleven o'clock, when the King used to receive everybody. Coming down from the stairs, he perceived Brühl's *porte-chaise* and it angered him.

'Patience,' he said to himself, 'these are their last efforts, for they would not dare to shut the door in my face. We shall see—'

He went to Ludovici's office and found him pale and confused.

'The papers? Have you the papers?' asked the Count.

'I have not got them up to the present; there is something mysterious about the way the officials treat me—it does not portend anything good to us.'

'I understand,' said the Count laughing, 'they see their near downfall and lose their heads. I have not yet seen the King; they told me he was very busy. They must hold council what to do with Sulkowski, who ruins all their plans.'

He laughed; Ludovici sighed but did not dare to tell him that he was mistaken.

The Count hesitated as to whether or not he should call on Brühl, who ought to have already paid a visit to him. That was also a kind of a declaration of war.

'His conscience is not clear,' he said to himself, 'he does not dare to see me, he is packing his baggage, sure of dismissal.'

Ludovici that day was not communicative, he sighed, became pensive, paced the room and moaned. It made Sulkowski laugh.

As he had nothing to do he determined to pay a visit to the Countess Moszynski in order to see whether he would be received, and to enjoy the Countess's fright.

Accordingly he went to the Countess, but she begged to be excused, as the hour was early and she not dressed. He returned home where he found his wife very uneasy.

Joking at her useless fears, he told her that he was going again to the King. It was a quarter to eleven when Sulkowski went again to the castle. There were very few people in the ante-room.

As Sulkowski approached the door leading to the King's apartments, a page rushed out and told him that the King was in the Queen's apartments. He had no desire to go to the Queen, for there he would not be received without being first announced. Not knowing what to do with himself, he went to his *porte-chaise*. His first idea was to return home, but thinking that such an early return would frighten his wife, he preferred to go elsewhere.

The second failure to see the King made him thoughtful; naturally there was some intrigue but he did not believe it could have any result. He determined to overcome all difficulties by patience and constancy, not to show any impatience; and he was sure that he would conquer.

Faustina's house was on his way, and he determined to call on her. He knew how much the King admired the singer and he hoped to be able to learn something from her.

Already in the ante-room he heard such a noise that he thought of withdrawing, not wishing to find himself in improper company. All at once the door opened and out came Amorevoli, Monticelli, Abbuzzi, Puttini, Pilagia and a few Frenchmen, talking very loud and quarrelling. Catching sight of Sulkowski, they became silent, giving way to him and bowing humbly.

Faustina, who drove them out, stood on the threshold; she became confused at sight of the Count, but smiling she asked him to come in.

'When did your Excellency return?' she exclaimed, 'for I did not know you were back.'

'Well, up to the present I am half *incognito*,' said the Count smiling. 'Just imagine, my beautiful lady, that since yesterday I have not seen the King. I!' said he pointing to himself. 'Twice they would not admit me to his Majesty. I began to believe that my absence made me forget the customs of the court, and I came to beg you for some explanation.'

'The Count is kind enough to joke with me,' the singer replied, looking at him with a mixture of commiseration and fear. 'I only know the stage court. On the stage I am either a Queen or a goddess, but when I am off the stage I know nothing of what is going on in the world.'

'But,' said Sulkowski in a low voice, 'tell me, have you heard anything? Am I really threatened by your friend Guarini?'

'I do not know anything,' said Faustina, shaking her head. 'I have enough of my own theatrical sorrows. It is very probably that they are plotting against you, but you, Count, you need not be afraid.'

'Neither am I afraid, but I would like to *tirer au clair* and to know what it is.'

'It is jealousy and competition,' Faustina rejoined, 'In theatres they are very common, we are well acquainted with them.'

'And the remedy?'

Faustina shrugged her shoulders.

'Some people would withdraw; those who wish to fight it out, must stick to their guns, for they will never find peace.'

Sulkowski did not dare to remind her of the warning she had given him; her speech and manner were now quite different; she was afraid.

Seeing that he would not learn much from her, the Count asked about the new opera, about Hasse, and took leave of her.

He determined to go straight home. Notwithstanding the confidence which had not yet left him, he was depressed and obliged to keep a close watch on himself, lest the impatience which was taking hold of him should show itself.

In front of his palace he found a court carriage. The Baroness von Lowendhal, daughter of the Grand Master of Ceremonies was with his wife. Sulkowski entered the drawing-room.

The two ladies were sitting on the sofa and chatting with vivacity. The Baroness von Lowendhal, a very lively though not very young person, and always the best informed about everything, sprang from the sofa and greeted the Count as he entered. On her face one might discern much distraction and nervousness.

'Count, you will be able to tell us the latest news, she said shaking hands with him, 'what is going on at the court? Some changes are expected, and we do not know what they may be.'

'But where does such a supposition come from?' asked the Count.

'An hour ago,' said the lady animated, 'the King sent for old General Bandissin, who is suffering with gout and commanded him to come to the castle. The general who could hardly walk across the room with a stick, begged to be excused, giving his illness as his reason; notwithstanding that they sent again for him and I saw him going to the castle.'

'I do not know what that means,' answered Sulkowski quietly. 'I went twice to the castle and could not see the King; it's extremely amusing.'

He began to laugh, while the Baroness prattled on.

'They say that Bandissin, who has already asked several times to be pensioned, will get his release at last. He needs rest. But the worst thing is, it seems that my father is going to be dismissed.'

'I do not believe it,' said Sulkowski, 'but as I was absent from Dresden for several months, I am not *au courant* of affairs just now.'

The Baroness looked at him.

'It is very easy to guess. The positions are required for others.'

'Better not talk of these things,' said the Countess 'I am afraid to say a word.'

The Count shrugged his shoulders.

'Vain fears,' he said, 'all that will soon be changed.'

A lackey rushed in.

'His Excellency the Grand Master of Ceremonies, Baron von Lowendhal and His Excellency General Bandissin,' he announced.

All looked at each other, the Countess grew pale.

'Show them in,' said the Count advancing towards the door.

The guests entered, and Lowendhal, having noticed his daughter, looked at her as though in reproach at finding her there.

The greeting was stiff, Sulkowski received them coldly, not being able to explain their visit. He motioned to them to be seated, when Bandissin said:

'Count, we wish to speak to you without witnesses, we are sent by the King.'

Sulkowski's face did not change, he pointed to the next room.

The ladies, who could not hear the conversation, remained seated, frightened and curious.

The Countess trembled, feeling that this boded no good.

The Baroness wished to leave, but the Countess retained her by force, and she had not the strength to resist.

When the men entered the other room, Bandissin, an old and obedient soldier, took from his pocket and with evident pain a warrant signed by the King.

He handed it in silence to Sulkowski, who, in passing the threshold of that room, seemed to have strayed into another world, and stood pale and as though thunderstruck.

He took the paper with trembling hands, read it, but did not understand.

Lowendhal, who pitied him and wished to get it over as soon as possible, seeing that the Count did not understand what it was all about, passed behind him and read the warrant aloud.

It was very short and ran as follows:

'His Majesty the King, having noticed that the Count Sulkowski has several times, and especially at the last interview forgotten himself and lacked the respect due to His Majesty, has determined to take from him all the appointments the Count has held at the court, and dismiss him from all duties. In consideration of his long service, however, His Majesty leaves him the pension of a general.'

Sulkowski expected something worse from the fate which other men had met; therefore as he now understood the meaning of the warrant, he recovered.

'His Majesty's will,' he said, 'is sacred to me. Although I feel unjustly hurt, evidently by the machinations of my rivals, I shall bear my lot. If I have ever forgotten myself towards his Majesty, it was because of the love I have for my King, and not from any lack of respect.'

Neither Bandissin nor Lowendhal replied. Sulkowski, before whom not long ago they had almost kneeled, noticed the effect of his disgrace first upon them.

Their former affability was gone. Bandissin looked at him as on an inferior. In the faces of both gentlemen one could see that all they desired was to get rid of him as soon as possible.

Both bowed coolly, and distantly. Sulkowski returned their bow and conducted them back to the drawing-room. Here they saluted the ladies from a distance and went out as soon as they could. The Count politely escorted them to the ante-room and returned so serene, that his wife could not read in his face what had happened.

The Baroness Lowendhal waited hoping to be enlightened, and dared not ask him.

Sulkowski looked at his wife whose face betrayed anxious curiosity.

'Thank God,' said he, in a voice which trembled slightly, 'we are free. His Majesty has pleased to dismiss me from my duties. Although I regret to be obliged to leave my beloved lord, I do not feel at all hurt. It would be difficult for an honest man to remain at the court under existing circumstances.'

His wife covered her face.

'My dear,' said the Count, 'be calm, pray. The reason for my dismissal is this. It seems that I forgot myself in the respect due to his Majesty, in that I spoke the unadvisable and unpleasant truth; the King is kind enough to leave me the pension of a general and give me precious liberty—we shall go to Vienna.'

The Baroness Lowendhal looked at the Count with admiration. She could not understand the equanimity with which he received the news of his downfall from his former high position. The fact was that Sulkowski's pride permitted him neither to feel nor to show that he was hurt. After the first shock he pulled himself together and accepted his fate in a truly lordly way.

It was possible that he still had hope.

The Countess cried.

The Baroness understood that her presence was superfluous, for she could not offer consolation and her presence prevented them from consoling each other; she silently pressed her friend's hand and slipped from the room.

The Countess continued to weep.

'My dearest,' exclaimed the Count, 'I pray you to be brave. It is not advisable to show that we are hurt. We have to be thankful to the King that I was not sent to Königstein, and that instead of confiscating my estates they leave me a pension. The banishment to Nebigan is not very dreadful and does not exclude all hope—of overthrowing all that scaffolding built by my honest, sweet, faithful friend, Brühl! Pray, be calm—'

But the woman was not easily consoled.

Sulkowski looked at his watch, offered his wife his arm and whispering gently, conducted her to her room.

If there is anything that can arouse the greatest contempt for mankind it is the sight of the sudden downfall of the favourite of fortune, who, not long since, was idolised by his fellows.

There is in that something so vile and degrading, that the heart shudders; but in such situations a man learns to value others at their right price and tests his best friends. No one who has not passed through a similar crisis, can understand how bitter is the feeling that arises in the heart.

Sulkowski, who from childhood had been with Augustus and who was accustomed to be treated as his friend, bore his fate with dignity; he could not, however, restrain the scorn excited in him by the two gentlemen dispatched to him by the King.

He at once sent for Ludovici. The councillor owed him everything; but fear for his future, for his position, prompted him not to come, excusing himself on the plea that he was very busy.

'It will be necessary,' the Count said quietly, 'for me to pay the knave a visit and get my papers back, if he has not already given them to Brühl, in order in that way to purchase his pardon.'

In the afternoon of the same day, the Count went to the Castle. On his way he endured a veritable martyrdom.

The news of Sulkowski's downfall was already known in town, and although he had never wronged anybody, and could have sinned only by his pride against his subordinates, being even too good to many of them, all felt it their duty to show him how glad they were to hear of his disgrace.

He passed by Brühl's offices; the clerks noticed him through the windows, and, putting their pens behind their ears, with their hands in their pockets, they rushed out into the street in order to sneer at their former master.

Sulkowski saw and heard what was going on around him, but he exercised so much self-control that neither by sign nor glance did he betray that he saw or felt anything. He passed on slowly, hearing their ironical exclamations.

At every step of the way he met those who only yesterday bowed humbly as they passed him, but today they pretended not to see him, or looked at him impertinently, in order to show that they might disregard him.

Carriages passed by from which heads would be stretched and eyes follow him. In the castle the apparition of a ghost would not have caused greater fear.

They dared not shut the doors in his face, but even the lackeys would not make way for him.

Sulkowski seeing this would perhaps have withdrawn but he determined to see the King once more.

Being familiar with the King's regular habits, he knew that he passed that hour in the Queen's apartments. It was possible that the servants would warn the King but he determined to take his chance.

He entered a certain room in which fortunately there was no one, and this man, whose orders were formerly obeyed by the whole court, stood modestly in a corner, thinking over his situation. At that moment the King entered with a chamberlain; when Sulkowski kneeled the King was frightened and wished to retreat.

The count seized his legs.

'Sire!' he exclaimed, 'do not send your servant away, without a hearing.

'Ever since childhood I have been fortunate in faithfully fulfilling my duties towards your Majesty.'

The King's face depicted the greatest alarm.

'Sulkowski—' he said, '—I cannot—I do not wish to hear anything—'

'I beseech your Majesty,' rejoined the Count, 'to listen to me; I ask for nothing, except that I may go away cleared, for my conscience is clean. Sire, kindly remember the years we spent together; have I ever forgotten myself or overstepped the boundaries of respect? Those who wish to get rid of me, are afraid that someone watching over them might discover their deeds, and they send me away because I am faithful to your Majesty—Sire—'

Augustus covered his eyes with trembling hands and tapping the floor with his feet, repeated:

'I do not wish to hear—'

'I only want to justify myself.'

'Enough!' cried the King, 'my firm resolution is to part with you; that cannot be changed. Neither to yourself nor to your family shall any evil befall—be at ease, but go, go, go!'

The King said this with evident fear, afraid lest he might give way should no one come in.

'Sire,' cried the Count desperately rising from the ground, 'may it be permitted me to thank your Majesty for the favours I have received from the King, and to kiss his hand for the last time?'

The King was near to tears, but there was a chamberlain present, a witness and spy in one; therefore he put out his trembling hand, which the Count covered with kisses.

'Sire!' he cried, 'that hand repulses an innocent man! I repeat that I am innocent, because I could have sinned only by the excess of my love towards your Majesty.'

The uneasiness and alarm on the King's face increased.

'Enough!' he exclaimed, 'I cannot listen to you, I command you to leave.'

Sulkowski bowed in silence and withdrew—Augustus rushed to the door leading to the Queen's apartment.

The count needed a few minutes to collect his thoughts and gather strength; he leaned against the wall, pressed his forehead with his hands, and stood there for some time; he was about to go when a chamberlain entered and told him in the most impertinent tone to leave the room.

'His majesty commands you by me,' he said, 'to leave the castle at once and not to show yourself at the court. His Majesty's will is that you live at Nebigan.'

Sulkowski glanced proudly at the man, made no reply and went out.

His last effort was frustrated, and there remained nothing, but to drink the cup without shrinking. A craving for revenge arose in his heart, but he quelled it, for he knew that his enemies had the advantage.

He returned home in order to tranquillise his wife and assure her that she need fear nothing worse.

The banishment to Nebigan, situated near Dresden, permitted the hope of meeting the King and of justifying himself. To this his wife replied:

'Brühl will not be satisfied with banishment, we shall be in his hands! He will find some reasons to renew his attack; let us leave this cursed Saxony immediately: let us go to Vienna, to Poland, anywhere you please, except remain here!'

During the whole evening, the people gathered round Sulkowski's palace, looking in at the windows, anxious to see the ashes of the sacrifice.

From time to time Sulkowski came to the window and looked at the vile crowd. Nobody called on him that evening. But an official document was handed to the porter, in which the King dismissed the Count from his duties of Grand Chamberlain and Grand Equerry of the court.

The Count laid the paper on the table.

The same evening there was a reception at Brühl's palace. The minister's face expressed uneasiness; he was tired after the fight. He threw himself into an arm-chair when his wife came into the drawing-room.

She looked at him scornfully.

'I ought to congratulate you,' she said, 'you are master of the situation, king of Saxony and Poland; Henniche is the lieutenant general; Loss, Hammer and Globig viceroys.'

'And you are the queen,' rejoined Brühl smiling, '*à double titre.*'

'Yes,' she said laughing, 'I am beginning to get accustomed to my situation, I find it quite bearable.'

She shrugged her shoulders.

'Provided it lasts longer than Sulkowski's reign.'

'I should add, that you are very clever, having laid your throne on women's shoulders. The Queen, I, the Countess Moszynski, and Fräulein Hernberg—not counting Abbuzzi, for she is a supernumary.'

'It is your fault that I must seek for hearts outside my own house.'

'Ah! hearts! hearts!' interrupted his wife, 'neither you nor I have any right to speak about hearts. We have fancies, but not hearts; we have senses, but not sentiments, but—it is better so.'

She turned from him.

'One word,' said Brühl, 'later the guests will arrive and I shall not have a chance of talking to you.'

'What is it?'

Brühl bent close to her ear.

'You are compromising yourself.'

'The idea!'

'That young employé from my office—'

She blushed and said angrily:

'I have my fancies! Nobody can stop them. Pray do not mix yourself up in my affairs, as I do not mix in yours.'

'Madam!'

Here the Countess Moszynski entered: she was beaming with animation. She put out her hands to Frau Brühl and said:

'There is victory *sur tout la ligne!* In town they speak of nothing else; they wonder, they tremble—'

'They rejoice,' added Brühl.

'I am not certain of that,' the Countess interrupted, 'but we are pleased at the downfall of that proconsul. Once and for all we are *en famille* and are not required to bow to that proud lord.'

'What news? What does he intend to do?' asked Brühl.

'If you know him,' the Countess said, 'you should readily guess. Naturally he will go to Nebigan, where he will shake his head as he used to do and try to see the King, and to intrigue in order to regain his favour.'

Brühl laughed.

'Yes, it is very probable; but, dear Countess—from Nebigan it is not far to Dresden, neither is it far from Königstein—I doubt—'

At that moment a new-comer, Countess Hernberg, the wife of the Aus-

trian envoy, entered. She was a beautiful, black-eyed Viennese, with aristocratic features, who was also Brühl's Egeria, and said without any greeting:

'I make a wager that they go to Vienna.'

Brühl made a grimace.

The two ladies began to converse together and the Countess Moszynski
took Brühl aside.

'You make a mistake,' she said. 'Never do anything by halves; you ought
to have shut him—'

'The King would never consent,' said Brühl, 'by asking too much, we
might make him resist, and Sulkowski would have our heads cut off. Then,
I know the Count too well, and that is why I do not fear him, he is a
weak-minded man, he cannot make a plot. Before he leaves Nebigan I
shall find proofs that he appropriated two million thalers and then Königstein will be justified—'

'Brühl!' laughed the Countess, 'two million thalers—and you—'

'I do not have one single penny for myself,' exclaimed Brühl, 'only for
the receptions, by which I endeavour to do honour to my King. I am in
debt.'

Then he whispered:

'Do not think that I am so stupid as to let the prey go before it is killed;
but I was obliged to do it with two blows. I shall get him away from
Nebigan as soon as I wish. In the meanwhile I gather proofs. In a few
weeks' time the King will consent to anything.'

He laughed strangely, when the Grand Minister of Ceremonies, entering, obliged him to leave the Countess, who joined the ladies.

'How did he receive the news?' asked Brühl.

'At first he was dismayed, but after a time, bravely and proudly.'

'But the Chamberlain Frisen told me,' hissed Brühl, 'that having surprised the King in the castle, he crawled to his feet.'

'It is possible,' said Lowendhal, 'But—'

He did not have time to finish the sentence, for the butler made signs to

Brühl from the door, and he was obliged to leave his guest and go and find out why he had been called. He passed through the drawing-room with some uneasiness, for although the King was carefully watched, he feared that the former favourite had succeeded in stealing into the castle.

Henniche was waiting in the study, sitting comfortably in an armchair. Although he made some movement as the minister entered, one could see that he played with him, knowing that he was more necessary to Brühl, than Brühl to him.

'What is this urgent business you have to communicate?' said Brühl reproachfully. 'The people will think that something has happened.'

'Let them think,' said Henniche impatiently. 'Your Excellency amuses himself and I work; I cannot satisfy your fancies.'

'Are you mad?'

'I?' asked Henniche quickly.

'You forget yourself,' said Brühl.

Henniche laughed.

'Let us drop that; to others you may be a great man, but not to me.'

He waved his hand.

'To what would you amount without me?'

'And what about you, without me?' cried Brühl vehemently.

'I am a fork, with which every minister must eat; it's quite different.'

Brühl quieted down.

'Well, tell me, what news?'

'Instead of thanking me, your Excellency scolds me. It is true that Henniche was a lackey, but precisely for that reason, he does not like to be reminded of the fact.'

Saying this he unfolded some papers.

'Here is what I have brought; I made Ludovici drunk, I have assured him that we shall appoint him a councillor in the secret department, and I guarantee that he shall keep it in such secrecy that nobody shall learn about it! I have already some accusations. There are sums taken from the custom house, there are receipts of money not paid to the army. Ho! ho! plenty to accuse him of. How could he buy estates otherwise?'

'You must have proofs,' said Brühl.

'Black and white,' Henniche returned.

'When could you have them ready?'

'In a few days.'

'There is no hurry,' said Brühl, 'the King must rest after his first effort. Faustina shall sing, Guarini shall make him laugh, we shall shoot; the incident in the corridor will be forgotten, then we shall be able to act. The essential thing is to keep all in secrecy; he must not suspect anything and run away.'

Henniche, who looked attentively at his master, added:

'We must watch him at Nebigan; we must tell some of our lackeys to enter his service; they will act as spies.'

'Very good,' said Brühl.

'I should think it is very good, as I never suggest anything bad,' rejoined Henniche.

'If he escapes to Vienna, or to Prussia, even to Poland,' said Brühl thoughtfully, 'it would be a very unpleasant and dangerous occurrence.'

'Yes, dangerous,' said Henniche fixing his wig, 'for although he is not very cunning, it is never wise to despise an enemy.'

'Then it is understood,' whispered Brühl, 'you collect proofs of guilt. It would not be proper for me, who succeed him, to act openly against him.'

Before leaving he added:

'Listen, Henniche, you cannot go away, it will be better to send Globig. Such a man as Sulkowski cannot be put in one room, especially when it is probable that he will remain there a long time. Do you understand? Tell Globig to go to the commandant and let him choose a few good rooms for the Count, that he may be quite comfortable. They might clean the rooms and have them ready, but they must not know for whom they are destined.'

Henniche laughed.

'Your Excellency forgets that for such a game I must be rewarded.'

'When he is in the cage,' Brühl said. 'And it seems to me that you do not forget yourself.'

'We are both alike,' rejoined Henniche folding the papers. 'Why should we cheat each other? We know each other well.'

Brühl, although the ex-lackey treated him so brutally, did not dare to answer; he needed him.

The minister returned with a serene face to the drawing-room, where the card tables were quite ready. The Countess Moszynski, tapping the table with her fingers, waited for him.

'Sit down,' she said, 'at this hour all business goes to bed.'

The last days of the carnival were more merry than in former years, because everyone tried to make the King cheerful, on whose forehead could often be seen something like sadness and yearning.

He yawned very often during the afternoon, and Guarini's jokes could not make him laugh. They asked Faustina to sing the King's favourite songs. Frosch and Horch were promised a reward for good tricks. They induced the King to shoot every day at a target. The entertainments at the castle were very brilliant. Brühl would hardly leave the castle; he would stand at the door trying to guess the King's thoughts. Sometimes Augustus would be in a better humour and would smile; but very often too, during the laughter, a cloud would come and the monarch's face would become suddenly gloomy; then he would turn to the window, and appeared not to see or to hear anything.

The next day Sulkowski received an order to go immediately to Nebigan. He was obliged to leave Dresden. The people were waiting for him on his way in order to jeer at him.

His little dog Fido was running after his carriage; someone shot him. It was done in the day time, in the town, and no one said anything. The Countess cried, the Count said not a word, he bore it stoically, pretending to know nothing about it.

The vile mob accompanied him beyond the bridge, running and shouting after him. The coachman urged the horses, the Count looked into the distance and did not even move—he felt superior to it all.

Brühl was told all about this; he only smiled.

At last the new minister learned through his spies that Sulkowski's downfall aroused in the court rather regret and fear than pleasure. They murmured everywhere.

The only remedy for that was to isolate the King so that no unauthorised word could penetrate to him. During the next few days, immediately the new officials were appointed, Brühl's brother became the Grand Marshal of the court, the pages and lackeys whom they suspected of having any relations with Sulkowski, were changed.

Augustus got everything he was fond of, but he was strictly watched. He felt happy, since he could satisfy his habits and besides that, desired nothing else.

It was impossible immediately to think of restraining the Queen's influence, but it was in Brühl's plans to do so. He determined to act through his wife alone, for he feared that Guarini would not consent to use such radical measures. Brühl felt omnipotent, and his viceroys, as they called his councillors, grew more and more arrogant.

They were still afraid of Sulkowski and it was necessary to finish with him once and for ever. Henniche collected proofs of money appropriated. The action that now had to be put through was, to confiscate the Fürstenburg Palace, given to him by the King, to take from him Nebigan Castle, and lock him up in Königstein. As there had been many similar examples in the reign of Augustus the Strong, Brühl expected to be able to carry out his plans very easily. Sulkowski, free, was dangerous. Sulkowski in Vienna would be threatening.

Brühl was still more alarmed that the Count did not seem to be crushed by his misfortune. He ordered his furniture to be brought from Dresden to Nebigan, and the beautiful situation of the castle made sojourn in it quite bearable. From his window Sulkowski could see the tower of the King's castle, in which he had been such a powerful man.

The carnival drew to its end, the Count did not leave Nebigan.

Every day his steps were dogged by spies, but they could not learn anything. Nobody visited him from town. Every day the Count's servants would go to Dresden for provisions, but they had no intercourse with anyone except the shopkeepers.

The Count would spend whole days reading, conversing with his wife, and writing letters, but the spies never learned how they were sent.

One morning Brühl entered the King's room with a pile of papers. The King hated the mere sight of papers, and talk about intrigues. One word would make him sullen.

Brühl would shorten the disagreeable duty by handing to the King documents ready for his signature. Augustus III would sit at a table and would sign them like a machine, not looking at the documents; his signature was always the same, clear, precise, majestic and quiet.

That day, the King, having noticed the papers, was preparing to perform his onerous duty, but Brühl stood motionless, and did not unfold the documents.

An enquiring look made him speak.

'Sire,' he said, 'I have today such a disagreeable affair that for the sake of my lord's peace I should like not to speak about it.'

The King twisted his mouth.

'I would have preferred that somebody else should have done this, but nobody would take my place,' said Brühl sighing. 'Consequently I must speak myself.'

'H'm?' said Augustus.

'Your Majesty knows well,' Brühl continued, 'that I am not mixed up in Sulkowski's affairs.'

'It is over! Enough of it!' interrupted the King impatiently.

'Not altogether,' rejoined Brühl, 'and that is why I feel so unhappy. I took his duties, I am an honest man, I was obliged to investigate everything.'

The King stared at Brühl; there was something alarming in that look.

'Among his papers were found some letters accusing your Majesty's ungrateful servant; there were many abuses; deficits in the accounts—'

The King cleared his throat.

'But I still have money?' he asked with energy.

'Yes, but not as much as there ought to be,' said the minister. 'But the worst is this, that the letters exchanged between Sulkowski and some foreign courts condemn him as a most dangerous man. If he goes to Poland he will be protected by the laws of the republic; should he go to Vienna, he might be a menace to us there. In a word, wherever Sulkowski might go—'

Brühl looked attentively at the King's face as he said this, but although he knew his character well, he could not guess what impression he had made on Augustus by his speech. Augustus looked surprised, gazed round the room, grew red and pale by turns, appeared confused, but did not say a word.

The minister waited for the answer. Augustus cleared his throat, coughed loudly and looked challengingly at Brühl.

'Your Majesty,' Brühl continued, 'knows that I am against severe measures. I also loved that man, he was my friend as long as he was faithful to my lord. Today as a minister, as a faithful servant, I must act against my heart.'

It was evidently an understood thing between Brühl and Guarini, that the Padre was to enter during this conversation, and in he came. But the King made quite a different use of his presence and asked after Faustina.

'She is very well,' answered Guarini laughing. *'Chi ha la sanita, è ricco, e se no 'l sa.'*

But Brühl stood there like an executioner. 'Will Your Majesty permit me to finish my unpleasant business?' he said. 'Father Guarini knows all about it.'

'Ah! He knows! Very well!' said the King and turning to the Padre asked him: 'And what do you think of it?'

The Padre shrugged his shoulders. 'I hold the same opinion as my gracious lord,' he said laughing. 'I am a priest, it is not for me to judge these things.'

There was a pause; Augustus looked at the floor; Brühl was frightened.

'During the reign of Augustus the Strong, Sulkowski would by this time have been in Königstein,' said Brühl.

'No! No!' said Augustus, looking at Brühl and growing pale; then he rose and paced to and fro.

Guarini stood sighing.

'I never insisted on treating anyone severely,' rejoined Brühl. 'I was and I am for clemency, but there are proofs of such ingratitude—'

The Jesuit raised his eyes and sighed again. He and Brühl both watched the King's every movement and did not know what to think. Never before had he been a riddle to them, knowing him they were sure of being able to make him give in, but the question was, how to do it without wearying him, for then he would be angry with them for tiring him. Brühl looked at Guarini as though urging him to finish the matter. The Padre looked back at the minister with the same silent request. Augustus directed his gaze steadily to the floor.

'What are your Majesty's orders?' asked Brühl persisting.

'What about?' muttered the King.

'About Sulkowski.'

'Ah! yes—yes—'

And again he looked down at the floor.

At length he turned to Brühl, and as it seemed with a great effort, pointing to the table, said:

'Leave the papers until tomorrow.'

The minister grew confused, for he was not willing to leave the papers. Although he was sure that the King would not read them he was cautious, and being afraid that something unexpected might happen, wished to finish the business at one blow. He looked at Guarini.

'Sire,' said the Jesuit softly, 'it is such a bitter pill that it is not worth while to taste it twice. *Alcun pensier no paga mai debito.* Why think it over?'

The King did not answer; presently he turned to Brühl and said: 'In the afternoon shooting at the target in the castle.'

The order was significant, Brühl was confounded.

'The last reindeer tired us,' added the King, 'but it was worthy of our efforts.'

He was silent again.

'And the last died,' he added sighing.

The clock pointed to the hour at which the King was accustomed to go to the Queen; he ordered a chamberlain to be called.

Brühl was dismissed, having gained nothing, and his efforts were frustrated. He did not know why the King resisted him. The King hastened off. They were obliged to leave him, and Brühl called the Padre into the next room.

He threw the papers on the table.

'I am at a loss to understand it!' he cried.

'Patienza! Col tempo e colla paglia maturano le nespole!' answered Guarini.

'Wait till tomorrow; you could not expect to do it so soon. The King must grow accustomed to the idea, and as he dislikes every fresh attack, you will succeed.'

The minister relapsed into thought.

'At any rate, it is bad,' he said, 'that he is still so fond of Sulkowski.'

They began to whisper, taking counsel of each other. The Jesuit went to the Queen, Brühl returned home with the papers.

The King being fond of regular habits, while smoking his pipe in the afternoon, would never see anyone except those who could amuse him. Even Brühl was then obliged to forget his duties as prime minister and assume the rôle of one of the King's fools. But, as there was no danger on those afternoons, the minister showed himself very seldom. The King amused himself with his fools, and was not permitted to send for anybody outside the court, for even if Brühl's creatures received such an order, they would find some pretext for not fulfilling it, until they had consulted the minister.

From the time of Augustus the Strong there remained in the court the famous fool Joseph Frohlich, who wore a silver chamberlain's key on his back containing a quart of wine.

Brühl, who distrusted him as much as the Baron Schmiedel, tried to get him dismissed, but Augustus would not permit him to drive off all his father's faithful servants. Frohlich had his own house beyond the bridge, was well to do, and seldom appeared at court; but every time he came, Augustus would laugh as soon as he caught sight of his round face.

That afternoon Brühl was not with the King. Frosch had a swollen face, the result of a blow from Horch, and could not come to amuse the King. Therefore no one was surprised when the King told the page to go and bring Frohlich.

The fool was very much surprised when he received the order to go to the castle. He quickly donned one of the three hundred dresses purchased for him by Augustus the Strong, hung his famous key on his back, and rushed through the bridge thinking by what joke he could best amuse the King.

Even fools have hours in which they do not care to laugh. Frohlich, *semper nunquam traurig,* as the motto ran on a medal struck in his honour, was in such a mood that day that he was not *fröhlich* but sour as vinegar.

He would not confess it, but he liked the times of Augustus II better than those of his son.

But the habit of being amusing to order enabled him to be merry when he appeared before the King.

Besides being witty, Frohlich was a very able conjuror, and it was just then more easy for him to begin by some trick than a witticism.

Kneeling before the King, Frohlich said that he ran so fast that his throat was dry. He took off his key and asked if his Majesty would be kind enough to permit him to strengthen his forces by a draught of wine. The King clapped his hands and told a page to bring a bottle.

In the meantime Frohlich employed himself cleaning his key which was a little rusty, and from which he was going to drink, complaining that he seldom used it now. The page stood with the bottle ready to pour in the wine, when Frohlich looking at the bottom of his key, grew frightened at seeing something in it.

'Who would have expected,' he exclaimed, 'that a bird would build a nest in it?' And a canary flew out of the key. The King laughed; but that was not all; there was still something more in the key, and the fool took out a pile of ribbons, six handkerchiefs, a candle, and a handful of nuts. Then he said that not being certain that there was not an enchanted princess in the key, he would prefer to drink the King's health from a glass. After some refreshment, the fool began to amuse the King by imitating well-known actors.

The entertainment lasted about half an hour. The King laughed, but Frohlich noticed that in spite of his apparent mirth, he was uneasy, perplexed and distracted. He wondered what the cause could be, when, to his surprise, the King went to the farthest window, and motioned to him to follow.

There was something so mysterious and unusual in this that Frohlich was alarmed. He followed the King, however, to the window, where he was standing, looking round undecided and alarmed.

The fool could not solve the riddle.

'Frohlich, listen,' said the King in a whisper, 'h'm! laugh aloud, laugh, but listen to what I am going to say, Do you understand?'

As yet the fool did not understand, but he began to laugh so loudly as to deafen the loudest conversation. The King took hold of his ear and drew it almost to his lips.

'Frohlich is faithful, honest, will not betray me,' he said. 'Today, go secretly to Nebigan. Understand? Tell him, understand, to escape at once to Poland.'

Frohlich could not understand why the King should use him as a secret messenger. It did not strike him to think of Sulkowski. He made a gesture that he did not understand. The King bent again over his ear and said one word only: 'Sulkowski!'

Having said this, as though frightened at having mentioned a name forbidden to be spoken at the court, he drew aside, Frohlich could not laugh any more. He was so frightened that he did not yet comprehend.

His face must have expressed the doubt, for the King told him again to laugh, aloud, repeating the order precisely.

He spoke quickly, incoherently, but at length the fool understood that the King told him to warn the Count of his danger, and bid him escape to Poland.

In order not to arouse suspicion Augustus continued for a time to listen to the fool's jokes and then taking a handful of gold pieces from his pocket, put them into Frohlich's hands.

'Go!' said the King.

Frohlich, after being permitted to kiss the King's hand, went out and ran home as fast as he could.

He hardly grasped what had happened to him. It was necessary to collect his thoughts and take counsel with himself, how he could best fulfil the King's order, for he was afraid of his entourage.

He fell into deep thought, and sighed. The task was difficult. Even had he been less familiar with the life of the court and the fate of favourites, he could easily guess that there were plenty of spies round Nebigan and probably also in the castle.

Frohlich was a well-known person, but happily the frequent fancy-dress balls, given during the reign of Augustus the Strong, accustomed most people to the art of disguising themselves. Frohlich closeted himself in his room and without losing time commenced to work at his transformation.

It was early in February, the river Elbe was covered with strong ice, and it seemed to Frohlich that access to Nebigan was easiest and safest from the river. It was too late to travel on foot, so he hired a sledge at Briesnitz, and having promised the driver high pay, was driven swiftly to an inn in the village of Nebigan. Telling the driver to wait, he went out through, another door and walked towards the river.

He felt that only by some good luck could he fulfil his dangerous mission. On arriving at the castle he hesitated, then he entered the courtyard and ran as fast as he could to the hall. It was dark and no one was about. Sulkowski never kept many servants and now he had still less. The stairs were dark, and only on ascending them did he hear voices. In the ante-room the servants were quarrelling over their game of cards.

At the sight of a strangely dressed man, coming at such an unusual hour, they sprang to their feet, asking him what he wanted.

Frohlich said that he must see the Count at once. The butler first searched his pockets, fearing that he might carry arms, or might have come with some evil design, then went to the Count to announce the stranger.

There was some stir in the castle: the wig, the clothes and the handker-chief with which his face was covered did not permit them to recognise Frohlich. They showed him into a drawing-room, just lighted for the pur-pose. Sulkowski was pale but quiet and as proud as if he were still prime minister. The visitor requested that the servant might be dismissed. The request aroused some suspicion and alarm, but the Count did not betray his feelings. As soon as they were alone, Frohlich uncovered his face.

'Two hours ago,' he said, 'I was called to the King; I shall repeat his own words: "Today, secretly, go to Nebigan—tell him to escape at once to Poland."'

Sulkowski listened indifferently.

'The King told you this?' he asked.

'Yes, and with fear lest he might be overheard, as though he were a slave and not a king.'

'He is a slave and will remain so for ever,' sighed Sulkowski.

He became pensive.

'May God reward you,' he said presently, 'for the trouble you have taken for me, or rather for the King. How can I show you my gratitude?'

'Only by this, that your Excellency fulfils the King's will tonight.'

The Count stood as if riveted to the ground. Frohlich went out to find his sledge, while the Count still stood undecided as to what to do.

He knew enough of Brühl to understand that his wisest course was to follow the King's advice.

The next day as the King was returning from chapel, Guarini came to him to wish him good morning. To this the King would usually answer by sounds similar to those produced by clearing his throat, laughter or hiccoughs. The King's face indicated excellent health, which he inherited from his father, and as he did not abuse it, it served him admirably.

Guarini with other courtiers accompanied the King.

The King looked at him inquisitively several times, as if trying to learn something from the expression of his face; at length he said laconically: 'Cold.'

'I feel it, for at best I am an Italian,' said Guarini, 'but notwithstanding the cold,' he continued in a whisper, 'there are people who do not fear to travel. A certain Count whose name I will not mention, for he was unfortunate enough to fall into disgrace—started last night, so I heard, to an unknown destination.'

The King as though not hearing made no answer.

Brühl was waiting in the King's room with the documents, but he was distracted and morose.

Augustus came to him quickly. 'Brühl! those papers of yesterday; we must finish with them.'

'All is over,' answered the minister, sighing.